The Truth About Vampires

THERESA MEYERS

MILLS BOON

First published in Great Britain 2011
by Mills & Boon,
an imprint of Harlequin (UK) Limited,
Large Print edition 2011
Eton House, 18-24 Paradise Road,
Richmond, Surrey TW9 1SR

© Theresa Meyers 2011

ISBN: 978 0 263 22378 1

Harlequin (UK) policy is to use papers that are natural, renewable and recyclable products and made from wood grown in sustainable forests. The logging and manufacturing process conform to the legal environmental regulations of the country of origin.

Printed and bound in Great Britain
by CPI Antony Rowe, Chippenham, Wiltshire

Raised by a bibliophile who turned the family dining room into a library lined with bookshelves, **Theresa Meyers** has always been a lover of books and stories. First a writer for newspapers, then for national magazines, she started her first novel in high school. In 2005 she was selected as one of eleven finalists for the American Title II contest, the *American Idol* of books. She is married to the first man she ever went on a real date with (to their high school prom.) They currently live in a Victorian house on a mini farm in the Pacific Northwest with their children, a large assortment of animals, and an out-of-control herb garden. You can find her online at her website at www.theresameyers.com on Twitter at www.twitter.com/Theresa_Meyers or on Facebook at www.facebook.com/TheresaMeyersAuthor.

To my grandmother Helen Jane Palmeri Sauro Stokes—for giving me a small part of your indomitable Sicilian spirit and a true zest for life. You've made more of an impression on me than you'll ever know and always made me feel I was special. Thank you.

To Karla Baehr, Jennifer Hansen and Rachel Lee, for your steadfast friendship and love of tea. Thanks for helping keeping me grounded and being my cheering squad. You girls are the best.

To Cherry Adair, for being a fantastic critique partner and all around brilliant sounding board. You're greatly appreciated.

To Holly Root, agent of awesome, and Tara Gavin, editor of fabulousness, you took a chance and changed my world. Thank you.

For Regina Emig Mathews Ronk, who never got to read this book, but without whom it never would have came to exist in the first place. Thank you for teaching me to read when no one else thought I'd learn how. I miss you, mama.

And for Jerry, because you believe in me even when I doubt myself. Thanks for all you do to make my writing possible.

Chapter 1

The bodies concerned him. There were too many for this to be merely a coincidence.

A toxic mix of rotting trash and old urine drifted out of the alley between the brick buildings. The stench, underscored by the slightly sweet scent of death, seemed a thousand times stronger to his preternaturally sharp sense of smell than to the human cops inspecting the scratched and dented Dumpster. And underlying it all was the scent of three, possibly four, unfamiliar vampires.

"There has to be more to it," Dmitri Dionotte muttered to no one in particular. Why would a vampire leave behind such a blatant calling card as a string of bodies void of blood and missing vital organs? Why kill a donor that would come back to give more? And what the hell did a vampire need with organs anyway? If he or she—or judging by the number of bodies, they—needed additional sustenance, why not liquefy the organs with their venom and leave the outer body intact? And more importantly, why leave them where they could easily be discovered in downtown?

Revenge. That was always an option. So was justice. Hell, everything as basic as blood lust to something as complicated as insanity could be a motivation to slake thirst. The lack of blood he understood, but the missing organs?

He ducked behind the edge of the brick building to avoid being seen as the police zipped a black body bag over the latest victim found among the heaps of plastic trash bags.

What did you discover? The voice of the clan laird, Roman Petrov, echoed clearly in his head.

It is another. Same situation. No blood, chest cavity split, organs missing. The police arrived before I finished my observations.

Damn.

You can say that again. Someone is tipping off the mortals before we can remove the bodies. Dmitri walked at a steady pace back toward the club, the wind off Puget Sound whipping his black trench coat around his jean-clad legs and pushing strands of his dark hair and sunglasses hard against his face. Despite the cloudy sky and intermittent sunlight, the glasses helped prevent him from getting a migraine from the intensity of the light.

You know what this means?

Yes, my laird. They'll be looking for answers.

Followed directly by pointing fingers, Roman said dryly.

Dmitri's shoulders tightened as memories of a peasant mob, people he'd known and led, their faces twisted with fear and hate, flickered before his eyes. They were armed with pitchforks and lighted rushes, and rough-woven garments hung from their skeletal, starved forms. It took so very little to incite madness. A little fear, a dash of superstition, a pinch of anger and you had the perfect cocktail for chaos.

Mortals, so damn predictable, Roman scoffed.

Dmitri considered pointing out that once they had been mortals too, but held his tongue. *My laird, since we already know there is the possibility of exposure, should we not work to ensure we're presented in a positive light while we conduct our own investigation?*

An excellent suggestion. I shall convene the council.

An hour later, Dmitri still hadn't heard a single word from the council or Roman. Sitting in his office at the nightclub Sangria, he scrubbed his hands over his face, then closed down the tracking program on his computer screen.

He had enough to do with running the club, making sure that the donors who came in kept their anonymity and that the vampires who came in minded their manners. If there was one thing he was fastidious about in accommodating the vampires of Seattle, it was that humans weren't changed unless they wanted to be. Blood exchange wasn't allowed. Donation, yes. Drinking, yes. But no random conversions.

Despite being a vampire himself, he never believed in his kind's divine right to change humans as they saw fit, never giving a thought to whether the human wanted to be an immortal damned to a hellish eternity bound in blood.

He squeezed the bridge of his nose, warding off the pressure building there. Beyond the club, he didn't need or want any further entanglements with mortals. As *trejan* for the clan, responsible for governing their secrecy, security and safety, he had more than enough to occupy his time and resources. But the Bloodless Murders, as the local media had dubbed the four bodies found in the past two weeks, were the kind of high-profile exposure his clan didn't need or want. Dmitri rolled his shoulders.

As long as the clan kept itself exclusive, only admitting a few select mortals who knew to keep their mouths shut, vampires got along fine with the community. Ordinary people went about their happy, blissfully ignorant little lives, completely content with their confidence that mortals were at the top of the food chain. Imbeciles. If they only knew.

The Cascade Clan maintained order and discipline. Mortals were not cattle, they insisted. They were symbiotic partners. So the vampires that lived in and around Seattle followed the code lain down as law by the clan council. Or they left or were executed.

Dmitri?

Yes, my laird. He edged forward in his black leather desk chair, waiting.

It has been decided. The council suspects there are reiver vampires within our territory. As trejan, *you are to find out the truth of this, and what they want. Do what you can to seed the community with a positive view of our kind, if indeed the police or reports seem to be pointing in our direction. It would not do for there to be chaos. It may indeed be time for us to reintroduce our kind to mortals.*

Come out into the open? Are you certain?

The council seems to think it may be best, especially if we need to form alliances against the reivers.

I'm on it.

Dmitri pushed away from his desk and strode through his private door into the main body of the club, his mind swirling with the implications of the assignment. This was a chance for his kind to solidify their status among mortals, to stop living in the shadows. But it was equally a chance for sheer insanity and mob mentality to rule if handled badly.

What happened within the walls of the club would help determine their future in this city. Too bad the interior of Sangria looked like a swanked-out version of the Bat Cave or a B-movie version of an uptown hell, minus the roaring flames.

With the modern black-and-chrome fixtures, plush crimson velvet booths, black lacquered bar uplit with red neon and oblong red glass globes suspended from the ceiling, Sangria qualified as an upscale trendy theme bar.

It was the strategically placed and lighted stalagmites jutting up from the floor and stalactites that dripped down in giant stone daggers from the ceiling that gave the place its underground appeal. They encircled the cozy booths, bracketed the length of the bar and encased the row of crimson curtains leading to the private rooms off the side of the dance floor.

He was used to the slightly unpleasant stench

of overcooked steak and the acidic smell of cheap red wine, but those good-to-mortal smells were tainted with something caustic. Bleach. He'd have to talk to the staff about that. It wouldn't do to offend the incredibly sensitive noses of his best clientele.

A ridge of pressure built around Dmitri's eyes, pressing against his sinus cavities, forcing him to inhale a very potent scent, one that made the bleach inconsequential. His eyes narrowed, tracking the source. A mortal.

A curvy blonde in a conservative ice-blue button-down shirt and black slacks picked out a high-backed bar stool. Her shirt was cut for a man, based on how the shoulders looked a little too large and the buttons across her chest strained a little too hard. Dmitri felt a tug low and deep in his gut. A yearning he hadn't experienced in aeons crept over him, insidious and needy, causing his fangs to press insistently against his gums for release.

Thank God the club was nearly deserted at this time of day. The wave of need that slammed into him could have turned deadly in an instant had any other vampire strode up to her. As it was, the black lights caused the huge overlapping three-circle design inlayed with pale wood to glow amidst the dark wood of the empty dance floor. The mark of the Cascade Clan. It was still too early for most of his regulars to be here. Hell, half of them had yet to wake up at this hour. Only mortals were enticed into seeking out happy hour prior to sundown.

The woman gazed at the various bottles of deep ruby-red, clear and amber liquids lining the glass shelves behind the chrome-topped bar. Or perhaps she was observing herself in the mirror backing the shelves. A fall of long honey-blond hair cascaded over her shoulder, half masking a far too angelic face. At least too angelic to be in a place like this.

She reminded him of an image out of Botticelli's paintings. Ultrafeminine and ripe with wide expressive blue eyes, a delicate but determined chin and a lush mouth made for kisses. Dmitri wasn't sure for a moment if she truly was an angel or a succubus. The fallen sometimes did come to the vampires first. Immortals seeking out other immortals of dubious nature. And she was certainly the type that could lure a mortal into giving up his soul.

He tried to reach into her mind, to see precisely why she was there. *What the*— Blocked. Interesting. It didn't happen often, but when it did, the mortal was intently focused on something. Normally it was only other vampires who could block their thoughts, and one whiff of the delicious mixture coursing through her veins told him she was definitely not a vampire.

"What can I get you?" asked Anastasia. Tonight the raven-haired bartender was laced up in a black leather vest. A small diamond stud glinted in her nose, but her thickly outlined hazel eyes were far too old and world-weary for her young face. Anastasia was over six hundred years old but still looked twenty-two.

"Do you have a special tonight?" The silken-smooth quality of the mortal's voice gave Dmitri a pang of memory. The pure quality of a soprano in the church choir, lifted above the people, a sliver of light and beauty inside a great cathedral. He released the curl of his fist. Forced himself to relax. That was another time, another existence, far too long ago. Best to focus on the here and now.

The bartender's eyes flicked toward him from across the room. *She wants to see the manager.*

Well, here I am.

Careful, Dmitri. I think she could be trouble.

He smiled. *Really? How entertaining. I'll see what I can do about it.*

In an instant he crossed the room and stood right behind their visitor without so much as causing a current of air.

Watch it!

Dmitri lifted a brow. *Careful,* piccola. *It's best not to speak so to your elders.*

But you shouldn't move that fast where mortals can see you.

And did any of them notice?

No.

Then quiet your mewling.

Tendrils of spiced vanilla and cinnamon swirled around the blonde in an invisible cloud that beckoned him closer, daring him to touch her cheek to see if it felt as soft as it appeared. Saints preserve him from temptation. From the scent, he bet her blood tasted like hot cinnamon rolls. Why were such wonders as this wasted upon the living?

"Why don't you get her a Vampire." The sexy-as-hell male voice, with a slight Italian lilt, soaked into Kristin Reed's skin and elicited a flutter in her stomach.

She glanced behind her and found herself face to broad chest. Encased in a crisp white shirt and fitted black jacket, the plane of muscle led to a deeply tanned throat, firm jaw and sinfully sculpted lips. She turned her gaze upward and found herself staring into a set of intense brown eyes, so dark they looked nearly black, and so deep they seemed soulless. A jolt, like caffeine from a double shot of espresso, raced down her spine and made her limbs tingle.

"Don't look quite so appalled," he offered in a deep, rich voice laced with amusement. "I think you'll enjoy it. No, put that away, this drink is on the house. Anastasia, please prepare a Vampire for our guest."

Kristin returned her wallet to her purse.

"Thanks." Lord, he had a great mouth. What would it feel like to brush her mouth against his? To have his mouth crush hers in a soul-stealing kiss? Whoa, put on the brakes, she warned herself. This guy is a total stranger. Sexy and great to look at, but still a total stranger.

He put out his hand, and Kristin suddenly found her fingers enveloped in the coolness of his. "Dmitri Dionotte, manager of this establishment." He brought her hand up to his mouth, brushing dry lips across her skin. A shiver, part fear, part fascination, raced down her spine.

Still holding her hand, he lifted his head, his eyes all pupil as he held her gaze. He was like no one she'd ever met before. Darker, more imposing in a way that filled up the room, not just with his size, but also with the power radiating off him in pulsating waves.

She'd never had her hand kissed in her life and the contact alone was making her body buzz. "Kristin. Kristin Reed." Her pulsed kicked up double time, as if she'd made several trips up and down the staircase to the newsroom. Kristin swallowed and pulled herself together, kicking her brain back into gear, and withdrew her hand from his. She was here to find a lead. That's what she should be concentrating on. Not Mr. Tall, Dark and Delicious.

"Want that Vampire?" The bartender jarringly interrupted the silent connection shimmering between them.

Eyes still locked with his, Kristin pushed out something vaguely intelligent, though her brain had shut down and her body went into lust mode. "What's in it?"

The mountain-size guy beside her answered, "Chambord, peach schnapps, red Vampyre Vodka, a splash of 7-Up and some cranberry juice." The words were prosaic enough, but he made them sound like seduction.

The drink sounded harmless enough. The man was anything but. "Sure, I'll try it."

The bartender slid across a hurricane glass filled to the rim with ruby-red liquid and capped off with a black straw and a pair of plastic vampire-costume fangs on the rim. Cute, but a little tacky.

Kristin took out her wallet, pulled out a ten and

tucked it in the tip jar. Good information was hard to come by and the man at her side was more a distraction than a good source. She forced her attention away from him and back to the bartender. "Have you worked here long?"

The bartender popped her gum as she sliced lemons and limes and dropped them into a container behind the bar. "Since they opened in October."

The sharp smell of citrus overwhelmed some of the mouthwatering cooking scents, which were making Kristin's stomach grumble. She'd forgotten lunch again.

She swizzled the straw in her crimson concoction, casting a glance under her lashes at the hunky guy beside her. "Yeah, I heard you had the best Halloween costume party in town."

"We get some real characters in here," the bartender confirmed.

As she took a sip of her drink, the fruit flavors burst on her tongue. A delicious combination of sweet and tangy. She glanced at the manager and gave him a little smile. "Hey, I think I like Vampires. Thanks for the suggestion."

The bartender snorted.

"You say that now," he said. The smoky quality of his voice both tempted her and put her on edge at the same time. "But watch out. They seem harmless, but they've got some serious bite."

Kristin paused a beat. There was no point in seeming too eager to talk with him. She took another sip, then looked up at him. "I'll try to remember that."

"Welcome to Sangria."

He sat down on the stool beside her, his focus on her so intense it wrapped around her like a warm down jacket. Comfortable. Heated. Welcoming.

"Interesting decor." She glanced around, taking another sip of her drink, acutely conscious of him sitting beside her and how it was making her light-headed. Maybe it was the alcohol on an empty stomach, but somehow she doubted it.

"A place for the curious."

"You mean vampire wannabes."

His lips stretched into a subtle smile over very white, very even teeth. His eyes made her feel as if he was reaching inside her. Searching the deepest corners of her mind, her heart. "Not exactly."

His wavy dark hair curled over the edge of his collar and she resisted the urge to slip a ring of it around her finger.

Maybe that Vampire drink was stronger than she thought. A wave of dizziness crashed into her and Kristin sucked in a gulp of air. She smelled the clean scent of starch, the spiciness of cloves and something darker, rich and sweet like brandy laced with dark chocolate. It reached out and coiled about her senses, both arousing her and making her wary of how relaxed she seemed to be.

"What are you really here for?" The tenor of his voice stroked her skin, making her shiver and, odder still, making her desire to tell him everything. Every secret she'd ever kept. Every thought she meant to be private. "A man?" His eyes glittered with invitation.

"No, information. I'm just curious."

"So you've heard about the club."

She nodded, then peered intently into his eyes. "Only a few stories. But I hear that you cater to people who are a little more exotic in what interests them."

"Really, like what?"

A rush of heat washed over her skin. Just how much should she reveal? Interviewing was a delicate balancing act. Give too much and you got nothing. Give a little and sometimes you got a lot more.

She turned and peered at the kaleidoscope of colors in the bottles that lined the back of the bar and wondered for a moment what exactly was in them. Some of the red ones appeared more dense and opaque. Her source had said people with vampire fantasies, or kids into cutting, were regulars at the club. Either way, blood was a big deal. It had seemed like the best place to find a lead to the weird Bloodless Murders, since the cop shop had been less than helpful. Again.

Perhaps she ought to go for broke. "Is that blood?" She indicated a bottle of opaque dark red liquid on the shelves behind the bar.

He didn't even flinch. "We try to appeal to all our customers."

Her curiosity spiked. "And is any of that from donors?"

Dmitri stiffened, turning guarded. Bingo. Her

pulse sped up, this time not from attraction but from excitement. If she could score a lead on the Bloodless Murders, even just enough to write up one article, it would give her time.

"So you're interested in the backroom activities we offer?"

"Perhaps. I'm a little picky about who I'd partner up with."

He inclined his head. "Naturally."

"And I'd like to know a little bit more about what you offer before I decide if I just want to watch or would rather participate."

Oh, God. Had she just said that? *Smooth, Reed. Real smooth.* She covered her flub by taking a last sip of the drink and found herself loudly sucking air instead.

"You really do like Vampires." He motioned for the bartender to refill her glass.

Kristin held up a hand. "Oh, I don't need another right now." His eyes bored into hers, searching, weighing, but revealing nothing. Kristin gave what she hoped was a smile rather than a grimace. "So, about these other activities?"

"Of course."

He held out his hand. Grasping it, her hand tingled. She slid off the high bar stool, and quickly released his hand. What was up with that? Sure, she'd met cute guys before, but her body was in overdrive and it shocked her. Grabbing her purse, she slung the strap over her shoulder and tried to cover how flustered Dmitri Dionotte seemed to make her. He led her to the row of crimson-draped rooms on the far side of the club. "These would be our tasting rooms."

"Tasting what?"

"Our clientele is interested in unusual vintages. Hard to obtain wine like, say, a 1945 Mouton Rothschild Pauillac that retails for about nine thousand dollars a bottle, if you can find it."

"Oh." Who had swung by and stamped a giant *L* on her forehead? Her reporting career seemed to be shriveling before her eyes and her tongue was completely uncooperative. For some insane reason, she'd hoped she would stumble upon a solid connection to the murders, a lead that could take her somewhere with the story and save her ass in the process. Her editor, Rex Hollander, had been very specific—get a front-page investigative story or get a pink slip.

Dmitri lifted one of the heavy velvet curtains aside and gestured her ahead of him. As a last resort she straightened her shoulders and tried the vapid smile that got her far more information than direct questioning ever had. Especially from a guy like this—cool, reserved, with just enough swagger to think, or rather know, that he was worth a second look.

"It's pretty," she said, keeping her voice artificially high-pitched, shaving another ten points off her IQ. She glanced around the room, pressing as many details as she could into her memory. Honestly, it was more like some Goth sitting room tricked out in crimson faux leather on the walls, soft black leather couches and lounge chairs, chrome-and-glass tables, with an enormous flat-screen television on one wall. A tall black lacquered cabinet stood in one corner. "What's in there?"

"Supplies. Glassware, napkins, trays."

"May I see?"

He moved his hand with a flourish. "But of course."

He didn't move to open it, so she took it upon herself to do the honors.

The doors hid a bit more than napkins and glasses. Hermetically sealed razor blades, tubing, individually wrapped packets of gauze, tape. She picked up a plastic-encased blade between her fingers. "And this would be for slicing…"

"Olives."

"Riiight." She tapped her finger on the cabinet door.

"They make the best practice," he added, his lips tipping up in the corners in a knowing way.

Kristin's stomach dropped to her shoes. "Come again?"

"If people are interested in blood activities, we have them first practice on olives, or grapes. Either tends to simulate the necessary balance between pressure and precision that's required."

"For…" Kristin rolled her hand, wishing she could pull the words out of his mouth faster.

"Some people like to drink blood."

"Annnnd we're back to the vampire wannabes."

He stepped closer, making the room seem all of a sudden way too small and intimate for her taste. "Not all of them." He slipped the cabinet door from her fingers and lightly closed it, the clicking sound echoing through the hollow in her chest. Kristin could feel her heartbeat fast and thick in her throat.

His lips twitched and his eyes seemed to take on a golden glow. A trick of the light, Kristin was sure.

"Some are wannabes. Some, my dear Miss Reed, are the real thing."

Chapter 2

"Are you telling me there are honest-to-God, actual vampires in this city?"

"Would you rather I lie to you?"

Suddenly Kristin found it hard to breathe. Her brain swarmed with thoughts, buzzing and insistent like mosquitoes on a hot summer night. Deep down she suspected if Tall, Dark and Delicious was telling her this, it was either because he was trying to hit on her or he was hiding something else. Or he had a rich fantasy life that involved a thing for vampires and wished he was one.

Since she was absolutely certain a guy like this didn't need to hit on women, so much as beat them off with a stick, option one made no sense. Chances were good he was hiding something; after all, everybody had secrets. So option two was looking credible. Vampires, of course, weren't real. And if she tried to slip that little ditty into her editor's in-box she'd get hit in the head with a pink slip the instant she turned around to walk out of his office. Scratch option three.

"Um. No. It's just that—"

"You don't believe in vampires."

"Well, yes, that and—"

"You're afraid."

Kristin crossed her arms. She was perfectly capable of finishing her own damn thoughts. "No. If vampires really existed, I'd be more concerned that they were responsible for our recent rash of Bloodless Murders."

His eyes narrowed almost imperceptively. "Just exactly what do you do for a living, Miss Reed?" The way he said her last name left enough chill in the air to bite into her skin.

"I'm a reporter for the *Pacific News Tribune*." Kristin tilted her chin up a bit.

He leaned forward, his broad chest nearly

brushing her breasts, his sexy as hell mouth just a few inches from hers. Kristin couldn't stop the quick inhale of surprise or the quick uptick in her pulse. He was definitely in her personal space.

"I see. So are you here because you really are interested in the club, or are you here for a story? No. Wait. Don't answer that." His feral smile made her legs feel decidedly unstable. "I already know the answer."

Before she could stop him, he grabbed her hand and led her out of the tasting room toward the front door of the club. "I can't tell you anything about the Bloodless Murders. But if you're interested in finding out the truth about vampires in this city, call me." He let go of her hand and with a flick of his fingers reached inside the breast pocket of his suit jacket, pulling out a business card that had the same intertwined three-circle logo emblazoned on it in dark red.

With his free hand he yanked the door open. The filtered early-evening sun seemed unnaturally bright after the dim interior of the club, and the rattle of car engines, squealing bus breaks and shush of tires across pavement from rush-hour traffic at her back seemed suddenly deafening.

He stepped toward her, and Kristin stepped backward in response. She snatched the card and found herself outside on the curb, staring at a firmly closed door.

Perfect. Just perfect.

Now she was going to be late on her deadline, and she had nothing to go on except a funky club, a place where people pretended they liked to drink blood and a gorgeous club manager with some whacked-out notion that vampires really existed.

No matter how you sliced it, she was screwed.

Her pocket vibrated and she dug out her phone, walking to her car as she read the incoming text message: STAFF MEETING IN 5. WHERE R U???

Damn. She'd gotten too distracted to keep track of time.

Fortunately, the newspaper office was only a few blocks south. Driving through the five o'clock traffic was a challenge, but she got there as fast as she could. She tossed her keys to the lot attendant who knew her, and ran flat out, up six flights of stairs and through the heavy metal door, her cell phone buzzing at her hip. The third page in five minutes. Who needed a gym membership when they worked for the most demanding editor at the *Pacific News Tribune?*

The visit to Sangria had potential, but Rex Hollander wouldn't care. When he set a meeting for five, you damn well better be there at 4:55.

Out of breath, and with a stitch in her side, she barreled through the narrow walkways created by the labyrinth of gray cubicle partitions, and headed straight for the glassed-in office on the opposite side. Phones rang, people chattered and printers whirred, the noise echoing off the concrete ceiling and industrial fluorescent lights. The newsroom operated in a constant state of controlled chaos, so no one even noticed her rushing by.

She sucked in gulps of air laced with the scents of stale coffee, fresh newsprint and the sugary fat-soaked temptation of doughnuts. But there was no time to stop despite the fact that her stomach gurgled in protest to the alcohol without any food. Hollander was waiting.

"Where in the hell is she?" His booming voice rattled the sheets of tinted glass that made up his office. Around the table the news staff fidgeted. Only one chair sat conspicuously empty.

Kristin smoothed down her blond flyaways and made sure her shirt was tucked into her slacks right before she slid into the back of the room, her heart pounding in her ears.

Hollander speared her with a no-nonsense glare, which competed with the blinding glare of the early-evening sun shining through the window behind him and bouncing off his balding pate. "You're late, Reed. Take a seat."

She nodded, and did what he said, but didn't comment. It had taken only a week on the job to learn that she-who-commented got her head bitten off. That had been six years ago.

"People, I'm going to be blunt. We're in trouble." Hollander sighed, brushing his hand over his fleshy face. "The bean counters downstairs don't want me to tell you this, but unless we can bump up our sales, we're headed down the can. I need some stories. Great stories. Something that's hard-hitting and will make Associated Press sit up and take notice. Something that will make papers fly off the newsstands. What've we got? Think, people. Think. Anderson?"

Arthur Anderson, the mid-forties man sitting next to her, with a heavy beard and a penchant for sucking down three packs a day, twitched. "Working on a piece looking at attacks of zoo animals on their keepers."

"Weak, but work on it. Peters?"

The late-twenties golden boy of the newsroom grinned. Daddy had bought Bradley Peters a job on the paper and he took every advantage of it he could. "Looking into the closing of stores in the market, seeing how the economy is affecting Pike Place as a local icon."

Yeah. And he was likely shopping on the clock at the same time, Kristin thought as she shifted in her seat.

"Great. Reed?"

Kristin flipped open her notepad. It pissed her off that Hollander played favorites, but she'd earn her kudos by her own work. "Working on that bakery piece about how their recipe for rye bread was picked up by a major national retail chain. Feel-good story for the week and ties into local economy."

Hollander frowned, his bulldog jowls sagging even farther. "Ditch it. I need something hard-hitting. What about the Bloodless Murders? I thought you and Blake were working on that."

"He's been out with the flu. I'm still investigating and I should have a draft by Monday."

"You'd better. Thomas?"

Kristin raised her hand as Dillion Thomas, the dark-haired skater kid who was interning, started rising up out of his slouch. "Yeah, I've got a story—"

Hollander interrupted. "What is it, Reed?"

"I could get you a draft tonight if you didn't mind it being on a parallel line of investigation."

"Like what?"

"Vampires in Seattle." The awkward moment bloomed into a full-on tragic episode. Kristin could feel the weight of every stare in the room firmly fixated on her and even hear a few snickers.

"Did you say vampires?" There was no mistaking the skeptical edge to Hollander's voice.

"Yes, sir."

Hollander paused, cupping the back of his head, then ran his hand over his bare scalp. "We're looking for a concrete lead on the murders, not fiction fantasies. What've the cops said?"

She knew that the cops weren't going to tell her anything. The blonde girlie reporter wasn't *smart* enough to follow along, which had led to her being pissed and burning more than a few bridges. More like left her stranded on a desert island. "Sir, I just think—"

Hollander leaned forward, his entire head turning an unhealthy purplish shade of red. "You aren't paid to think, Reed. You're paid to investigate and report. Now get the damn story on the murders, or you'll be holding a pink slip instead of a pay stub!"

Damn.

Why in the world couldn't she have been a sportswriter? Kristin swallowed past the sickeningly huge lump that had welled up in her throat and nodded. Because sportswriters didn't win Pulitzers. That's why, she reminded herself.

She tugged on the cuffs of her shirt as Hollander grilled the remaining staff on their story assignments and continued his irritating habit of talking in clichés and snapping pencils between his thick hands.

For as long as she could remember, Kristin had craved a Pulitzer. Her father had run a small-town paper and she'd grown up in the offices. While other kids drew pictures of their dog, she drew mockups of her own imaginary newspaper. She didn't sell Girl Scout cookies; she'd sold subscriptions. And when she was old enough to ride a bike, she'd taken on a delivery route, and been the only girl doing it.

If they opened her up, they'd probably find a half-and-half mix of printing ink and blood in her veins. Pulitzer was the golden ring. With it, her dad could never again tell her that she ought to settle down. He could never dispute that she was just as good, and just as hard-hitting, as any male reporter.

So if an investigative report on the Bloodless

Murders was what Hollander wanted, he was going to get it in spades, whatever it took.

Hollander dismissed them and Kristin got in line to file out the door.

"Hold up a moment, Reed." Her boss was going to give her the I'm-giving-you-a-golden-opportunity pep talk after he'd torn her down in front of the all-male staff.

"Yes?"

"What I said about the pink slip? That's not bull. They're asking me to cut the staff by a quarter by the end of the month. I need you to prove to me you can pull your weight."

Her body temperature spiked a few degrees higher. Kristin tried to keep her voice firm and even, so her anger wouldn't show. "So you're thinking it would be me and skater boy who get cut first?"

"No. You. We don't pay skater boy. He's an intern."

Oh, for cripe's sake.

"And what about Peters or Calloway? I've got seniority over both of them."

"You know my hands are tied with Peters. And

Calloway got us that piece that won the award last year. You're good, Reed, but you don't take any risks. You turn in solid stories that are all small potatoes. This is your chance to prove you're out to play with the big dogs."

Kristin dragged in a long slow pull of air to stave off the pounding starting in her temples and wished for an instant she smoked. So much happened out on the rooftop where the smokers met that she often felt completely out of the loop. Calloway getting that assignment on the immigrant adoption scam was likely a result of being out there, while she was inside.

"Got it. Anything else, Chief?"

Hollander eyed her for a moment, then shook his head. "Go hit me a home run with this Bloodless thing. Remember, a good reporter uses every advantage they can. Don't just rely on that melon of yours."

"You mean the melon on top of my shoulders, as opposed to the two on my chest?" She clenched her hands as tightly as she could.

He winked at her. "That's a girl. Go get 'em."

Kristin spun around on her heel and strode out

of the office resisting the urge to swear. How in the world chauvinism could be so alive and well in this day and age completely stunned her. But there it was. And everyone knew it. That's why she was the only woman on the news staff. Other women only lasted a year or two before they were so annoyed, they left. It wasn't as if Hollander was sexually harassing anyone. He just thought men were smarter. Period.

Just like her dad.

She swung into her cubicle and grabbed her BlackBerry out of her pocket. Who did she still have decent contacts with downtown?

Bradley leaned over the four-foot partition that separated their cubicles. "So, Hollander give you any last-minute tips?"

"Buzz off, Peters. I'm working here."

He gave her an orthodontically perfect grin that looked too white in his fake-and-bake tan. "You know, if it's too much pressure for you, you don't have to work here. You're pretty enough. I'm sure you'd make great tips down at the Toys bar down on Second."

Kristin tipped her head to the side. "I'd hate to have to compete with your mother."

Brad's brow bent with irritation.

From the cubicle behind her, skater-boy intern laughed. "Burn, dude. She got ya with a 'your mama.'"

"Shut up, Thomas," both she and Bradley said in unison.

"Look, Brad, if I wanted your help, I'd ask for it. I've been doing this since before you graduated college, so how about you let me do my job and get out of my face?"

He held up his hands in mock surrender. "Fine by me. Just don't come crying when Hollander hands you a pink slip and you end up working at Toys anyway. I'll even be a good sport and stop by with a nice tip for you now and again."

Late that night Kristin found herself in the dicey section of Pioneer Square in Seattle's downtown just a block away from Toys, dressed in a tight, short red leather skirt, low-cut black silk blouse and screaming-red peep-toe FM heels. But she wasn't there for a job interview.

She'd cruised by the cop shop only to get told what she already knew. The police had no leads and no suspects. Weird murders. Victims drained of blood and vital organs removed. It was like some twisted version of the Operation game. She'd put her money on some surgeon or a medical researcher with a sideline…or a strange fetish. Someone with a taste for blood, literally.

Overhead, the red neon sign reading Sangria strobed on and off, with a heartbeat-like rhythm. Vampires. What the hell was she thinking when she pitched the idea to Hollander? She sighed.

It was the best lead she had. Hell, it was the only lead she had. She took a deep breath and pushed through the door.

Unlike earlier, the place was packed. The deep bass of the music rumbled in her chest and competed with the hum of countless conversations. Kristin threaded her way through the crush, heading for the familiar face at the bar.

"Back already?" the bartender asked, her diamond stud winking red in the lights overhead.

"Guess I got a taste for Vampires." She paused for a moment trying to recall the young woman's name. People seemed more comfortable if you called them by name. "Hey, Anastasia, is Dmitri around?"

"Not that I've seen. He's usually pretty busy until 3:00 a.m. Anything I can help you with?"

For a moment Kristin was sorely tempted to ask the bartender what she knew about the vampires Dmitri had alluded to. But her gut told her the woman wasn't likely to be much help. "Just the drink for now."

The leather-clad bartender mixed and poured, then slid the hurricane glass in Kristin's direction. She picked it up. At least with the drink in her hand, no one could slip something into it. Sure, it was suspicious of her, but given what she was investigating, being extra careful couldn't hurt. She peered over the rim of the glass, watching the people that filled Sangria.

They all seemed young. Some sported contacts that gave them colored pupils of red, violet, bluish-white, even yellow cat's eyes. There were people dressed in everything from high-end fashion to denim to Goth black. Even the flash of a cloak or two straight out of the Halloween Dracula costume.

Taking her glass with her, Kristin slowly and deliberately made her way toward the tasting room Dmitri had showed her earlier that day, mingling with people here and there. Asking questions. Was this their first time to the club? How did they find out about it? Did they believe in vampires? She managed to get enough quotes and material to flesh out an article about blood lust in Seattle and how seemingly normal people considered themselves donors for the real vampires of the city.

What a racket. Chances were they were donating their blood and somebody was selling it, getting rich in the process.

Glancing around, she inched back the curtain to discover a broad back. Jet-black hair and odd topaz eyes greeted her as the bouncer turned around to glare at her.

"Sorry, private party. Tasting rooms four and five are open for guests this evening."

Over his shoulder, Kristin thought she caught a glimpse of the mayor laughing, holding a glass of distinctly red liquid that clung in dark rivulets to the sides as he finished taking a sip. It might not be the inside scoop on the murders Hollander wanted, but coverage of the mayor would at least give her story some credibility.

Kristin widened her eyes slightly, tilted her head to the side and smiled at the oversize bouncer in front of her in her best imitation of a brainless bimbo.

"Dmitri invited me." She pulled his card out of her itty-bitty black clutch and flashed it in the bouncer's face. "Said I should show this card and it would be fine."

He took the card and for the instant that he looked at it, Kristin skimmed the list attached to the clipboard in his beefy hand. The thick brows drew together in a definite point. "What's your name?"

"Tessa Hartman."

His gaze darted down the list as he put a check next to the name. "Have a nice evening, Miss Hartman."

She flashed him another vapid smile and sauntered into the salon as if she belonged. No guts, no glory. Of course, given the nature of the murders, that thought made her stomach clench tighter.

In addition to the mayor, the room boasted the city's premier heart surgeon, a well-known hospital administrator and one of the local guys from the Centers for Disease Control.

Her mind started creating puzzle pieces to the story and swirling them around to see what fit where. What if there was someone in this room who really was out to take blood and organs, and not just for some ramped-up vamp fantasy? What if they were selling it off for transplants and transfusions through some front organization? Certainly there was the potential.

"It's absolutely amazing," the surgeon said. "I've never seen anything like it."

"True, but there's no supporting evidence this effect will last. You need to think about that, Stan," answered the guy from the CDC.

"All I know is that without it you'd be—" The hospital administrator clamped his mouth in a firm tight line the instant he spotted Kristin.

"Good evening, gentlemen."

The bouncer stepped up to her side. "This is

Miss Tessa Hartman. Mayor Stan McCallum, Dr. Eric Chung, Mr. Adam Paulson and Mr. Mathew Balor." Mayor McCallum's face broke into a wide inviting smile. Dr. Chung inclined his head in a bowlike nod and Paulson and Balor just stared, Paulson with boredom and Balor with avid interest.

Fixing her best party-girl look in place, Kristin nodded, waved her fingers in a shy little hello and batted her eyelashes for an added confirmation that she was no threat. She noticed right off that bouncer boy hadn't bothered to introduce any of the ladies in the room, a couple of whom gave her a nasty glare. Guess they were window dressing too.

Mayor McCallum patted the sofa by him. "Have a seat, Tessa. We'll have someone get you a drink."

Kristin was instantly grateful she'd brought her own and knew precisely what was in it. She lifted it in her hand and gave a little shrug. "Oh, I brought one from the bar, thanks." She sat down and made a show of sipping at her straw. Not two seconds later Mayor McCallum's hand was brushing up against her shoulder in slow circles. Kristin fought off the urge to pull away and instead focused herself on listening to as much of the conversation as she could.

"Until you've taken a few more tests, I wouldn't place too much faith in it," Balor, the CDC guy, said. "It might have worked for you, but we don't know what the side effects might be. There have been issues with others."

"Besides, there are a lot bigger problems at the moment," hospital administrator Paulson added. "We've got to prevent any cross-contamination from happening so only the people who want it, and are willing to pay for it, can get it."

Kristin didn't even realize she'd leaned forward until she caught a glimpse of Balor's tongue nearly hanging out and his gaze firmly glued to her cleavage. She sat back and noticed an odd scent coming from the mayor's glass. It was metallic and sickly sweet. Whatever it was, she'd bet it wasn't alcoholic, and it wasn't thick or pasty enough to look like tomato juice either.

"What's the latest news on the murder investigations?" Dr. Chung asked.

"Nothing yet," the mayor said flatly.

"Are you talking about the Bloodless Murders?" Kristin asked, making sure her voice was high pitched with just enough singsong quality to make her question seem utterly innocent. She gave a small shiver. "They're just so scary. What if it's some psycho like the Green River Killer?" Given her current state of dress and the serial killer's profile for picking out prostitutes, nobody even batted an eyelash at her comment.

One of the other women entered the group, bringing Dr. Chung a martini and draping herself over his shoulder.

"If it is, then he's going to slip up eventually," Balor said.

"Don't the murders concern you, Mr. Mayor?"

He placed a hand on her knee and gave it an affectionate squeeze. "You can call me Stan. Of course they do, sweetheart, but this is a big city. Every big city has problems with crime. You can't stop all of it. Our police force does its best and they've got top people investigating it."

Kristin resisted the urge to snort. Detectives McNally and Babcock were leading the investigation and neither of them had been much help beyond identifying the victims. She'd done her own research to find anything that might be connecting them. All the victims had visited Sangria in the past year. Two were regulars, the others just the occasional visitor. But it was a solid connection.

Dmitri's comment about vampires played back in her head. "Do you think vampires are real?" She looked intently first at Dr. Chung and then at Mayor McCallum.

The mayor's eyes narrowed just a fraction. Kristin could see his pulse beating faster against the collar of his white shirt. He chuckled. "There are plenty of strange things out there, why not vampires?"

"But could they be causing the Bloodless Murders?"

Balor coughed so hard he sounded as if he was choking, and Dr. Chung began to beat on his back. As soon as he could breathe normally again, Balor started laughing. "You've got one seriously active imagination to go with that hot body."

"Too bad Miss Hartman already has a date." The familiar Italian lilt and dark tone curled over her skin, making Kristin flinch. She knew she'd been taking a chance that Dmitri might find her here, uninvited. But even if he threw her out now, she'd still have enough for a good story to hand in to Hollander.

She swiveled her head around and gazed directly into Dmitri's eyes. The deep brown had gone so dark it was espresso black. "Hi, Dmitri."

He smiled. Her stomach did a backflip in response.

"I was wondering where you were hiding." He extended a hand in invitation. Beside her, the mayor stiffened just enough that she could feel the friction in the air and nearly smell the testosterone.

Kristin slid her hand into Dmitri's. It closed firmly around hers, sending a zing of electricity up her arm. She would have been a fool to challenge him and stay longer, but her unusual response to him surprised her. Without missing a beat, she turned around, smiled at the quartet and lifted her glass. "It was nice to have met you."

They nodded their goodbyes, but Dmitri was already full steam ahead pulling her past bouncer boy, who he gave an I'll-deal-with-you-later glance, and through the curtain.

She barely had time to register that the curtain led not back out into the noisy, busy club, as it should have, but instead to a dark, empty hallway.

Dmitri moved quickly, pinning her against the wall with his hard body, his muscular arms locked in on either side of her. She gasped, dropping her drink, the glass shattering on the painted concrete floor.

"I told you if you wanted to talk about vampires, to come and see *me*." This wasn't a reminder, or a threat. This was an order. Kristin bristled.

"Perhaps I wanted to find out things you wouldn't tell me."

"My invitation did not imply that you could lie to my staff or accost my very best customers."

"Did they look like they were bothered?"

"Would you have noticed? Because you certainly *bother* me."

His face was so close, she was certain if she stuck her tongue out she'd be able to graze it on the dark shadow of stubble along his jaw or bite him. She wasn't sure which would be better. The scent of dark chocolate and brandy swamped her senses. Her heart was pumping hard enough that it vibrated in her ears and between her thighs at the same time. Kristin placed the flat of her hands against his chest and shoved hard.

Nothing. Nada. She might as well have pushed against the side of a mountain.

For the first time in her life, she realized that this was the kind of guy her father had warned her about. A man no woman could match. There was no going head to head with a guy like this. Power radiated off him like a shimmering wave of heat she could almost see but definitely feel. He was too much. Too much of everything.

Underneath her fingers his chest flexed, the muscles bunching. Her mind automatically filled in the gaps of what he probably looked like under that proper starched white shirt. "Either way, I got what I wanted."

His eyes burned with a hungry intensity that stole her ability to breathe. "Maybe you think that only because you weren't aware of your other options." Skilled fingers threaded through the hair at her nape, sending shivers skittering down her spine.

She'd had guys look at her. She'd had plenty of kisses, but this was different. Far different. The world didn't exist outside the two of them, and his focus on her was pure, undiluted and intoxicating. His eyes said that in that moment nothing else but her mattered. She couldn't hear anything above the roaring rush of her pulse.

"Maybe you should enlighten me." The words came out far more needy and raw than she'd intended. Her lips suddenly felt too dry and she sucked in her bottom lip.

He stiffened against her, one hand cupping her shoulder, then caressing down the length of her arm to come to rest at the flair of her hip. She could sense he was holding back and it made her wonder why. Was he just caught up in the moment? Was his anger mixing with attraction? Was he second-guessing?

His other hand glided along her neck, his fingertips resting on her pulse point. The pad of his thumb seemed rough as it skimmed her damp bottom lip, causing a throbbing ache to build at her core and radiate outward so that each finger and toe felt the demanding beat of her pulse. Kristin realized that she wanted him to kiss her. Needed it.

She sucked in a breath. "Or p-perhaps—" she stammered. She realized that he seemed totally cool, nearly unaffected, while she couldn't seem to stop herself from talking. His pulse wasn't raging like hers. His breathing was slow and rhythmic. Only his eyes betrayed him, telling her he was just as hungry as she was for something more between them.

His thumb slid over her entire mouth in a rasping arc. "Shh."

"Aren't you going to kiss me?" she whispered against his thumb.

His mouth grazed a path along her check, nibbling, tasting her. "You talk too much."

Chapter 3

Kristin narrowed her eyes. "Well, better all talk and no action, than no talk and no ac—"

His mouth crushed down, hot and firm, on hers. A perfect fit. The sizzling sensation that started at her mouth traveled through her veins to every cell in her body. Her mind went fuzzy around the edges as her world centered on his touch.

He crowded her back against the wall, pressing her body between the cold concrete and the heat of his hard body. She was aware of moving her hands to his broad back, pulling him closer. She knew she should be peppering him with questions, but as soon as the thought appeared it vanished again, wiped away by the shiver he elicited from her body.

His clever hands caressed her. She shuddered as his thumb brushed the edge of her breast, making both of them ache and tighten. Her short skirt slid dangerously high as she wound her leg around his, as she rode the cresting wave of heat spiraling upward inside her.

Breathing hard, she surfaced to drag in a gulp of air. "I don't—"

"Talking again." The words shaped against her lips then his tongue darted into her mouth, stroking as he deepened their kiss, bringing with it the slick heat she craved. The thump of the music from the club throbbed through the wall at her back, and the delicious aromas filtered into the deserted hallway from the nearby kitchen, reminding her of exactly where she was. For an instant she realized a club employee might appear at any moment around the stacks of flattened cardboard boxes and shipping crates.

He pulled back, just long enough for her to breathe, his dark gaze locking onto hers. "No one will disturb us." Had he read her mind? She shuddered as one hand cupped her butt, pulling her hard against his erection.

There was no mistaking the hard press of his arousal against her stomach, or how it pulsed against her. Inside she contracted, melting, needing, and ground her mons against him. She'd had flings before, but not in a very long time, and never like this. *I don't usually do this with guys like you.* The words sat useless on the tip of her tongue. Aggressive guys usually got a sharp putdown, but that would require her to be able to think, to breathe, and she wasn't certain she could do either with the inferno Dmitri was feeding. She gasped. "I don't—"

Her words faded into a moan as her head tilted back against the wall and his mouth seared away the rest of the thought. Dmitri's hot mouth kissed down her collarbone to the swell of her breasts. Boneless and pliant in his hands, she stretched, inching her leg up higher on his hip, hoping, praying, he'd touch the throbbing ache building between her thighs. His hand curved over her bottom, his fingers tracing the crease between her thigh and buttock.

"Don't. Stop." Each word came out a puff of breath. She was more than ready, aching.

He pulled back suddenly, bracing his hands on the wall on either side of her head, his eyes black as he looked at her.

Exposed to the chill of the air in the hallway, Kristin struggled to bring her mind back into focus. No easy task when her entire body trembled and screamed out for his touch.

His eyes closed and he turned his face away from her, but it was enough that she got the message loud and clear.

"I shouldn't have done that," he said quietly.

Her heart contracted at the words, shriveling, aching with confusion and doubt. "Regrets so soon. Wow, that's a record. Usually that doesn't come until the next morning." She could see that he was far from overwhelmed with lust for her. His breathing was nearly imperceptible, his pulse so rock steady, she couldn't even detect it. Her pulse and breathing were rapid and uneven as she tried to pull herself back together. For a brief moment it had all seemed so right, so utterly perfect. She'd never questioned that he might not feel the same way.

Boy, did I read that wrong. She knew she wasn't a whiz when it came to men. She'd been one of the boys so long that the minute one showed her attention like she was a girl, she usually jumped in with both feet. Well, she had both times they seemed sincere. Not only out for a good time. Dmitri was just so intense she'd mistaken it for something more.

"It's my fault." She scraped a shaking hand across her bangs, pushing them aside, along with any thoughts of how incredible he felt. "It was just a kiss. All right? No big deal." Her skin was still way too warm. Of course it was from embarrassment now, rather than a sizzling case of the hots. But if he could act as if it was no big deal, then so could she. All her life anything a guy could do, she could do better.

Dmitri locked his gaze with hers. She was dangerous to his carefully balanced world. Everything about her screamed "take me now."

Yet he'd clearly heard her say the words *don't* and *stop*.

Aroused and frustrated, Dmitri wanted to grab her and shake her. Hard. Then pick up right where they'd left off and sink into her. But he was a man of honor. Any kind of negative verbal response from a woman, no matter how many positive signals her body gave, meant he stopped what he was doing and pulled back.

Despite her very clear words, the signals she was throwing at him said anything but hands off, adding to his confusion. Hot cinnamon-tinted female arousal saturated the air so heavily he could have sworn he was in a damn bakery—in the oven, with the cinnamon rolls. His ears picked out the rapid, frantic beating of her blood rushing sweet and thick through her veins, and his fangs responded, pushing, begging for release—just like the rest of him.

Why wasn't she impacted by the flames that licked and raged through him? Saints! That was just a kiss? Hell. It had taken every ounce of his discipline and control not to take her there in the hallway. He blamed himself. He should know better. Being a vampire with a conscience sucked.

The very essence of him was programmed to change to suit her most intimate fantasy. Even the scent of a vampire altered to suit their quarry. They were the ultimate predator, perfectly designed to lure their victim. At least he'd mastered enough control over the centuries to keep his fangs at bay, no matter how aroused he was. As long as they stayed retracted, the venom couldn't flow.

He took a deep breath, more to calm his mind than fill his void, useless lungs. He'd practiced long and hard over the centuries to appear to the untrained human eye as though he were breathing, but sometimes, like now, he had to consciously think about it.

"I think it would be best if you went home now." The words stuck like bits of dirt and gravel in his throat. He forced his hands down to his sides and took a step away from her. Away from temptation. Her heat, her scent, the very rush of her pulse, were an insanely addictive drug he could barely resist.

The cool facade that dropped over her beautiful face hit him like a physical blow.

"Does the offer still stand to tell me about vampires?" She stepped around the shattered remains of her drink.

"Back to business, are we?"

She leveled her gaze at him, and her knuckles went white in the hand where she held her small clutch purse so tightly. "Yes."

"Of course the offer still stands."

"Then how about tomorrow night?"

"What would you like to do then?"

"An interview. With you. Here at the club."

"Agreed." He nodded. "Let me show you back inside."

She bit her lower lip and the rosy stain the pressure caused nearly drove him to his knees with blood lust.

"Do you have a back exit I could use instead?"

Rather than reply, he turned on his heel and led her down the hall. "Would you like me to walk you to your car or call a cab for you?"

She waved away his concern. "I should be fine." Clearly she had no sense of self-preservation.

First taunting a vampire, then venturing out into the dark alley alone. Either she was supremely confident or very naive. He opened the door, the odors of rancid meat and wet pavement from the dark alley wafting into the hallway on the night air.

She shivered, then glanced up at him. "See you tomorrow."

He stood there in the open door and watched her sweetly curved derriere outlined sinfully in red leather until she was safely out of the alley. How women in this day and age got away with dressing like that in public still astounded him, but that didn't mean he didn't appreciate the view.

And if Miss Reed thought the earliest she'd see him would be the next day she was sadly mistaken. When he'd found her in the company of Mayor McCallum, Dr. Chung, Balor and Paulson using an assumed name he'd wanted to rip the bouncer's throat out first, then theirs. Thankfully, he could tell by scent alone none of them had touched or drunk from her. None of them had marked her as his own.

If she were insistent on pursuing her investigation of the Bloodless Murders, he was going to have to keep a closer watch on her. Starting tonight.

Kristin drove home a little too fast, determined to write up her story while tonight's experience was still fresh in her memory. As soon as she walked in the door of her apartment she pushed the button on the microrecorder she'd hidden in her purse, rewinding it to the conversation in the tasting room.

There was something odd about those four men. Clearly something was going down with the CDC that had to do with contamination of some kind. And from the presence of Paulson and Dr. Chung, she'd bet her position at the paper that it had to do with the medical community.

And had her eyes been playing tricks on her? It looked like blood in the mayor's glass. It had even smelled like it. And the mayor looked awfully good for having stage-four cancer following a triple bypass two years ago.

She shimmied out of her silky top, leather skirt and heels and into a soft, much-washed dark blue

Mariners T-shirt three sizes too big that she'd gotten as a Christmas present from her dad several years ago. As she organized her quotes and massaged her aching feet, the first lines of the article started to trickle through her brain. She planted herself in front of her laptop. Her fingers flew, moving fast to keep up with her mind. She connected the pieces so they followed along in a logical path, plugging in quotes to make the assertions seem viable.

Two hours later, she scanned the story, looking for holes, looking for anything Hollander might shoot down. Everything seemed in order, but a funny, niggling sensation still tickled at the back of her neck.

If she hadn't spent the last two hours up to her eyeballs writing, she'd have sworn someone was watching her. Of course, every time she'd taken a sip of her diet cola and glanced around, she was still the same as she'd been for years. All alone.

She saved the file, both to the hard drive and her flash drive, then sent a copy to Hollander's email box. By the evening news tomorrow, the story of the mayor's fascination with vampirism and the willing donors at the club would be in black and white and read all over. So would the club's connection to the victims of the Bloodless Murders.

Satisfied she'd done the best she could, Kristin stretched, scraped her hair into a sloppy ponytail, brushed her teeth and fell into bed. Four hours' sleep was going to barely keep her alive tomorrow.

From the corner of the room, Dmitri waited until her breathing evened out before he moved. He'd had the ridiculous urge to pull the covers up over her, but knew it would be best if she didn't know he'd been watching over her shoulder all evening as she typed.

The intensity he'd seen in her had made a little bit of pride well up in him. He'd suspected her silly, bumbling persona was just a ruse. Her eyes had been too keen, her questions too sharp for him to believe she was a nitwit.

Her apartment confirmed his suspicions. No matter what games she played, or part she portrayed, or the sexy hint of cinnamon and vanilla that cloaked her skin, she was a serious person with a no-nonsense manner at the heart of things. Her utilitarian apartment didn't sport lacy frilly things or girlish fripperies.

The furniture was solid, the counters and table-tops clear of clutter, and the colors limited to blue and white. Instead of paintings or pictures, she had decorated the walls with newspapers enclosed in glass frames. He peered at the papers, recognizing an issue from the sinking of the *Titanic,* another from World War II and one from some small local paper.

The only picture he could find was on the night table by her alarm clock. It was of a clearly younger Kristin with an older man who had the same stubborn tilt to his chin she did.

He toyed with the idea of entering her dreams to see precisely what was running through her head. Without the intense concentration that blocked him before, it might be possible. He kneeled on the floor beside her bed, closed his eyes and reached into her mind.

Oddly enough she was still replaying the evening, especially their kiss in the hallway. Dmitri smiled. Perhaps she wasn't as immune to him as she'd seemed.

It was no difficult matter to twist the dream, making her clothing vanish and their actions go far beyond a mere kiss, to a full-fledged mating complete with him lapping at the blood coursing from a thin red line in her skin that caused her to orgasm over and over again.

She thrashed in the bed in front of him, her breathing fast, her nipples puckered and hard beneath the T-shirt. For an instant there was a flash of guilt. Dmitri shoved it away. Early training in the church still managed to suffuse his base reactions. But that time was passed. There was nothing wrong with her enjoying the sensations he could offer her. And nothing wrong with him enjoying them too.

She's quite beautiful.

Dmitri tensed at Roman's intrusion and glanced behind him. *What are you doing here, my laird?*

Roman, his shoulder propped up against the doorjamb, gave a smile, his elongated fangs tipping over his bottom lip. *Going out for dinner. What about you? She seems a tasty enough treat.*

She's a reporter that came to the club twice today. I've been watching her write up a story about blood fixations, the mayor and our club.

And was the article flattering?

Not really. Interesting in a juvenile manner. She really hasn't accepted that vampires exist.

Roman leaned forward to inspect a sleeping Kristin more closely, hunger flaring in his eyes. *Perhaps I ought to educate her.*

In a blink Dmitri was in front of him, a hand firmly on Roman's chest. *Leave this one to me. She's part of the assignment you and the council authorized. I'll see that she's dealt with and watched. This is my duty.*

Roman's tongue flicked over one of his fangs. *Do as you must, brother. I trust you'll enjoy this assignment. As for me, I believe I'll dine at the club tonight.*

In an instant he'd left the same way he'd come in, by the sliding glass door on her second-story balcony. Dmitri shifted his gaze from the billowing white curtains to Kristin.

The smooth pale arc of her cheek made the fan of brown lashes seem darker. She looked far too innocent, her flaxen hair bundled into a girlish ponytail, but her article would be like a match to a bonfire.

Of course there was no way he could let her

print the piece as it was. There was too much that she'd noticed about the mayor and the rest of that quartet and she'd obviously gotten a lot of people in the club to talk easily with her about what they did and why they were there.

He couldn't pull the story out of her editor's email. But he could write an article himself, casting aspersions on her reporting, and convince her editor with a little mind manipulation to run it side by side with hers.

She was going to be irate. He'd have to remember to have the fire extinguisher handy for his meeting tomorrow night. Considering what he now knew about Kristin's true nature, sparks were likely to fly and cause a full-out conflagration once she realized what he'd done.

Satisfied that she was safe until the morning light, Dmitri gave her one last lingering glance before he let himself out onto the balcony. He carefully shut and locked the sliding glass door behind him from the outside with a flick of his mind. Then he stepped up to the railing and jumped into the night.

Chapter 4

Kristin strode into the newsroom, snagging a chocolate-glazed doughnut with sprinkles on the way to Hollander's office. Turning in a knockout story put an extra bounce in her step.

Sometimes hitting a home run with a story was better than sex. Okay, she decided, wiping sprinkles off her lips and going in for another chocolaty bite, perhaps better than *average* sex.

After the kiss in the hallway last night, she was certain that nothing Dmitri Dionotte did would fall in the average category. It would be extraordinary, supernova fantastic. That was if he was still even interested in her.

Good Lord! She was thinking about having sex with a virtual stranger. There was just something about him that drew her like a meteorite going down in flames into the gravitational pull of a planet. Of course, there was always the possibility she wouldn't survive something that white-hot.

She took another gooey bite of her doughnut and hit the cream filling inside.

After last night she doubted she'd have the chance to find out. One minute he couldn't get enough, and the next he was pushing her away as if she'd said or done something unforgivable. She preferred her life to be simple. Dmitri was anything but simple. He was dark and complex, and she suspected, far too experienced for her tastes. Better to focus on today's win than last night's loss.

She rapped at the open door. Hollander's bald head caught the light as he looked up. Annoyance for the interruption switched to approval when he saw her hovering at the door. With what he thought passed for a smile, he beckoned her inside. He rose, opening his arms wide. "There she is. My star reporter."

A little shimmer of satisfaction and pride blossomed in Kristin's chest as she approached his desk. She glanced at a towering pile of file folders and days-old newspapers nestled in the only other chair and decided against moving it just to sit for a moment. Instead, she rested her hip up against Hollander's desk.

"So you liked the piece?" It wasn't gloating. Sometimes a girl needed to hear she'd done a great job—especially when she worked for a guy like Hollander. He could be an abrasive perfectionist, an I-dotter and T-crosser, with no tolerance for error or half-baked reporting.

"You nailed it."

"Did it land above the fold?" Front-page placement where everyone could see your byline was the gold star she was aiming for. Hollander looked away and her gut toppled from golden-yummy glow to sour and squishy.

"It was good, I give you that. Good enough for the front of the op-ed section in tonight's edition."

"Op-ed!" The damn doughnut flew out of her hand as Kristin gestured with frustration. She watched it skitter across his desk, leaving a trail of chocolate icing and cream filling. She tried to quell her disappointment over the story placement and the loss of her doughnut.

"That was a solid piece, not opinion." And apparently, *not good enough.* Again. "It should've at least made the news section and you know it."

Hollander's fleshy mouth transformed into a flat line as he scooped the doughnut with the edge of a piece of paper into his trash can. "First of all, Reed, I don't have to explain my decisions to you."

Whoa. Time to back up a pace. "Granted," she said, striving to keep the disappointment from her voice. "But I'd still like to know why."

"Something else came in early this morning that was a direct contrast to your piece. Thought the two-dogs-over-one-bone setup might pump up reader interest, so I ran them side by side in the opinions section."

Someone else at the paper must have thought her idea wasn't that lame in the meeting or they wouldn't have been writing about vampires. Bradley? He was sneaky enough to try something like that. "I thought you didn't even want to run a piece on vampires, and now you're telling me you ran two?"

"It's popular culture. Latest fads and what people think of them, why they get into them. How far they're willing to go into their fantasy. Fascinating stuff. Readers will eat it up."

Kristin locked her gaze with her editor. "Who was the other reporter?"

"Freelancer. Dmitri Dionotte."

A sizzle of anger and heat speared through her, splitting her in two. She'd let that jackass kiss her, touch her, when all the while he'd been planning to undercut her with an article to her very own paper. He was devious, hot, underhanded, hot, completely untrustworthy, hot, and in for a big piece of her mind. He'd stolen her story idea plain and simple. *Dammit.*

Kristin didn't even bother to respond when Hollander yelled for her to turn in another home run by tomorrow's deadline as she stalked out of his office.

Twenty minutes later she was sitting outside Sangria still fuming. "Low-down, rotten..." She threw a withering glance at the closed door as she climbed out of her car. Taking a deep breath, she pushed on the club door. Locked.

That snapped a little of the wind out of her self-righteous sails. Of course the club wasn't open at nine-thirty in the morning. Confronting Dmitri would have to wait until tonight. Which wasn't nearly soon enough.

She strolled in from the night as if she owned the place, her long legs encased in tight dark denim finished off with black high-heeled boots. A soft red sweater skimmed the swell of her breasts and slouched off one shoulder, exposing so much of her neck and collarbone that it screamed vampire bait. She looked sexy as hell and decidedly pissed as she scanned the semicrowded room. Dmitri hid a smile.

It was a good crowd for a Thursday night. Too early for most of his clientele, but enough people to make Kristin have to work at finding him in the darkened room as he sat at the bar.

He'd anticipated her anger. In truth, he'd counted on it. She stalked straight toward him, a delicious pink suffusing her skin. He felt the throb of her blood, heard the thudding as her heart pounded in both anger and anticipation. A surprising mix of hunger and lust rumbled deep in his gut. He hadn't been prepared for *that*.

He shoved the sensation away, focusing instead on the intensity of her blue eyes. *"Ciao, bellissima."* He didn't dare move from his seat at the bar. In this agitated state, he'd likely move too fast and scare her.

She tossed her purse onto the bar and glared at him as she slid onto the bar stool, bringing them eye to eye. Lightning flashed in their depths as she leaned forward. "Why'd you do it?"

"Perhaps if I knew what the accusation was regarding?" he murmured coolly, picking up his glass to drink. Her gaze flicked to the red liquid for an instant before locking onto his face once more.

"The article you wrote for *my* paper."

"Ah." He set the glass down, running his finger around the rim of the crystal and making it sing.

She crossed her long legs, her booted foot bouncing with impatience. "When did you develop an interest in journalism?"

He fixated on her eyes. Cobalt blue rimmed in a darker blue the color of a midsummer midnight sky on the edges of her irises. The artists of the Renaissance would have been enchanted with her. "About the same time I met a journalist worth being interested in."

She seemed to soften under his stare. He could easily call her to him, make her forget every other thought in her mind if he willed it. But that was a game for other vampires. Dmitri broke the lingering gaze between them. Until now he'd successfully avoided having any kind of infatuation with mortal or vampire, a kind of self-inflicted penance for being something he'd never wanted to be.

She brushed the wispy bangs from her eyes, her fingertips resting against her forehead. "Look, I don't try and run your club, so I'm asking you nicely—butt out of my newspaper."

This softer side of her rattled him, bringing out protective urges he didn't need or want. Having her angry with him, active and vibrant, was much easier. He couldn't resist the urge to goad her. "*Your* paper, is it? Funny. Hollander seemed to be the one in charge, and he liked my article well enough to run it today."

The heated tint returned to her skin and with it, his own blood lust. Her eyes sparkled with challenge, reflecting the flash and strobe of the lights off the dance floor. There, that was better.

"This is my job. This is what I was born to do, and if you think I'm going to let you louse it up, you're in for a big surprise, buddy boy."

"I thought you might react like this." He picked up the glass and took another sip. The packaged blood barely took the edge off his increasing thirst. The scent of cinnamon that cloaked the air around her was hotter, spicier than he recalled. He remembered what it had felt like for his heart to pound at the sight of a beautiful woman. Remembered it only intellectually. His ribs curled around a cold stone replica of what remained of his actual heart. But his sexual interest in this woman was startling, and not welcomed. Not here. Not now. And not her.

"Angry. You bet."

"I was thinking irrational, but angry works too."

"Irrational? How about we stick to the facts

here. Fact one, you knew I was working on a vampire story. Fact two, you undercut me."

She was fighting the anger, trying to be rational, striving for calm. But he could feel her frustration and aggravation vibrating in the air, spiking it with the hint of pepper. "I see." And he did. She was all about the job, just like him. Focused. Dedicated. And not about to have anyone, particularly him, undercut her or stop her upward climb at the newspaper. "So you're afraid of a little friendly competition," Dmitri needled.

Kristin huffed. "If this is how you treat your friends, remind me never to sign up to be one."

He threw her a thousand-watt fangless smile. "Would you like a drink?"

"Is that supposed to be some kind of apology or a peace offering?"

"It can be both, if you like."

Her shoulders relaxed and Dmitri found he couldn't resist the urge to touch her. He grasped her hand and began massaging small circles into her palm. Her skin was hot and a thousand times softer than silk under his sensitive fingers.

"Why *did* you do it?"

"Maybe I wanted to get your attention."

She snorted and glanced away for a moment, clearly uncertain what to do with his obvious interest. "I doubt you have to work to get most women to pay attention to you."

"Ah, but you aren't most women, are you?"

Her eyes narrowed, raking over him, assessing him. Appreciation was there. So was desire. Despite her rejection of his advances the night before, she was as intoxicated by him as he was by her. Ultimately it could come to no good. It was just one of the reasons many vampires didn't often choose a mortal mate.

"So where do we go from here?" she asked, her tone betraying her warring interest and distrust.

"That depends entirely on you."

Kristin got the feeling from the way he was looking at her that he was talking about far more than just her investigation or the article. His eyes were hot melted chocolate, and she had the completely irrational desire to dip herself into them. Hell, he even smelled like dark chocolate. He was far too rich for her blood. Kristin tried to think of all the reasons she should abstain from chocolate.

And sexy men. And competitors in the newspaper business.

It was going to be hard to stay away from Dmitri because she needed him. Needed him for this story. The story she hoped would win her the coveted Pulitzer, let alone the front-page-above-the-fold position that was quickly becoming a subsection of her holy grail.

"Look," she said evenly, keeping her eyes on his nose instead of drowning in chocolate or looking lower to his all-too-sexy mouth. "We can help each other. You obviously have a thriving club here. But who would say no to more business? A bigger crowd? I can do that for you. Stir up interest in vampires, make people curious enough to come and see for themselves how this is all so—" she waved a hand vaguely "—interesting. You know more about what's going on with this subculture than anyone else I've run into. What's the harm if I give you a little coverage?"

He didn't answer right away, just gazed at her, which unnerved her. She'd never had a man look at her so intently before. "People are threatened by things they don't understand."

"So basically you're saying you'd rather people didn't know the truth."

"That's not what I said at all. Obviously I need to be a bit more specific for you." He leaned in closer, crowding into her space and bringing his sexy mouth far too close for her comfort. Her skin suddenly seemed a size too small and her lips tingled. "You're meddling in things you can't possibly understand. You could get hurt. And I'd like to avoid having that on my conscience."

Kristin snatched up her purse. She was still boiling mad that he'd gotten her bumped to the opinion page, and a bit pissed at herself for being so undeniably attracted to the guy. There was only so much civility she could muster, especially when he was blocking her access to another story and tampering with her libido. "You know, under that slick cultured exterior you're a Neanderthal just like the rest of them."

His eyes narrowed dangerously. "Them who?"

"Men. You think you can take whatever it is you want, do whatever it is you want, and womankind is just supposed to step aside and let you because of your—" She sputtered, waving her hand in the general direction of his groin. "That. Well, news flash. Male or not, I'm good enough at my job to be able to find out what I need to know with or without your help."

Faster than she could blink, Dmitri had her hard up against him, his arms locked around her in a way that made everything within her squirm.

"What do you—" she shoved at his hands "—think—" she pulled at his fingers "—you're—" she dug into him with her fingernails "—doing?" Nothing worked.

She glared up at him, but his face was perfectly smooth, his manner unruffled, as if she was no more than a kitten fidgeting about in his grasp. His dark eyes seemed to deepen, widen, sucking her in and making everything else in the room fade away.

"I'm keeping you from making the most dangerous mistake of your life. Listen to me. You're going to go home now. You're going to leave the Bloodless Murders up to the authorities to figure out, and you are going to stop writing nonsense about vampires."

She blinked. Then giggled. "I'm sorry, I don't

mean to mess up your macho-guy routine, but that isn't going to work on me. I'm going to do whatever it takes to do my job, and you can't stop me." Hell. The glamour had been completely ineffective on her. Her mind was far stronger than he'd anticipated.

His arms slackened enough that she was able to pull out of his hold and walk away. She glanced back, but the bar stool where Dmitri had been only an instant before now sat vacant.

"What did you expect, Sunshine?" she muttered to herself, using her dad's favorite pet name for her. "You wanted weird, you got weird." She shook her head and made for the door.

The crowd pushed in and a large man dressed in a black leather duster and sporting a shock of brilliant, nearly platinum-blond spiked hair and startling red eyes, knocked into her shoulder. She stumbled back a step with the force of the blow and went down, landing on her butt.

He turned, offering her a long tapered hand. "Sorry, my apologies." He pulled her to her feet, then gave her a quick nod, before disappearing into the crowd, his long duster blending in with people dancing and swaying to the music.

She moved to brush herself off and realized there was a crumpled slip of paper tucked into her hand. The guy had slipped it to her when he'd helped her up.

Kristin spun around, searching for his distinctive hair somewhere in the crowd. How many Billy Idol look-alikes could there be in this bar? Like Dmitri, he was nowhere to be seen.

That was until she turned around to face the door. Dmitri suddenly stood between her and the exit. To say he blocked her way wasn't accurate. He was bigger than any linebacker she'd seen in the NFL. There was no way around him. She instantly moved her hand with the note behind her back, not trusting him as far as she could throw him.

"Let me see it."

She cocked her head to one side. "See what?"

He peered at her, his eyes boring into hers. "The note in your hand."

"What are you talking about?"

"*Tsk, tsk.* Really, Miss Reed, lying hardly becomes you." He'd captured her hand before she had time to take another breath and had pried it open, despite her best efforts to keep it clamped onto the scrap of paper. His touch burned like ice, and made her shiver.

"Let's see what your secret admirer had to say."

Kristin rose up on her toes to read over his substantial bicep.

WANT THE TRUTH? FIND WHAT YOU'RE LOOKING FOR. Below that was an address to the industrial section of town.

He growled. Literally growled.

Kristin inched away from him and closer to the door.

"Where, precisely, do you think you're going?" He wasn't even looking at her when he said it.

"Me? Home."

He spun around and grasped her wrist firmly. "I may not know you well, but I know you well enough to know you have every intention of going to that address at the first opportunity."

Kristin glanced at her cell phone. "It's ten-thirty and that address is in the industrial section of town. Just how stupid do you think I am?"

"Not stupid. Hungry. You want to break a story so badly you'd probably sell your dog to get it."

"I don't have a dog."

His mouth lifted at the corner in a mocking grin she suddenly had the urge to smack off his face. "And I didn't sell him either," she added.

"Regardless, I'm going with you."

"Oh, no. You screwed me out of a front-page slot once, buddy boy. I'm not letting you do it again."

"So you're afraid that if I sent in an article to Mr. Hollander he'd choose mine over yours this time?"

Kristin snorted. "Not a chance." Deep down he'd hit a sore spot. She knew she was a good writer. That wasn't the problem. But was she better than Dmitri? She hadn't even had the chance to see what he'd turned in that had tackled Hollander's good sense.

"Let's call a truce. We'll go together and each write our own story. Then let Hollander decide. May the best man, or woman, win."

"I don't partner up."

"Obviously."

"What's that supposed to mean?"

He raised a brow as if to say, *I have to explain it to you? My, you are in dire straits.*

Kristin huffed. "All it means is this series is my baby. I'm doing the work, so I'm taking the credit," she said.

Dmitri put up a hand in mock defense. "By all means. I'm just going along for the ride to make sure nothing strange out there is more than you can handle."

"Because you're supernatural yourself?"

He stared at her.

Kristin pushed past her anger and worry. As badly as she wanted to give him the slip and go to the address, she knew going alone would be risky. "Fine, but you don't get in my way and I won't get in yours. Deal?"

"Agreed."

"And I get to drive."

Something flashed in his eyes, then quickly disappeared, making her heart pump a little harder. "If that is what is required," he said.

"Good. I'll meet you out front."

He didn't let go of her hand. Kristin glanced

down. "You can let go of me. I said we could go together."

She looked up and met an unwavering dark gaze. "I do not take you for a fool, Miss Reed. Please do not mistake me for one."

His hand around her wrist, he walked her out to her car, his touch sending arcs of electricity zinging up her arm with every fast-paced beat of her heart.

By the time she'd driven there, and left a message on Hollander's voice mail, giving him an update, it was eleven. The temperature down by the docks was noticeably cooler and tinged with the smell of kelp and fish wafting off the water. She shrugged deeper into her coat.

Using the small flashlight she kept in her car's glove compartment, she completed a quick scan of the warehouse building, confirming she had the right address. "This looks like the place, but I don't see anything." She crumpled the slip of paper in her hand. She hated leads that didn't pan out. "What a waste of time," she muttered.

She glanced at Dmitri. His gaze was fixated on a dark corner of the building facing the narrow gap between two warehouses. Kristin threw a beam of light in that direction.

That's when she saw the foot.

A pair of scuffed business shoes peeked out from the alley, the toes pointed toward the sky. Kristin swallowed the hot acidic spurt of bile in the back of her throat. She seriously doubted that they were attached to a homeless person sleeping it off, but she hoped anyway.

"Excuse me? Hello?" No answer.

"He's dead," Dmitri said flatly.

"Thanks, Sherlock. I think I figured that out." She crept closer, her flashlight in front of her, her gaze darting around and scrutinizing every shadow.

Trailing the orb of light from his feet up to his face, Kristin gave a sharp squeak of recognition. Mathew Balor, the man from the CDC, the one who'd been in the mayor's little quartet, stared blankly at nothing, his mouth slightly open in a rictus of pain, his skin a bloodless waxy white.

Oh, God. Oh, God. What do I do?

"You recognize him."

"Yes. From the club. He was with the mayor."

Dmitri stiffened.

The man's button-down shirt lay loosely closed, but sank inward. Kristin could tell without even checking that his body had been opened and now sat like an empty husk, drained of blood and missing his organs just like the other victims of the Bloodless Murders. She slapped a hand over her mouth to stem the gag reflex kicking in hard.

"What is that?" Dmitri pointed at Balor's face. An odd flash of white in his mouth drew her attention.

Dmitri carefully sidestepped closer to Balor's body.

"Don't touch it!" Kristin demanded. "You're messing with a crime scene."

He threw her a wry glance, then plucked the piece of folded paper out of Balor's mouth. "Trust me, Balor isn't going to mind. If someone went to the trouble of inviting you here, you might as well know why."

He handed her the paper. With shaking fingers she opened it.

Chapter 5

WANT TO KNOW WHAT STARTED THIS SPREE? ASK YOUR BOYFRIEND, KRISTIN.

The salty tang in the air seemed sharper, more sinister, as she sucked in a startled breath. She pressed a fist to the icy chill lodged in her lungs. "Holy crap—" The murderer knew her.

"Wait. What boyfriend?" Clearly they didn't know her *that* well.

Dmitri cleared his throat. "I believe the note is referring to me."

"You're neither a boy nor a friend," she pointed out with asperity. If someone had been spying on them, though, he or she might have taken the relationship as a given.

Whatever had flared up between them in the club last night couldn't be relied on to protect her against the personal well-wishes of the psycho responsible for the Bloodless Murders. The police wouldn't be happy if they knew the crime scene had been tampered with. Still, she was grateful that it was Dmitri, and not the police, who'd found and read the note, which clearly involved her in the murder.

"We need to call the police. But before we do, I want some photos of the crime scene." There was no telling if she was missing an important detail because this entire scene had her on edge. Kristin stuffed the note into her pocket, trying very hard not to think about where it had just been. She flipped open her phone and started snapping pictures.

Dmitri didn't need pictures to tell him precisely what had happened. He tasted the air. Three, possibly four, unfamiliar vampires had been present in the alley in the last hour. Border reivers. There was no sign they lay in waiting. Had they been, Kristin would've been dead before she'd ever read the note.

The image of her bloodless body, ripped apart, left him feeling hollow. If he'd been mortal he'd be in a cold sweat. As it was, he had to force himself to continue to appear as though he were breathing. He would not, could not, allow harm to come to her. Especially from his own kind.

Looking down the long narrow slice of darkness, he telescoped his vision so that he could see tiny details invisible to the human eye. He easily read yesterday's date on a crumpled newspaper a hundred feet away, and observed the slide of a rat's tail in the stygian darkness beside a Dumpster. The dark was no barrier to his vision, in fact it made it easier to see. Objects appeared refined and clearer.

He focused his thoughts on Roman. *There's been another slaying, my laird. Not one of ours. Three, possibly four, unknown assailants.*

Have you contacted the mortal authorities?

Not yet.

Good. Bring the body to us.

That's a little more complicated. I have a mortal with me.

Alive?

Yes. The reporter.

By all means, bring her with you.

Dmitri glanced at her. She'd have to change that damn sexy red come-eat-me sweater that barely clung to her shoulders and breasts. There was no way he'd take her to their clan, let alone the council, with so much of her exposed. It would be like bringing in a platter of desserts to a party and refusing to let anyone have a bite.

Are you certain that it's wise?

Come now, Dmitri, we're civilized enough not to pounce on her.

Dmitri bristled. He'd seen the look in Roman's eye that night in Kristin's room. By all the saints, he'd felt his own fangs slip through the folds of his soft gum tissue, extending with aching thirst. He could barely resist the radiant, sweet cinnamon confection under her delicately pinked skin. How could he expect the others not to want to feed? Saints, he needed a drink.

The difference was, in their clan, intellect reigned over instinct. By the look of the corpse, the killer had held no such illusions about the symbiotic relationship between mortal and vampire. They were the kind who saw mortals as foil juice pouches to pierce, drain and toss away.

"Earth to Dmitri?" There was an edge of irritation to her tone.

His gaze snapped to meet her eyes. He put up his hand to silence her. She froze in place, her brows pressing together at the center. All his instincts were balanced on a razor's edge. Listening. Tracking a scent. One of the reiver vampires had returned.

She sighed, fisting a hand on her hip, annoyance scenting the air with a kick of pepper. "You can't avoid my question by ignoring it. Look, you're the local vampire expert here. Is this something a vampire wannabe could have done?"

Her voice sounded far away as he concentrated on the subtle movements of the vampire crouched against the dark roofline of the neighboring warehouse.

"No. Not an impostor. The real thing. Get down. Now." He shoved her to the pavement behind him none too gently.

With an inhuman shriek, the vampire sprang from the shadows. His red eyes glowed in the night like a wild creature spat out of hell, fangs bared, dark hair flying.

Dmitri tore the large silver dagger from the sheath on his thigh, its tip dripping sluggish brown-red liquid, and lunged at his attacker. Behind him Kristin muffled a scream.

The attacker dodged the knife, and landed with a deft tuck and roll on the pavement before bouncing up to the balls of his feet. "I see we've gotten your attention," the vampire said. The deep graveled voice of a three-hundred-year-old chain-smoker seemed at odds with his twenty-something appearance. He circled, his red gaze darting from Dmitri to Kristin.

"You're trespassing." Dmitri growled low, shifted his blade to the other hand, making sure he stayed between the vamp and Kristin.

"Perhaps. Perhaps we've come to challenge you for rights to the territory."

"With four of you? That's hardly a force to be reckoned with," Dmitri taunted.

"Four?" The man laughed. Caustic. Haughty. "We've many more than that. With more arriving every day. More being *created* every day.

Maybe I'll turn your girlfriend next—and you can watch."

Flick. Dmitri's fangs descended instantly. Almond-flavored venom swirled heavy and thick over his tongue.

He lunged for the reiver.

The vampire grabbed Dmitri's wrist with one hand, stopping the blade an inch from his eye. The liquid on the blade dripped on his alabaster skin, burning a red tearlike streak down the vamp's cheek that made the skin bubble and blister.

"That's dead man's blood on my blade," Dmitri growled through his fangs, his own eyes blazing as he forced his blade a millimeter closer to the man's eye. "One nick is all I need to take you down."

The vampire hissed, venom dripping clear and thick from his fangs as they grappled with each other. "I'd like to see you try," he spat as he twisted Dmitri's wrist, making the bones crackle.

Dmitri pulled back hard and snapped a kick at the vampire's chin, sending his dark head flying back with a sharp crack. His body crashed into the warehouse, leaving a dent the size of a small truck in the metal sheeting. Flipping the blade to his undamaged hand, Dmitri dove forward, but the attacker leaped to the top of the warehouse in one fluid movement.

"You've grown slow and weak," the man taunted. "A product of your clan's deviant ways. You've forgotten who's at the head of the food chain. Now it's going to cost you."

With a roar, Dmitri leaped to the roof. A fist, sledgehammer solid, caught him in the side of the head. His vision blurred, doubling for an instant.

He tucked his chin down and plowed forward, head butting the vampire and sending him staggering backward. The fiend skittered down the angle of the roof, jumping off the edge to land neatly on the pavement below.

He glanced upward at Dmitri and grinned, his fangs flashing too white in the darkness. "Shall I take her now or later?" he called up, becoming a blur as he made a dash for Kristin.

Dmitri took a flying leap and landed, feet solid, in the vampire's path before he could reach her. He slashed hard at the reiver's chest. The other vampire cursed, then glanced down at his gaping shirt and the dark line splitting his pale skin. Vampire ichor, black and thin as ink, dribbled from the cut. The skin around the wound began to pucker, blackening and curling away from the slice like burning paper.

Outraged, the vampire gasped before he fell to his knees. Dead man's blood acted as a swift-moving poison and would immobilize a vampire for hours, but one had to pierce the skin to activate it. The silver of the dagger only sealed the deal.

"Valuing human choice is not weakness," Dmitri said, sheathing his dagger. "Denying it is not strength."

The vampire glared up at him, his eyes red maliciousness. "Make no mistake, vampire. Your clan will fall to us." The last word turned to a hiss as he passed out at Dmitri's feet.

Kristin emerged from behind a stack of wooden crates against the building and stared at the reiver, her face pale and hands shaking. "How'd you jum—" Her face puckered as she glanced at the fangs retracting on the unconscious man.

"They're real. Holy crap. Vampires are real." Her words came out as a rasping breath. When she looked up at him her eyes were glassy and unfocused. "And you're one of them."

Her eyes widened a moment before they rolled back and her knees gave way. He caught her as she began to crumple and gently lowered her to the pavement, her head relaxed against his chest.

The smooth white column of her neck and curve of her collarbone lay exposed by her slouching sweater. It took everything within him, every shred of mortal mentality that remained locked inside his agile brain, not to give in. The primitive urge to taste the hot vanilla-cinnamon mixture rushing through those delicate little blue veins pounded in him like a heartbeat.

Dmitri forced his fangs to retract, then swallowed hard against the demanding dust-dry sensation in the back of his throat. He would feed later, but not from her.

Her eyes fluttered, as did her light, sweet heartbeat. He pushed her upright with a gentle hand. "Tuck your head between your knees. Now breathe."

"Maybe I should go home now."

That was humorous. Was any place safe if these reivers were intent on preying on a frail, all-too-mortal human? Especially if they were already leading her on a game of cat and mouse, where she would be the especially tender mouse.

"I think it would be best if you came with me."

"Back to the club?"

"No. To the clan."

She scrambled to her feet. "Oh, my God. I mean, I thought that you might have a vampire fetish when I saw you drinking that stuff tonight, but I never dreamed you really *were* one. Why haven't I seen your fangs before? Would you show me? You're going to take me to a bunch of real vampires?"

Saints preserve him. Did she always tend to prattle when she was nervous? "First, fangs aren't something we normally just whip out in public for display. It would be better if you didn't ask any of the others to do so, unless you're inviting them to taste you. Second, the clan is the safest place you can be at the moment."

"Surrounded by bloodsuckers?"

He arched a dark brow. Clearly she didn't know just how offensive that sounded. "The vampires who did this wouldn't dare try to hunt you there. This one—" he nudged the unconscious vampire with his toe "—and the others who did this, are not from my clan. They're reivers hunting uninvited in our territory."

"They're hunting me?" she squeaked. "Why? I haven't done anything!"

"You know about them. You're investigating the murders. That's enough. And they may not be hunting you. You just may be the bait for something larger they have planned."

"Vampires are real. Who would've believed it?" She sounded a bit breathless. Likely shock, he thought.

"Well, now that you are aware of the truth, it would be foolish of you not to investigate it thoroughly."

She nodded vigorously. "I'm ready."

Dmitri eyed the red sweater. "Not quite." He snapped his fingers and her racy sweater phased away, replaced by a black cashmere turtleneck.

"Much better. And safer. Best not to make an offer you don't intend."

Kristin held a hand to her throat. "Oh. I guess you're right. Hey, how did you do that, and the jumping thing?"

"Ask me later." Dmitri held out his hand and Kristin slipped her much smaller one into his. Her show of trust humbled him. For a moment he was shocked by how fragile she seemed. So breakable, so mortal. He could hear the shushing of her blood in her veins and feel the fast throb of her heartbeat in her fingertips. Heat and need flared in him. "You may want to hold on tight. And close your eyes."

As difficult as it was, he focused his thoughts away from her and instead on the clan headquarters, transporting them to his suite of rooms, the unconscious vampire directly to the clan detention center, and Balor's body to the clan medical facilities. The familiar suck and pull at his midsection took over.

Her entire body became rigid and tight against him as they transported. She peeked through a slit in her tightly clenched eyes the second they arrived, then opened them both wide. "How'd you do that?"

He smiled at the wonder that lit her eyes from the inside, then stepped away from her and edged toward the bar. An invisible fist squeezed his chest. It had been a long time since anyone had gazed at him with anything close to admiration.

"Vampires have a lot of skills. Phasing and transporting seem instantaneous to you because we move so quickly and can materialize physical objects by calling them into being."

"Like magic."

Too bad her admiration was misplaced. "Hardly. If it were magic we wouldn't get so damn thirsty."

Kristin pulled the edge of her turtleneck up a little higher. "Have you had dinner yet?"

"No, but you aren't even on the menu."

"I'm relieved to hear it," she muttered, looking around. For all she knew they could have been at any high-rent condo downtown. Only one major difference stood out. There were no windows.

Adorning the rich burgundy walls were beautiful landscapes lush with color, and stunning black-and-white photography of Notre Dame and some nameless cathedral or abbey in what looked like the wilds of Scotland. Even an enormous flat-screen television. But no windows.

Dmitri poured himself a glass of thick dark crimson liquid. He glanced at her. "Did you want something to drink?"

She stared at his glass and shuddered, her stomach swishing uncomfortably. "No. Not unless you've got some diet cola around somewhere."

He held out his hand and a can of her favorite drink materialized along with a glass. She gasped a little breath. The corner of his sexy mouth tipped upward in amusement.

"Did you want ice with that?"

She nodded as her feet moved of their own accord toward the bar. Cubes of ice clinked into the glass from out of thin air as if dispensed from some invisible machine overhead.

"Wow. I guess being a vampire comes with some serious perks."

"And serious costs." The cola fizzed and foamed as he poured it over the ice cubes and handed her the glass.

Kristin took a sip. It was perfect. Of course it was perfect, everything around her seemed almost too perfect, which made it seem…weird. Like someone was trying too hard.

There wasn't a speck of dust to be found on the solid wooden mission-style furniture or a hint of dusty-bunny action on the dark wood floors. Even the stained-glass shades on the lamps seemed dustproof.

"Where are we? Still in the city?"

"Not in the city. Under it."

"Under Seattle?"

He gave her a lazy smile. "Tourists aren't the only ones who use the abandoned parts of the city beneath your feet."

"But I've taken the Underground Tour of Seattle. There's nothing down there but a bunch of old storefronts, dusty cobwebs and rusted-out antiques."

"And doors."

"Yeah, a bunch of— Wait, you're telling me that one of those doors leads to your lair?"

"Clan."

"I thought it was called a nest."

"Vampires who nest in mated pairs and small groups are closer to their feral nature. Uncivilized. One thing you may as well realize now is that not all vampires are the same. Some of us value mortals. Others don't. Civilized vampires live in a clan, like the one we have here."

"But how—"

"We were here when Seattle burned in the late 1880s, living among the settlers like anyone else. And when more than twenty-five city blocks burned to the ground and people wanted to re-build, we helped them—and ourselves."

"So you have, like, a whole city to yourself down here?"

"Our very own version of Seattle." He tipped back the remaining red dregs in his glass and drained it.

"Wait until Hollander hears about this!"

He grasped her hand as she was about to take a sip of her drink. His touch sent sparks shooting up her arm, making her warm all over. "How about you wait to file that story until I can show you around a bit more? That way you'll have all the facts."

Kristin nodded. "Okay. I can wait a few hours. Where are you going?"

"I need to confer with our leaders on what to do with the vampire we encountered."

"What'd you do to him anyway?"

"Just transported him here, as I did you. He hasn't been harmed. The poison should be wearing off in an hour or three."

"Can I come wi—"

Dmitri held up a hand, cutting her off. "Just stay here. And don't do anything stupid. I'll be back in a half hour. Find something to entertain yourself. The remote to the television is on the coffee table and I'm sure there's a movie or two you could watch."

Kristin damn well knew that nothing, not even a speck of dust, let alone the remote, had been on the coffee table when she'd last looked at it. But when she glanced over her shoulder there it was. And as she watched, a bowl of popcorn materialized as well. She glanced back over her shoulder, but Dmitri had already disappeared.

The hot buttery smell of it made her stomach rumble. One chocolate doughnut and a cream-cheese bagel didn't hold a girl over. What time was it anyway? She looked for a clock to check the time and found there wasn't one. Anywhere. Kristin flipped open her phone. There wasn't any reception, but the clock read five after midnight. Perfect timing for a midnight snack.

She walked over and plunked herself down on the couch. For as solid as it looked, it was surprisingly comfortable. She snuggled in and picked up the remote. The television flickered to life. Kristin reached forward and grabbed a handful of popcorn, popping it into her mouth.

One minute she was looking at the TV, and the next at a golden mountain of a man. With fangs.

The popcorn stuck uncomfortably in her throat. She scooted back into the depths of the couch. "Who are you?"

He sniffed the air appreciatively, his green eyes glittering in a way that made her stomach drop to her shoes. "And, who, my delicious little morsel, are you?"

Chapter 6

"Not yours." The distinct Italian lilt of Dmitri's voice flooded her system with relief.

He phased in beside the strange vampire, his form at first a swirl of dark smoke, which suddenly transformed into solid muscle and bone and that dark gaze that stole her breath away. Dmitri's dark hair and olive complexion created a direct contrast to the blond locks and bronzed skin of the intruder beside him.

He shot the other vampire a cool glance. "I'll thank you not to frighten my guest, Achilles."

"Guest? You're certain she's not takeout?" He snapped his teeth and Kristin flinched. He chuckled.

"Stop that. Can't you see she's been through enough tonight?"

Achilles gave her a wicked grin. "She doesn't look too scared. You don't find me scary in the least, do you?" he purred like a giant cat, powerful, beautiful and radiating a deadly grace that Kristin could feel saturating the air. "You find me fascinating."

It was as though he was trying to hypnotize her. Distinctly uncomfortable, she glanced away. "Has anyone ever told you that you look a lot like Brad Pitt in the movie *Troy?*" Kristin said.

He moved closer. "Who do you think he copied, sweetling?" Dmitri shoved him aside and sat down beside her, putting his arm over the back of the couch, his fingers brushing her nape before he lay his arm on the cushion behind her. A silent signal from one male to another. Territory staked. Back off.

Despite the fact that normally she found such male posing annoying, at the moment she took a certain comfort in Dmitri's possessive posturing. In fact, small sparks started firing all over Kristin's skin, just having Dmitri close.

"Achilles was just leaving." Dmitri's tone matched the warning look in his eyes.

"I could stay—"

"Say goodbye, *amico*."

Achilles ignored him to give her a good-natured wink. "If he is too pious for you, come find me. *Ciao,* sweetling."

He disappeared like a hologram image, there one moment, gone the next.

"Who was that?"

"My *tutore*. Mentor, teacher."

"That's a mentor?" He looked ten years younger than the man beside her.

Dmitri shrugged. "He's about a thousand years older than I am. Not that he ever acts his age. He was assigned to guide me through the change and instruct me in the ways of our kind. He likes to follow current trends, no matter how things change. But be warned, *tesoro*, Achilles plays at seducing women the same way old men in the park play chess. It's all about out maneuvering your opponent and reaching checkmate first."

"So you're warning him off—"

Dmitri removed his arm from the back of the

couch, irritation rolling off him. "Probably not the smartest move. He'll take it as a challenge and try harder."

"Great."

His eyes bored into hers and suddenly the room smelled like the inside of a dark-chocolate bar and something even more seductive, sucking her in, setting off all her senses at once.

"You don't have anything to fear. I'll make certain of it."

She swallowed. She should be frightened of him. The strength of her reaction to him made no logical sense. It was as though he exhaled sex appeal. She leaned in closer to him, against every logical impulse that stammered in her brain.

"So, your mentor showed up here because…" She was close enough now that she could feel the heat of her breath bouncing off him. Her body squirmed. Tightened. Her heart beat against the confines of her chest.

"He wanted to meet the mortal who's revealing our existence to the world. Not every day you get to scrutinize a legend."

"Legend?" she breathed.

Dmitri brushed a strand of hair away from her cheek, his thumb caressing her skin. Jolts shot down her spine, to the tips of her breasts, turning her nipples hard. His eyes turned impossibly dark. If desire had been smoke, the alarms in the whole damn building would have been going off by now.

He cracked a smile, his sexy mouth all but daring her to kiss him. "You'll be a legend. The woman who discovered real vampires."

That sounded good. Better than Pulitzer good. But the buzzing sensation under her skin wasn't about being a legend. It was all about the mojo he was throwing off like an intense light from a million-watt bulb. Just being this close to Dmitri amped her up, all circuits firing. She licked her lips with the tip of her tongue.

God knew whatever eddied in the air between them—whether pure unadulterated lust or just some wacky chemical pheromone thingy between human and vampire—hit home. And hit deep. She ached to feel every inch of him against every inch of her. She intentionally leaned in further,

her sensitized breasts pressing against his rock-hard chest.

He flinched. "Don't." The darkness in his eyes swirled with secrets.

"Is this the part where you're going to tell me you're dangerous? Because I kind of already figured that out."

"But you don't know—" He looked away.

Kristin cupped his hard jaw in her hand, forcing him to face her. "I'm a big girl. I know what I want. And right now I want you to touch me."

His resolve crumbled right before her eyes. His seductive mouth locked down on hers. Hungry. Decisive. He seemed to saturate the air, that blend of dark chocolate, citrus and something utterly masculine seeping through her skin and into her bones, melting them.

For a second she couldn't breathe. She cursed the turtleneck, her bare skin screaming to feel him. He kissed along her jaw, growling in her ear, his hands threading into her hair. Kristin arched, letting her head fall back.

He inhaled the heady cinnamon-vanilla scent of her blood now spiked with the lush combination of honey and jasmine. Innocence and female desire. The pressure inside him was cresting, begging for release. But if there was one thing Dmitri excelled at, it was the art of denial.

The priests had beaten the lessons into him so well as a lad he'd never forgotten it. Just because you thought you needed something like your next breath didn't mean you truly needed it to survive. But one taste was all he wanted. Just one.

"Kristin…" He breathed her name like a fervent prayer. Her artery throbbed at the base of her jaw. But this was a hunger that could well drive him insane. It clawed and tore at him, a wild thing in his breast, demanding every shred of his attention.

He had to be careful, so very careful not to let the taste turn into death. His hand slipped beneath the soft cashmere as he kissed her, indulging in the delicious fullness of her soft lips. His fingers spread over her skin, which was far softer still. And hot, like sunlight on silk.

"Touch me."

He phased away the fabric, leaving her clothed from the waist up in nothing but the night air. He kissed the delicate shell of her ear and lower. Her throaty moan was like flipping on a switch. With a flick, his fangs extended.

Instantly her body tensed. "What was that? Was that your fangs?"

Dmitri pulled back and locked gazes with her. Her fear tinged the air with the musty odor of decay. "You don't have to be scared. I'm not going to feed from you."

She scooted back, pulling out of their tight embrace, covering herself with crossed arms. "Then what's with the fangs?"

Her sudden coolness was mercilessly cold to him. He phased the black turtleneck back over her bare skin and retreated from her. "It happens sometimes. Vampires can't always control when their fangs extend. Most often when we are angered or aroused."

Kristin reached forward, tentatively sliding a finger down the length of his right fang. Dmitri closed his eyes, a shudder rippling through him. It was by far the most intimate place she could have touched him, even more so than her hand running down the length of his shaft. But the mixed messages of hot to cold and standoffish versus intimate were too cluttered for him to sort through at the moment. He blew out a frustrated breath and turned away from her. He had no right to claim her. He was supposed to be protecting her, acting as her guide, not her lover.

"Does that hurt?"

He glanced at her. "No. Just the opposite." The ragged edge to his voice betrayed him.

"Oh." She blushed and the pretty pink in her cheeks pierced him with desire and need. Dmitri swallowed hard against it, determined to deny the call.

"What did Achilles mean when he said you were pious?"

Dmitri's gaze flicked to the photograph of the abbey ruins shrouded in mist on the wall. He hesitated. "In my mortal life I was a priest."

"A *priest?*" she murmured, stunned. "Becoming a vampire must have been an enormously hard decision for you, then."

He moved so quickly she barely had time to take a breath before he pinned her against the couch. His unyielding, rock-hard chest pressed against hers, his mouth a mere inch from hers, the tips of his fangs gleaming in the light.

The anger and fire erupting behind his eyes told her more than words ever could. "I never chose this life," he spat out.

She blinked and he was across the room, facing her.

"I'm sorry," she said. "I didn't mean to bring up a bad memory for you."

His laugh had the brittle, crumbling edge of a piece of termite-rotted wood. Suddenly he seemed far more a shell of a man than a real man, or a blood-eating monster, for that matter. His fangs had receded, leaving his teeth looking perfectly normal, even and white.

It had been a shock to discover that Dmitri was a vampire. Her father—good grief, everybody she'd ever known—would see them as an anathema, an evil, an embodiment of the devil. The living dead. Bloodsuckers. Dracula and things that go bump and murder people in the night.

And now they'd somehow randomly selected her to introduce them to society? A light throb started behind her left eye. This was a way bigger story than she'd ever anticipated. Deep down in her stomach swished a bad cocktail of uncertainty and ambition. Did she have the chops to cover something this huge and not muck it up?

But looking at Dmitri, at this moment, she could see that, like people, not all vampires were the same. Good and bad fell somewhere in between the cracks, in the gray. There were likely a million different stories. The challenge would be putting a face to this story, making humans care about vampires. And give vampires a chance to prove that they could peaceably coexist with humans.

Her reporter instincts kicked in. She stood up and started walking toward him. "Do you mind if I record our conversation?"

He gestured with a pale, elegant hand. "Please, be my guest."

She took out her digital microrecorder and clicked it on. "Just how old are you?"

His inscrutable brown gaze locked on hers. "I was born in 1370 and died in 1400."

"Died?" Just hearing the word from this strong, vital man made her wonder exactly what she was getting into. She reminded herself that she was a reporter. A reporter with the most amazing, incredible story to tell. This had Pulitzer written all over it. She could smell it.

"But you're standing right here, breathing, talking to me."

"We are the undead." Dmitri leaned back in his chair. "My appearance at breathing is merely that, an affectation that took me years to perfect so I could appear normal to mortals. Vampires do not need to breathe. We do not need oxygen. Blood alone, the life energy within it, sustains us."

"Do all of you drink blood?"

"Yes."

"Human blood?"

"When it is available."

"And when it's not?"

"We make do with other sources."

"Like…"

He simply stared at her. Time to change tactics.

"Look, I'm just trying to understand. People are going to freak out. They are going to feel threatened by your existence. Don't you think it might be a good idea to assure them there are other sources than little Emma and Jacob sleeping snug in their beds?"

He sighed and glanced again at the abbey. "Nothing is going to assuage them all. Fear is a given."

"But if you could give me a straight answer, it might help."

He matched gazes with hers. His was deep chocolate-colored brown and sucked her in, making her forget exactly what they'd been talking about.

"We can survive on warm-blooded animals and packaged blood."

She shook her head to clear it, then noticed the grimace bending his brow into a distinct V. "But it doesn't taste good," she prompted.

"It's not so much the taste. It's the feel. Fresh human blood makes you feel alive, invincible, like a drug-induced euphoria. Animal blood is like drinking a virgin cocktail. It may look the same, it may taste similar, it'll even satisfy your thirst somewhat, but it doesn't have any kick to it. It leaves you wanting."

"Interesting." And disgusting. But she tried not to show her feelings. He was doing his best to answer her questions honestly. She figured one man's tonic was another man's poison.

"Let me show you something else that might interest you." He offered her his hand and Kristin took it. Her hand tingled.

"Your skin is cold."

He quirked a brow. "Vampires are often several degrees cooler than mortals."

She looked him in the eye. "Do you still see yourself as human? I mean, you were human once, weren't you?"

The room around her swirled out of focus and a strange sucking pull started in her middle, making her feel as if she were a sweater being pulled inside out as it was taken off.

"We all were," Dmitri replied. "It's rather like asking someone who's had the chicken pox or HIV if they feel any different than they did before the disease entered their body. They've been chemically altered at a cellular level, but they appear to be the same. They function in society the same."

"Yeah, but they aren't dead," she pointed out, glancing around at the new location. They were standing in a brightly lit spa with a waterfall splashing and flowing over a rough rock wall to one side and a very Zenlike rock garden to the other. The well-groomed receptionist at the wooden podium smiled warmly at Dmitri, dipping for a moment in a curtsy, her chestnut-colored bob swinging slightly at her cheeks.

Kristin surreptitiously touched her arm to make sure she had transported in one piece.

"Undead. Clinically speaking," he said. "But more than our humanity or lack thereof, what's important to remember is that vampires have every bit as much intellect, desire and drive as mortals do. We are survivors, and oftentimes innovators."

"What exactly are you getting at?"

"Some of the brightest minds over the centuries, some of our most popular Hollywood and music stars, are vampires."

That stunned Kristin silent as she let it sink in.

Dmitri smiled at the receptionist. "We have an appointment to see Dr. Al Kashir."

She nodded, her nose slightly wrinkling, her gaze flitting briefly to meet Kristin's before darting back to Dmitri. "Is this for a conversion, my lord?" Dmitri's hand tightened slightly, forming a rocklike grip around Kristin's. "No. A tour."

"I'll let her know you've arrived. Please follow me."

"So vampires have integrated unnoticed with humans?" Kristin asked.

"Have for centuries. We blend in."

"Whoa." She shook her head. "Okay, getting back to the undead thing, how's that even possible?" she whispered as they followed the receptionist down the hall.

"Whatever age we are when we are changed, the biological aging process is arrested. We cease to die." Dmitri's eyes glittered with amusement. "And we have excellent hearing, so you don't need to whisper."

A raven-haired woman with dark expressive eyes and a complexion the color of caffe latte approached them with a smile that made her exotic looks even more pronounced, as if she held the key to some Middle Eastern secret of the ages. "My lord, how kind of you to favor us with a visit." She dipped in a curtsy.

Dmitri nodded, taking her hand and kissing the back of it lightly. "Dr. Zarah Al Kashir, I'd like to introduce you to Kristin Reed, a reporter for the *Pacific News Tribune*."

Zarah turned her gaze on Kristin and she suddenly felt awash in a sea of cloves and patchouli, with the distinct feeling of warm sand between her toes.

"A pleasure to meet you, Doctor."

Zarah nodded. "Trejan Dionotte has asked me to give you a tour. And, please, call me Zarah."

"What is this place?"

"A vampire holistic medical center."

"You mean like a fat camp or cleanup clinic?"

"Of sorts. Here, mortals who wish to be converted into vampires may do so in a clean and sterile process, or vampires needing specialized medical attention may find it."

They rounded the corner and came to a bank of frosted-glass walls. The doctor placed her fingertips to the glass and it became clear, with a view to the treatment room on the other side.

A woman in a hospital gown lay on a comfortable bed, a large quart of blackish-red liquid being fed into her, drip by drip, through an IV. Attending her was a person in scrubs with a metal nametag.

Kristin stared. "Wait, you mean you have humans who come here to become vampires?"

Zarah smiled warmly. "Of course." She touched the glass and once more it turned translucent. She turned and kept walking.

"Why?" Kristin pressed.

"Some do so voluntarily because they want to change their lifestyle. Others do so for medical reasons."

"Like…"

"Terminal illness, unsolvable medical injuries," Dmitri said.

They stopped in front of another plate of glass; this time a male patient was on the other side. He looked terribly frail, like a skeleton draped in papery skin.

"How does it work?" Kristin asked.

"Vampire ichor diluted with human blood heals their bodies to a whole and complete state more rapidly than anything current medical science can offer," Zarah explained. "Taken straight, and in significant quantities, the ichor can produce vampirism under the right conditions."

Kristin was catching on. "They're stopping the aging, or in this case, the dying process."

"Exactly." Dmitri eyed her with pride.

"What about their bodies? I mean, if they are wasted away to nothing when they change, is that the kind of body they're stuck with?"

Zarah touched the glass, cutting off Kristin's view to the man inside the room.

"No. The regeneration process allows them to build it to their desired state before the conversion is complete. Only after total conversion is the process arrested. This way, please."

They went through a set of double doors and entered a high-ceilinged room. It was airy, like a beautiful patio garden at twilight on a summer's evening. Even the ceiling looked like a star-filled night sky on one side and a setting sun on the other—like the changing overhead display at Caesar's Palace in Las Vegas. But this looked even more realistic.

Various patients mingled about. Some lifting weights, others getting a massage or talking over drinks or while getting manicures or pedicures. Kristin thought she even saw a few noted Seattle socialites, but couldn't get close enough to be sure.

"I can see the appeal. Stay young and have a firm, tight body forever. Look great. Have killer skills. No diet. No exercise."

Dmitri cleared his throat. "Well, there is a diet to consider. A rather strict one at that."

Kristin glanced at him. "Oh, yeah. I suppose so. When was the last time you had real food?"

"Last week. And it wasn't anything I'd go back for."

"Vampires can eat food?"

"If we want to. We just don't need to."

Kristin realized she was dead tired. A glance at her phone confirmed it was 3:00 a.m. "I know you probably pull all-nighters every night, but I've really got to get some sleep. Doctor, if I have more questions may I contact you?"

"Of course." Kristin noticed a glance pass between Zarah and Dmitri, almost as if they had an exchange without saying a word out loud.

That was the last thing she remembered.

* * *

Back in his rooms, Dmitri settled her on the couch, materializing first the Mariners T-shirt she favored, then a soft burgundy-colored chenille blanket to cover her. She mumbled something in her sleep as he mentally tucked the blanket around her. He leaned closer, watching her full mouth, his gaze skimming to the slow, steady bump of her pulse against her smooth skin at the base of her throat.

The next moment he was staring at the fine swirls in the burled-wood grain of Roman's desk.

"She isn't going to be a problem for you, is she?" Roman peered at him from the other side of the desk, his fingers steepled, his eyes sharp.

Dmitri straightened, standing up and looking at the laird of their clan who had transported him. A second later, Achilles materialized beside Dmitri in Roman's office.

"What was your observation, Achilles?" Roman asked smoothly.

"I think she's a wise choice. Observant, but guided easily enough."

"Then as long as she reports only the things we

wish her to, she poses no threat, and she may stay alive." Roman flicked his gaze back to Dmitri. "I want there to be nothing about the reivers mentioned. If we are revealing ourselves to mortals, it must be done flawlessly, with every assurance they are not in danger. One whiff of the reivers being connected to these local murders and we might as well stay in hiding another hundred years. Are we clear?"

Dmitri nodded his head. "Absolutely clear, my laird. However we will not be able to keep the truth about those behind the Bloodless Murders secret for much longer. Once our existence is revealed, the authorities are certain to implicate our kind."

Roman tapped the desk. "Achilles, have your men finished their interrogation of the reiver?"

"Yes, my laird. They are a group that has been moving up the coast from Santa Carla, California. But we have not yet found where they've been nesting locally."

"Find them. I would negotiate with their leader. If we cannot convince them to conform or leave, then we will take care of them."

Dmitri disliked killing his own kind as much as he disliked killing mortals. The clan rivalries, honor and vengeance ingrained into vampire society were common enough. But the idea of wiping out another clan or nest smacked too much of the burning times when thousands upon thousands died needlessly to satisfy a few in power. Deep down it rubbed against his earliest precepts like sandpaper, scrubbing away what little humanity he had left. But Roman's decree was more than ideology at work. It was survival. This was protecting their right to live.

He drew in a breath, not for the oxygen, but to steady his thoughts. God. Over six hundred years without really drawing a true breath, and yet the need was instinctive, the uncomfortable tightness in his chest real. "And what of the reporter?"

"See that she is kept under constant watch. What she knows could unravel everything we've spent centuries building in this country. Our efforts to create a democracy where all people could be equal, our first chance at true freedom, could be over before it begins."

Chapter 7

The one thing she couldn't get past was the blood. Great scarlet rivers of it flowed all around her. The viscous fluid filled her mouth and nose and stung her eyes. Her struggling lungs filled with its liquid warmth and her mind went blind with terror. She fought to keep her head above the suffocating tide. From the surrounding darkness red eyes glowed.

Sweating, gasping for a last sip of air, she woke from the nightmare, startled to be in the pitch dark. Not home. It didn't smell of her vanilla-scented candles or freshly washed cotton sheets, but of darker scents underscored with clean male.

Sitting up, she fumbled for a lamp. She almost sobbed with relief when her fingers bumped what felt like a lamp base. She flipped on the light and recognized Dmitri's windowless apartment. But there was no sign of Dmitri. Or her clothes.

She fingered the wash-softened fabric of her Mariners T-shirt. What had happened last night? And how had she ended up here in her sleep shirt?

Her purse was propped against the lamp. Grabbing it like a lifeline, she dug around for her cell phone amid shopping lists, receipts, yellow sticky notes, random pens and her small flip notepad. Her mobile file cabinet needed organizing. Finally she found the phone in a side pocket.

Flipping it open, she checked the time: 8:00 a.m. Hell. Hollander was going to be pissed. She'd already missed her deadline. Still, for *this* story, it would be worth the risk. When he knew what this piece was about he'd hold the presses and be willing to wait. At least she hoped he would.

She got up, and managed to find a computer in Dmitri's apartment where she logged in to check her email at work. Thank God vampires had internet and showers. She cleaned up, shoved her hair into a sloppy bun held together with a pencil, then began transcribing her notes from the recording.

"Working already?" Dmitri's voice slid thick and hot over her like melted chocolate.

She hadn't heard him enter, but twisted in her chair and smiled at him. The open collar of his black button-down shirt with thin blue pinstripes accented the deep caramel color of his skin. A pair of crisp black slacks fitted his lean hips to perfection, and she knew, probably fitted his perfect ass just as well. All in all he looked far too put together for a vampire up in the middle of the day.

Kristin clamped her knees together tighter, suddenly aware that she was wearing only a thin oversize T-shirt and a pair of underwear. Hell, next to him, she was practically naked. Her breasts became sensitive and tight and she crossed her arms to cover her nipples, outlined all too well by the thin cotton. "I hope you don't mind me using your computer to get my work done. Girl's gotta eat, you know."

"That's what I thought." He held up a white

bakery bag and her nose automatically sniffed out the yeasty sweetness of fresh doughnuts. Her gaze flicked to the cup in his hand. Modesty be damned. The man had coffee.

"You brought coffee too?" She walked over to him, taking the cup and inhaling deeply of the fresh-brewed aroma. She let out a groan after the first sip, sweet with sugar and heavy cream. "God love you." Which was probably not something she should say to a vampire, Kristin thought as the caffeine raced through her system.

"I realized this probably runs in your veins."

"Coffee and printer's ink." The coffee was exactly the way she liked it. Exactly. "But how did you know how I like it?"

His mouth tipped up at the edge. "That's still my little secret." He handed her the bakery bag. Inside was a chocolate doughnut with sprinkles and a chocolate éclair.

"How did you know I like chocolate?" His mouth tipped up in the corners in a sexy smile that made her lips tingle. Suddenly the chocolate had lost its appeal. As he leaned one shoulder against the wall, the buttons on his shirt pulled in protest to the shifting of muscle underneath. Kristin could barely swallow.

"Don't all women enjoy chocolate?" Of course, it was more than that. Dmitri had been picking up on her thoughts all through the night as he listened in on her dreams from his bed. Even though she was safe here in his apartment, he couldn't escape the nagging itch at the back of his neck telling him the reivers weren't just chasing her down about the Bloodless Murders, but about the plans to out the vampire world to mortals.

Her thoughts and dreams had shown him just how driven she was. And while Dmitri admired anyone who went after what they wanted, Kirsten's determination and curiosity were a heady, dangerous mix. Her dreams had shown him she was worried about her job; she was convinced it hinged on her article about the vampires. He had bigger concerns, like keeping her alive.

Her dreams, or drive, could very well be the death of her.

Roman had understated the fineness of the line she walked. Revealing their existence was one thing; exposing all their secrets was quite another.

He'd had Roman question his concern for mortals before.

Saving people from themselves seemed to be something of a specialty for him. As clan *trejan*, it was his duty to protect the laird and all those within the clan. But that was before Kristin. Right now, if he'd had a soul, he would have gladly surrendered it to feel her beneath him. She had the uncanny ability to turn his well-ordered world upside down, tempting him to toss out every tenet he held scared. Including his oath to protect his clan before all others, and his kind before mortals.

Heaviness pressed in upon him like a physical weight, but it wasn't just the unspoken burden of conscience and duty he carried. He could feel that daylight was out in full force aboveground, sapping his strength, making him ache to rest. She'd want to leave soon and go to work.

"I'll see you to work when you're ready."

"That's not necessary as long as I can call in to my editor and use your computer. And find my clothes, of course."

Good. "It would be safest for you to stay here.

You may use whatever you need. Your clothes are folded on the counter in the kitchen."

"How did they get there?"

"I phased them. And your nightshirt at the same time. I thought you'd be more comfortable sleeping in something familiar." She'd looked beautiful in repose, her golden hair a halo around her lovely face, her lips the pale pink of a newly opened rosebud. Too angelic to be with a vampire. When she discovered the brutal truth of how they survived, she'd see him as little better than a glorified parasite. The sweet softness that cloaked her features in sleep was long gone, her intelligent eyes far too penetrating and too wide-eyed innocent for his comfort.

Saints, he needed a drink. She recrossed her legs, exposing a brief flash of the creamy skin of her thigh, and his throat tightened even further. She tugged the hem of faded dark blue T-shirt lower, her fingers fidgeting.

Kristin fingered the pencil point in her bun. Apparently thinking about him stripping her of her clothing made her distinctly uncomfortable. There'd been a split second between phasing away her sweater and jeans and phasing the worn T-shirt onto her when he'd glimpsed her in nothing but her white lacy underwear. But that single glimpse was seared into his brain like a brand.

Touching the pale satin of her skin, tracing the flair of her hip, had been his first impulse, but it had been ruthlessly suppressed. No less tempting had been the subtle beat of her pulse in the femoral artery running under that smooth thigh. He'd held his fangs in place by sheer force of will.

But standing so close to her now wasn't helping. He needed to get away from her before he did something else he regretted as much as using her to control their unveiling to the mortal community.

"How do I get a hold of Zarah if I need to ask some more questions?"

He materialized a cordless phone and handed it to her. "Dial nine to make outside calls. Dial zero to reach our operator. She can put you in touch with the doctor or me."

"Perfect. What about the pizza-delivery guy?" She grinned. "Or are they afraid to make deliveries down here in the Underground?"

How could she think of food, when he suppressed the desire to feast on every inch of her?

Her spicy scent wrapped around him and he resisted the urge to inhale deeply, to let her essence fill him. He needed to feed and soon. "Call the operator and she'll connect you with food services at the clinic. They make an excellent chicken-and-artichoke-heart pizza with sun-dried tomatoes and a basil sauce you'd probably enjoy."

"What, I don't look spicy enough to be the pepperoni type?"

The way that T-shirt outlined the swell of her breasts and skimmed around the top of her thighs made it difficult for him to keep his concentration. "You don't want to know what you look like to me."

"Tell me."

"Temptation."

A man, mortal or vampire, could only bear so much before he broke. He turned on his heel and strode to the bedroom door, cursing himself with every step. He had his duty. His involvement with her would have to end as soon as expedient. Probably the sooner the better for both their sakes. "I'm going to sleep. See you in about twelve hours. If you need anything call the operator and she'll find someone to help you."

"Thanks, Dmitri, for everything."

He nodded, not trusting himself to say more. It had been too long since he'd fed and the thirst was too deep and too strong to be assuaged by bottled blood alone. The sooner they found the reivers and he got Kristin out of his home, the saner he'd be.

As the door closed behind him, Kristin shivered. She'd seen guys stare at her with interest, even lust, but what she'd glimpsed in his eyes had been rawer, more primitive, more ancient than that. A fine sheen of perspiration coated her skin. God, he was too hot for his own good. She pulled the pencil from her sloppy bun and chewed on it. Too bad he wasn't as into her as she could easily get into him.

Kristin turned back to her keyboard and sank into the article once more, letting the words flow and meld as she tried to capture the sights and sounds of the club, of the vampire clinic and of

Dmitri. The next time she checked the clock on her phone, two hours had passed. She bit her lip and called Hollander.

"You've missed the deadline for tomorrow's paper." She'd pegged Hollander's reaction. Pissed.

"I know. But I'm still doing interviews and research for the next vampire article. This is far bigger than anything we anticipated."

"How big?" Hollander pushed, the angry edge of his voice softening a touch.

"Pulitzer big."

He let out a long, low whistle. "When can you get it to me?"

"Probably on Monday. Don't you want any details?"

"Hell, of course I want details. Let's start off with where the hell are you?"

"In Seattle's main vampire enclave below the city."

"The Underground?"

"Yep. Turns out it's not just a tourist trap."

He sucked in a startled breath. "Holy shit on a shingle. They're real? Bloodsucking, fangs and all?"

"Yep."

"Are you okay? Have they tried to eat you?"

Kristin sighed. "I'm talking to you, aren't I?"

Hollander coughed a little. Clearly he was shook up.

"There are still some things I need to get details on—like how they feed, what's exactly in the vampire ichor that converts people into vampires, and the history of their race, and how else they are similar to normal people."

"Give me the address," he told her, and Kristin heard papers rustle. His desk was as messy as her purse. "Okay, shoot. I'll send you a photog right away. We need pictures. Plenty of pictures."

Now, wouldn't that be great? Too bad it wasn't going to happen. She wasn't exactly sure where she was herself. The Underground had to span more than twenty city blocks. "Not a snowball's chance in hell they'd allow that. Besides, I don't have a street address."

"What about the club?"

Dmitri wasn't going to allow that either; she was absolutely positive. She had a sudden interesting—no, make that fascinating—thought.

"Honestly, I don't even know if they'd show up in the image."

"Hadn't thought of that. See what you can get. We're going to need something."

She would try to get some shots with her cell phone, but the images would be crappy. Grainy and not good enough for the front page. Her mind spun a mile a minute searching for options and discarding them as fast as they popped into her brain. "If nothing else, maybe I can get the manager to let us take pictures of the decor in the club and perhaps some of the donors."

Hollander grumbled something indistinct under his breath. "You just take care of yourself. And report back in by Monday." Kristin was surprised to hear the concerned tone in his voice.

She spent the rest of her day working on the article and doing a little bit of online research into the late fourteenth century—the time Dmitri said he had lived before being turned. He came from the era of Chaucer and his *Canterbury Tales,* a time rife with superstition and dominated by the church. No wonder he'd seen his transformation as one huge negative.

She tried Dmitri's bedroom door, but it was locked. Instead, she trekked to the kitchen, where she found most of the cupboards bare. By dinnertime she was hungry enough to call the operator and order one of those pizzas Dmitri had mentioned.

It smelled like heaven as she peeked inside the box. Holding it with the palm of one hand, she lightly rapped on his bedroom door with the other. "Hey. I got pizza. You interested?" Nothing. Nada. Zip. Who knew, maybe he was a deep sleeper.

She knocked a little harder. No response. This time when she tried the knob his door swung open effortlessly. Her latent curiosity got the better of her. Exactly how did a vampire like to sleep?

She tiptoed in and found the dark room was vacant except for the massive bed covered in a simple tailored duvet in stark white and little else. It looked as if it hadn't even been slept in. It was a little disappointing when she'd somehow expected something far more dramatic, like a coffin.

The whole room radiated masculinity in a black-white way. Black carpet, black walls, white bed and white bathroom with sleek black-and-white tiles and chrome fixtures. The only picture was a black-and-white photograph of the same crumbled church from the other room, but from a different angle. The face of the stone angel carved into the fascia looked as if it had been crying. Dark tearlike stains from centuries of rain marred the stone's surface.

She turned away from the image and walked to the bed, reaching out to touch the pristine covers. A faint stirring of chocolate tinged with citrus and musk clung to them, but the covers were cold to the touch. He'd been gone awhile then. He must have transported while she'd been working.

A twinge pulled inside her chest. He was clearly avoiding her, but why? He was a contradiction of hot and cold. One minute he looked at her like a starving man, and the next he turned away as if she offended him.

Suddenly it seemed as if she was intruding on a personal place where she had no business. Kristin snatched her hand away from the covers and left the bedroom. She blew out a quick breath. Well, she wasn't going to just sit around and wait for him to return. That had gotten her nowhere fast in her experience. She had no idea when he'd be back and she still had questions she'd like answered before her next deadline.

She dialed the operator again. "Can you please connect me with Achilles?" She somehow doubted there'd be more than one.

His voice rumbled sleepy and languorous into the receiver. "Has he left you to your own devices so soon? Clearly I need to give him a refresher course on what one does with a beautiful woman."

While Achilles was no doubt the stuff of many a female fantasy, Kristin wasn't tempted in the slightest. Dmitri's darkness, both inside and out, were far more alluring to her. She shifted the phone to her other hand, and a whiff of the scent from his bedcovers tickled her nose, making her shiver thinking of him naked in that big bed. "Do you know where he is?"

"This time of night you'd usually find him at Sangria. Would you like me to take you there?"

Her heart stuttered for a moment. It was a risk, but one she needed to take. All she knew was that she needed to find Dmitri now. "How soon can we go?"

Chapter 8

Ten minutes later Kristin wound her way through Sangria toward the shuttered crimson velvet curtains Achilles had pointed out. But before she could pull them back, someone on the other side spoke.

"Go away."

The moment she heard his voice she knew it was Dmitri. Her heart pounded harder.

She yanked the curtain aside. Dmitri had a lithe young brunette snuggled up on his lap, her arms curved around his shoulders, her head arched back, his head nuzzled against her neck. A spark of anger flamed to life deep inside, but Kristin quickly snuffed it out. There was nothing between them. A kiss. That's all. And he'd done a fairly good job at avoiding whatever it was that was simmering between them whenever they were within eye contact of each other.

For a moment it looked like any other make-out session, until Dmitri lifted his head from the curve of the female's neck where throat met collarbone. Red glistened along the edges of his mouth like bright cherry lip gloss. Kristin's stomach twisted and she quickly turned away, fighting back the gag reflex pulsating in her throat.

Truth was she'd always been a bit squeamish when it came to blood. Others' blood, not her own. Her knees suddenly felt spongy. In a heartbeat all those useless warm, mushy things she'd been feeling for Dmitri disintegrated in her chest.

"Kristin—"

"You're busy. I'll see you later."

In an instant he was blocking her escape. He wiped the blood from his mouth with a black hankie, the red all but disappearing into the dark fabric. "I didn't want you to see it like this."

She stiffened as if he'd slapped her. "Oh, because you think it looks more civil if you use a straw? I don't give a rat's ass who you want to sleep with, or feed from, or whatever it is that you vampires do. It's none of my business."

His features darkened, looking more distant and more threatening all at once. A flash of fear skittered from her nape down her spine. She glanced behind her and saw the girl sprawled motionless in the chair. The swift shush of fabric made her whip around to look back at Dmitri. He had yanked the curtains closed, shutting them off from the view of everyone out in the club. He stepped closer, pushing into her space. She involuntarily took a step back. "I was only feeding."

His face, his mouth, which he'd just used to feed from a human being, were mere inches away from her own. She swallowed hard against the lump blocking her ability to breathe. "I thought all warm-blooded creatures could sustain you. That you didn't *need* to feed on humans." His face hardened into the same sad look as the stone angel from the black-and-white photograph.

"Sustain, but never fill."

"Please, don't let me stop you." She glanced

back at the brunette, who had a languid smile on her face, as if she was high. "Get whatever fill of her you need." She stepped sideways trying to avoid touching him.

He caught her arm, his fingers branding her skin. "For an unbiased reporter you're awfully quick to judge."

She spun around, yanking her arm from his hold and crossing both firmly over her chest. "You were freakin' eating her. What other explanation do you have for that? You want me to get a photographer in here to shoot it? Because, believe you me, if people get a shot of this alongside the article, there's no way they'll get to the article. A picture speaks a thousand words. They'll draw their own conclusions."

He pulled back, giving her enough space to breathe, but even then Kristin wasn't sure she could drag in enough air to stop her shallow breathing.

"Why don't you go ahead and interview Beth? Ask her how she feels."

"Yeah, like I'd interview a chocolate-chip

cookie. Besides, for all I know, you did your mind-control thingy on her."

"It's called a glamour and, no, I didn't. Many of our donors, like Beth, are willing enough. They don't have to be glamoured."

Somehow that was even less reassuring. "Fine." She turned back to Beth. The girl was cleaning the remaining blood from her neck with a damp washcloth, a big whacked-out smile on her face.

"Um, hi, Beth, is it? I'm Kristin." Kristin couldn't take her eyes off the two deep puncture marks on the girl's neck, but forced herself to look back into her face. "Dmitri's told me you're a donor, and I was wondering if I could ask you a few questions for an article I'm writing about the club."

Beth grinned. "Sure. Any friend of Dmitri's is a friend of mine."

Kristin glanced back at Dmitri, who was leaning against the door frame. At the moment she didn't feel too friendly toward him. An unfamiliar mixture of heat and uncertainty churned in her stomach. Jealousy? She squeezed her hand tighter. No, she certainly didn't want to be his juice box. But then, she definitely didn't like the idea of him snacking on some random woman either. It bothered her, but not in a way she could easily define.

His big brooding width filled the doorway completely, distracting her. "I thought you wanted me to interview her."

"Just pretend I'm not here."

Yeah. Like that could happen when the room fairly pulsed with the energy he was throwing off in her direction.

"I'd like to interview her alone, if you don't mind." She pulled a small spiral notepad out of her purse along with a pen.

He shrugged. "Suit yourself. I'll make certain you aren't disturbed." He slipped through the part in the curtain, then pulled it firmly shut, leaving her alone in the tasting room with Beth. The girl's eyes were closed, her head relaxed against the back of the black leather couch. God, she looked so young. She must be barely twenty-one.

"Beth."

"Ummm." The girl's eyelids fluttered, but didn't

open. Kristin reached out and gently touched her hand.

"Are you all right?"

Beth gave her a lazy, satiated smile, her eyes cracking open. "I'm great." Yeah, she bet. If this wasn't the aftereffect of a glamour, then clearly she'd been drugged.

"What are you on right now?"

"On?"

"Did he drug you?"

Beth sat up straighter, her eyes losing a little of their glow. "No! I stay pure for the experience. It's more intense that way."

"Why do you do it? Why do you let them drink from you like that?"

A small knowing smile curled Beth's lips. "You've never done it, have you?"

"I don't even like donating blood to the blood bank."

Beth bit the end of her index finger then smoothed the wet tip of it across her lips in a sensuous slide. "It's better than sex. There's no sweaty pawing or groping or sloppy kisses, just total orgasm one after another after another." She slowly closed her eyes. "And you don't even need a condom." She giggled.

"Really?"

Beth leaned forward as if confiding to a good friend instead of a reporter she'd known barely five minutes. "Yeah. It's probably the most erotic thing I've done in my whole life."

An uncomfortable hollowness settled in the pit of Kristin's stomach. The initial repulsion was replaced by something worse. Anxiety liberally doused with insecurity. If this was what feeding was like, how many others had Dmitri shared it with? And why did he seem so clear about not wanting to do that with her? Why did he insist it was merely sustenance when the exchange was clearly more? And what had she done during their kiss to so clearly turn him away?

"Is it always like that?" she asked the donor.

Beth ran her fingers into her hair, resting her head in her hand. "With the right vampire. You can feel their need. It's too intense when you're with one that's too hungry. Then there are the ones that can nearly suck you dry. Had that happen once and ended up in the hospital needing a transfusion because I was so drained."

Kristin shifted in her seat. The discussion about blood was making her uncomfortable in more ways than one.

"So when did you start being a donor?"

"When I was sixteen."

"And how old are you now?"

"Twenty-two."

Kristin scribbled a note on her pad. "How did you get into donating?"

"In high school my friend Envy was into cutting. She had heard about a cool place to hang out. She got us some fake IDs and we've been doing this at least once a month ever since. As long as we didn't try to get a drink at the bar, they let us stay until we were old enough to get in on our own."

A thought struck Kristin. "Do you think vampires can read minds?"

"Yeah, they totally do. Well, they talk to each other telepathically, anyway. But sometimes you can almost feel them reading what's on your mind too. That's why you can't lie to them."

Kristin's face burned with heat. Had Dmitri been reading her mind? She'd thought something was happening when she'd seen him look at the doctor at the vampire clinic, but she hadn't been sure at the time. If he could read minds, did that mean he could see into her dreams too? A cold sluice of mortification instantly replaced the heat.

"Hey, are you okay?"

Beth's question jerked Kristin back into the interview. "Have you ever transported with a vampire?"

By the way Beth's eyes lit up, Kristin could tell this was news to her. Interviewing was a delicate balancing act. You sometimes needed to give a little information to get more from a source. In this case perhaps she'd given too much.

"They can transport, you mean, like, 'Beam me up, Scotty'?"

Kristin tapped her pen on her notepad, schooling her features to reveal nothing but slight interest. She'd already revealed too much emotional reaction during the interview, as it was. "I was asking you."

"I've never had one take me from the club, if that's what you're asking."

Kristin nodded. "Are there any other perks, beside multiple O's, to being a donor?"

Beth let her smile get wider. "Sometimes they let you have a little vampire blood in return."

A sick, oily sensation slid through Kristin's stomach. Being fed off of was gross enough, but then turning around and sucking on the bloodsucker? No, thank you. She pressed her lips together hard at the thought.

Of course, she could understand the appeal was not in the act, but in the aftereffects. You felt incredibly strong, had better health and felt younger. Hell, in some cases, if Dr. Al Kashir was being honest with her, it could even heal terminal human diseases.

"And have you ever done that?" she asked Beth.

"Once. And it was the most incredible week of my life. Like being some kind of comic-book superhero."

Kristin was writing notes as fast as she could, the heel of her hand smudging the black ink slightly. The low buzz of conversation and the thump of the music intruded through the curtain. She shut them out so she could concentrate. Too bad she couldn't shut out the slight hint of chocolate, citrus and overbearing male that spiked the air.

But was it worth it? She still didn't know exactly how the vampire ichor worked on the body or, for that matter, how vampires were created from it. It seemed like an awfully big risk, but then so were street drugs, and it didn't stop people from risking everything for their next high. "Sounds interesting. I see how people could get hooked on feeling like they were invincible."

"Yeah. The problem is, they really aren't supposed to let you do that. I only got to because the vampire who let me doesn't always follow all the rules. Ya know?"

Kristin was getting a real good idea. "Does this vampire come to the club often?"

"No. Only seen him once or twice before."

"Could you describe him?"

"Blond, real blond, spiky hair. Intense red eyes. Cool black leather duster. Badass."

Bingo. Mystery note-slipping vamp identified.

"Do you know his name?"

"Vane."

A pair of glowing red eyes swam into Kristin's vision and she shook her head to erase the image so she could see clearly to finish her notes. She wondered if Dmitri knew who else had been snacking on his little chocolate-chip cookie.

"Thanks, Beth. I'll be in touch if I have any other questions."

Kristin got up from the chair and swung back the curtain to find Dmitri's broad back guarding the entrance. "I'm done. You can move now."

He turned, looking down at her over his shoulder. "I was merely ensuring your privacy. Since apparently the curtain isn't enough."

"Oh, and here I thought you might be merely trying to eavesdrop on the interview."

"It is my job to see to the security of our clan and all those inside this club." He glanced over at the bar, his tone taking on a distinct undercurrent of disapproval. "I see you came with Achilles. You could have called me on my cell and I would have brought you here."

"I think you were a little too busy to be bothered."

He glanced away, his mouth pressing into a firm line. He closed his eyes a moment, took a deep breath, then locked his gaze with hers.

"So, was it as bad as you had anticipated?"

"She seems happy enough with the whole thing. Did you glamour her?"

"I told you, I have no need to."

The truth was the girl acted as if it was one of the most fabulous experiences of her life, which bent Kristin's brain inside out. She just couldn't fathom how being eaten by another creature could be a positive experience. A kernel of thought popped into her head like the first to burst in a bag of popcorn, followed in rapid fire by more and more.

"Can I ask you a question?"

"Only one more? Are you certain?"

She ignored his sarcasm. "What happens when you feed? I mean, I know what you're getting out of it, but what is she getting out of it? What are you doing to her? How'd you get to be a vampire in the first place?"

He pulled her toward a booth, the stone stalagmites bracketing the edge of the booth, making it seem like their own private little cave. "So you've concluded there's more to the feeding than taking what we need. There is a giving too. If I were the good doctor, I could explain it medically to you, but as it is you'll just have to make do with a basic understanding."

"No. I don't want you to explain it. I want you to—" She grazed her fingers along her neck.

Dmitri's brow knit together. "You can't be serious."

Kristin huffed. "What's wrong? Are you full?"

His face turned stormy and dark a moment before he turned his gaze away from her. "I've already fed. I don't do so lightly."

She laid a hand on his. "I'm asking you as a matter of research. You don't have to give it your all. Just a little taste will do."

He shifted his hand, capturing hers in the cleft between his fingers and thumb, then he began tracing light circles on her palm with his thumb. "You're playing games with me."

The touch sent sparks racing into her veins.

Kristin pulled her hand away, feeling unbalanced, her tenacious need to know the truth turned fuzzy by the feeling of him next to her and the insistent, seductive scent that clung to him.

"My reputation as a serious journalist has never been a game. I need to know so I can accurately report on it."

"Come here, then." He held out a large hand to her.

Kristin hesitated, knowing what it would do to her, but slipped her hand into his, the coolness of his touch making a shiver travel up her arm and down her spine. A heady blend of fear and excitement pumped into her heart, making the beat frantic.

She'd never been one to take a personal risk like this. It was one thing to put yourself out for your work, another to put your body on the line, maybe even your heart. Kristin sucked in a breath. When did she start seeing herself with this man, this vampire, and craving his presence? Was she out of her mind to ask this of him?

One thing she knew for certain. There was no going back. She was crossing an intimate line with him, and at the moment it was exactly where she wanted to be.

"If I'm going to, it won't be here." Intimacy laced his every syllable.

"Where, then?"

He stretched his arm around her, and the curve of his powerful bicep and forearm pressed deliciously against her lower back, causing her insides to curl and contract with need. In a swirl of mist they were outside beneath the moonlit night sky. The waters off Alki Point whispered against the rocks, a rhythmic susurrus in the dark.

"You are certain?" he whispered.

She swallowed, anticipation making her lips tingle and her thighs press together a little tighter. "My editor would never forgive me if I didn't research this thoroughly." Truth be known, she wanted to research a hell of a lot more than just this. She'd already been fantasizing about what he looked like beneath his clothes.

Despite the shadow over his face, she could feel, more than see, his eyes darken to fathomless black. "But this isn't just research." Dmitri grazed his fingers down the curve of her cheek, down past her ear, tracing the lifeline that pulsed and throbbed. "You're curious."

The touch filtered through her skin, sending a bolt of cool light shimmering through her veins like liquid moonlight. Kristin gasped at the sensation, pressing her palms against the hard planes of his chest, wanting to feel him against her.

Her fingers picked out a rumble echoing deep within Dmitri. Despite the salted cool breeze blowing off the water, all Kristin could sense was the heat roaring in the quarter inch of space between them.

For a fraction of a second her logical mind protested. He must be controlling her mind. How else could she possibly explain the heady driving need blossoming within her? Her every sense, every desire, wrapped around the man, the vampire, against her.

He closed the gap between them, holding her against his rock-hard body with a firm yet gentle touch, his fingers twisting in the fall of her hair. "It's like silk. Beautiful, golden silk. And this—" his mouth brushed against hers "—this is perfection." The light touch sent her body spinning in a thousand different directions, making it difficult to concentrate. How in the hell was she supposed to put into words the sensations flooding her so that people could understand? The kiss turned deeper, more seductive, and Kristin forgot how to breathe.

She pressed herself against him, wrapping her arms around his neck tightly. She felt as if every pore opened up, wanting to soak him into her very skin, dying for him to be within her. His tongue skimmed the edge of her lip, then delved deeper, teasing her, stroking, tempting her to kiss him back and sending her senses scrambling.

"Stop thinking about it and just feel," he whispered softly, his breath caressing just below her ear. He nuzzled the sensitive spot there, inhaling deeply. She heard the distinctive flicking sound of his fangs extending. Unlike last time, instead of fear, a fierce desire tore through her. Her center coiled with delicious tension, spiraling, tightening, wanting.

"I've wondered if you taste as good as you smell."

She swallowed, barely able to catch her breath. "What do I smell like?"

"Hot cinnamon kissed with honey and vanilla."

The brush of his cold fangs against her hot skin made her shudder. "So you like sweets?"

He chuckled, the sound warm and deep. "Call it a weakness."

"A man after my own heart." She pulled back slightly, caressing one of his fangs with her fingertip. "But I bet your dentist hates you."

He sucked in a rattling breath. "Do you have any idea how many nerve endings are in the fangs?"

"Sensitive?"

"Incredibly."

"So how does it feel when I do this?" She leaned closer and swirled the tip of her tongue over the pointed tip.

Dmitri hissed, his eyes flashing iridescent in the darkness. "You make me hungry."

Heart pounding hard in her chest, Kristin leaned her head to the side and brushed her hair over her shoulder, exposing her neck. "Then what are you waiting for?"

Chapter 9

A gust of salty wind off the water buffeted them in the darkness, pushing her closer to him.

For a second her heartbeat stuttered to a stop, then took up a rapid beat again as he leaned in, his mouth inches from her throat. Goose bumps raised on her skin, following the trail of his fangs as the sharp points grazed a delicate path down her neck to where her pulse beat strongest. She shuddered.

The press and pop echoed through her whole body, like an orgasmic release, as he sank himself into her. A slow liquid heat ignited an exquisite ache that throbbed at the apex of her thighs and moved outward, pulsing in every cell. Kristin gasped.

Suddenly it felt as though his mouth, his hands, his perfectly sculpted body were touching her everywhere at once. A mouth hot and demanding against hers, his tongue teasing. Another tongue warm and wet laving her nipples into hardened points, even though he was still pressing his lips against her throat. Electric fingers stroking her breasts, making them tighten and ache. Wicked fingers sliding against the slick heat at her core, causing her to whimper with need. Strong hands pressing every inch of him against every inch of her. God, how many hands did he have? She could feel at least six pair. Sweat-slickened skin slid against hers even though they were both fully clothed. How was it possible?

Kristin moaned as the heat, the throbbing, beat in her blood, made her feel invincible, as if she too could leap buildings, hear the whisper of insect wings in the wind and see distant stars. The sensation spiraled out of control, focusing into a glowing epicenter between her thighs. It exploded outward, a tsunami that swept away everything but the feel of him within her, the sensations tumbling over her in sparkling wave after wave, making her shake and tremble.

She clung to him, panting, her legs unable to support her any longer. The moment his fangs slipped out of her skin, she wanted to pull him back. Tingling warmth lingered, radiating throughout her, but the waves of pulsating need and desperate desire receded until only sweet calm remained.

"Saints above, you're even sweeter than I imagined." He pressed his forehead to hers, his eyes luminous, glowing like dark amber lit from within. "How do you feel?"

"Like I've spent the day being utterly pampered at a day spa, had a full body massage, then spent an entire week being pleasured. But I still don't know if I can stand on my own."

He held her against him and she loved the way his hard body supported her.

"Why didn't you tell me you were type O?"

Worry crept in, slightly killing her buzz. "What's wrong with type O? Are you allergic?"

He shook his head, his tongue tracing lightly

along his bottom lip. "No. Just the opposite, in fact. Type O is the most addictive blood type there is."

Lucky her. Kristin found herself fixated on his mouth, the twin ivory blades gently indenting the soft skin of his bottom lip. Heat flooded her body. If type O was addictive for the vampire, it appeared that the vampire was addictive to the donor in return. "I can see how your donors might get insatiable." She didn't want to think about Dmitri doing what he'd just done to her to anyone else.

She flicked her gaze back to his face and found the firm features softened with a fleeting tenderness. "That's why our clan has rules. There's a fine line between feeding, death and conversion. What we shared…it isn't always this way."

"Really?"

His kiss-me-now mouth curved into a sexy smile, showing just the tips of his fangs. She wanted to melt into him all over again. "Sometimes, *tesoro*, it's better."

The dark-chocolate scent of his skin was driving her insane. She gingerly touched the side of her neck. Amazingly there was no soreness. "How can you do that? I mean, I know your mouth never left my neck, and you don't have that many hands, but I could feel you everywhere at once. All of you." Her face blazed with heat as she realized just how intimate the exchange between vampire and human could be. "And why do you always seem to smell like chocolate when you're around me?"

"It's one of the mysteries about us."

She pressed in even closer, letting her sensitive breasts rasp against his broad muscular chest and firmly ridged stomach. She wanted to rip off their clothes and feel his bare skin against hers. She wanted his hands on her, and his mouth. She wanted…him. "You can do better than that."

He broke his gaze with her, his brow crumpling and eyes narrowing for a second as he stared out at the dark water. "We change to become the deepest fantasy of our host." His tone made it seem as if he was revealing some dirty secret.

Whoa. Back that semi up. She took a step back from him, suddenly realizing just how lethal, literally, his sex appeal was to her personally. "So whatever turns me on most is what happens?"

He leveled his serious stare with her wide-eyed gaze. "Exactly."

A giddy smile tilted her lips. "Do you have any idea how many women would kill for that?"

He seemed guarded, his eyes assessing her. "You're not repulsed?"

How to answer? Everything she'd ever known told her to run like hell. He was the ultimate predator. But her heart told her differently. There was a hell of a lot more than just a physical connection shooting sparks between them. And it wasn't just the feeding. He intrigued her, made her feel as if she could fly and that nothing was impossible. Looking into his eyes she could tell her answer meant far more to him than he was letting on.

"Don't get me wrong, the idea of drinking blood still makes me woozy, but feeding you just makes me hot."

Relief flooded his eyes, relaxed the rigid planes of his face.

"Besides, I trust you."

He tenderly traced the curve of her ear, brushing her hair back in a gentle touch that made her shiver with anticipation. "You give your trust too easily. There's much you still don't know about us."

A warning bell triggered in Kristin's head, pricking at the back of her neck and down her spine. She did her best to ignore it. Of course vampires were dangerous. But everything in her promised that *this* vampire was different.

She brushed the plane of his cool cheek, the stubble rasping against the tips of her fingers. "And when you're ready, I hope you'll share that with me. In the meantime, I *do* trust you, Dmitri. God only knows, I feel as though I've just stepped out of an airplane to go skydiving and I'm not sure the parachute is going to open to cushion my fall. But I'm willing to take that leap into the unknown."

His eyes glowed with a fierce tenderness. "I don't want you to ever be afraid of me. I'll do everything in my power not to hurt you."

Kristin believed him, even though her heart was still giving off tiny bursts of fear. Ignoring the fading warnings, she wound her arms around his neck. "I know you will. Tell me something about vampires I don't know." She tried to come up with something innocuous, something that would allow her body to come down from the boil to a more comfortable simmer.

"Why do vampires have different eye colors?"

Sparks of appreciation danced in Dmitri's intense gaze. "I'm surprised you noticed. Most people can't tell."

"I'm a details kind of girl."

"Which is precisely what I like about you."

"So why is it?"

He cuddled her into his chest, and the solidness of him warmed her, making the cool breeze off the water unimportant. Moonlight glinted and sparkled out on the dark water and glowed in the snow on the distant Olympic mountain peaks. It was as though they were temporarily suspended in some sort of dreamworld. Just the two of them.

"You are cold. We should go indoors."

"Stop stalling."

His chest rose beneath her cheek with a resigned sigh. "Vampires have lineage like any other beings. We have makers who function like our mother or father, those who transform us into vampires. We have *tutores,* mentors who guide us through the process of learning to become a vampire when our maker cannot. And every lineage inherits the eye color of their line. In a nest they might all have the same eye color as they change to become more hivelike in their mentality, to the point where the strongest can control the will of them all. In a clan such as ours, though, we are accepting of others of different lines if they pledge themselves to the clan and forsake their lineage. They retain their own eye color because they retain their own will."

She pulled back enough to look in the mesmerizing brown depths of his eyes. "So, nesting vampires, the clanless ones, like the one you fought on the docks, are more dangerous?"

Dmitri's mouth flattened into a grim line. "Ruthless. They live to feed, rather than feed to live."

A shiver rippled through her. For the first time she understood how dangerous and fine a line she was treading between the reivers and Dmitri's clan.

For a moment they stood in companionable silence, watching ghostly clouds drift across the bright face of the moon. He slipped a strand of Kristin's hair through his fingers, enjoying the silky sensation. In the moon's light it was even more beautiful, like spun gold. The unique scent of her had saturated his clothes, creating the strange sensation of being both satisfied and even hungrier at the same time.

He'd not lied when he'd told her there was more. The mental gymnastics that vampires could perform during the act of feeding, sexually tampering with the mortal mind, was nothing compared to the actual act of mating. The taste of power a mortal received during feeding was minuscule in comparison to the full-fledged dose they received during mating, or if they fed directly on vampire ichor.

But the ichor was dangerous to mortals. That was where the virus resided, sustained on the pure life force energy that flowed through their veins. Vampires were the ultimate dichotomy of life and death. Pure life in the vein, pure death in the fang.

As long as mortals had only a vague under-standing of the creation process of vampires, then they'd be worried about bites, which where the most dangerous part anyway.

"How much of this are they going to let me write about?" Kristin's sweet voice startled him.

"They?"

"Your king or leaders, or whatever."

He secretly smiled. She was as brilliant as she was beautiful. "Perceptive of you."

"Comes with the territory."

"Our clan laird, Roman, has decreed that you may share enough to help mortals understand us. The council is concerned that if you release infor-mation about the reivers it will cause unnecessary panic. It is an internal matter, and we vampires would prefer not to air our bloody linens to the public."

He waited for her reaction to the edict. As strong as she was, and being a modern woman, she'd doubtless have a healthy opinion on the matter.

She twisted in his arms, putting her back against him, the sweet curve of her derriere press-ing against him in a way that made the blood lust more intense. "But what about the reivers' connection to the Bloodless Murders? Don't you think that we humans have a right to know?"

He wrapped his hands over her shoulders. "We will handle it and they will be brought to justice within our world."

Kristin turned slightly, her gaze not nearly so loving as it had been a moment before. "So they want it to remain an unsolved mystery to us." Irritation rolled off her in heated, swirling waves.

"As I said, perceptive."

She crossed her arms. "God, politics suck. Even in the vampire world." She pulled away and chafed her arms with her hands. While he could easily withstand the cold, she was still merely a mortal. He needed to get her back indoors.

Saints, he was a fool. It was one thing to protect this mortal as part of his sacred *trejan* oath, but it was a completely different thing to do so out of personal desire. Only once had he felt this way toward a woman before. But then he'd paid the ultimate price for his fixation.

The image of Larissa's dark beauty flared in his mind. In his zeal to lead the hunt by the church to destroy vampires, he'd been captured. She'd trapped him, seduced him, then changed him. Despite the fierce desire she'd raised in him, he'd tried to escape as soon as he'd realized what she intended. But it had been to no avail. In the end he'd been changed into the very thing he'd spent his young life fervently hunting.

But Kristin was so unlike Larissa, in every way but one. She tempted him to ignore his duty. Seduced him with thoughts that he could resist the natural order of things to capture a measure of heaven to hold in his own hands. But unlike Larissa she was mortal, not vampire.

He reached out to grasp her small fragile hand in his. The heat of her skin seared his. "It is for the best. Mortals will be worried enough when they discover vampires are real."

She looked up at the moon and sighed. He tried to probe her mind to understand what she was thinking, but found himself blocked. "So am I supposed to go back to your place tonight," she asked, "or can I go home?"

"You may go home, if I go with you."

She glanced at him and raised one sleek brow. "They put you up to that, didn't they?"

"My laird has nothing to do with it. I want you to be protected. When this is out, people will resort to their most base instinct—fear. You're far too removed from the times when superstition and fear ruled the world. It's an ugly thing, I assure you."

She glanced down at her feet. "Let's hope you're wrong."

"We can hope, but we cannot risk."

Kristin bit her lip. "Your couch is nice and all, but I think I'd rather sleep in my own bed tonight. And I still have work to do before that." It was a damn lie and she knew it. More than anything she wanted to curl up in a bed naked beside him. Her body was still vibrating from the sensations he'd brought out in her when he'd sunk his fangs into her.

"Not alone." He tucked her gently against his chest and rested his chin against the top of her head. "You are too valuable to me now. I can trust no other to watch you as I would."

In a swirl of white mist, the dark water and

night sky disappeared and Kristin found herself back in her own apartment. Even though it was pitch-black, she recognized the sweet vanilla scent of the votive candle on her end table, and the faint fragrance of freshly laundered clothes she hadn't put away yet still sitting in the basket by the counter. The tension that had coiled in the pit of her stomach started to unravel.

"Do you mind if I turn on the lights?" she asked.

"Give me a moment." She heard the shush of something against the fabric of his jacket.

"Go ahead."

She reached over and flipped on a table lamp. Dmitri wore dark sunglasses.

"Light bothers you that much?"

"I won't burn up, but I don't need a migraine."

"Whatever works for you. Would you like something to drink?"

Stupid question, Sunshine. He's likely had his limit. "Sorry, just automatic."

His firm lips tilted into a subtle smirk. "I could always try the other side if you're offering."

Instantly her hand went up to her neck, covering the twin marks that tingled there. A full body shiver rippled from head to toe and she had to force herself from stepping over to him. Wow. She wondered if vampires injected some kind of addictive substance, similar to caffeine or nicotine, into the body as they fed. Perhaps that would explain why she was so drawn to him that she'd willingly offer herself up again. Kristin resisted the pulsing urge deep down in her gut to go to him.

"As tempting as that offer might be—" and God, was it "—I'd better get to work."

She pulled her phone out of the pocket of her jeans and glanced at the time. It was 1:00 a.m. "I have enough time to get this written before the morning deadline." She needed something, anything to keep her focus off the sexy-as-hell vampire sitting a few feet away. Dmitri exuded pure sex without the slightest effort. His sex appeal came as naturally to him as breathing to a human.

Kristin grabbed the remote off the counter and tossed it to him. "Make yourself at home." He settled onto her couch. It never seemed too small before, but then it was meant for two, possibly three, normal-size people, not a guy the size of a bodybuilder on superhuman steroids.

"You sure you don't want to watch a late-night movie with me?" he asked casually as he flipped on the television.

Seriously? Hell, yeah. She wanted to curl herself up next to him, wrap herself up in his body, forget about the article and never leave. But that wasn't going to save her bacon with Hollander. This article would.

By 4:00 a.m. she felt as drained as Balor had been, metaphorically speaking, of course.

It had taken everything she had in her to put the story together piece by piece in a way that showcased both the humanity and the supernatural potential that the Cascade Clan possessed. Just as Dmitri had said, she'd left out the reivers attacking Balor. That could come later, when she had more concrete facts to go on.

She glanced at the vampire stretched out on her couch and wondered just how much deeper this was going to get. She sent the story in by email and reached her hands high over her head, working the knots out of her shoulders. "All done."

"For now."

Already he seemed to know her better than any boyfriend she'd ever had. She gave him a lazy grin. "A journalist's work is never done."

"You should go to sleep."

For a moment she toyed with the idea of inviting him to sleep in the bed with her, but she quickly discarded it. Things were moving too fast as it was. "You know it's not polite to tell a woman she looks tired."

"I meant no offense."

She shook her head. "Don't get bent about it. I was only teasing you. And you're right anyway. I am dead tired." Kristin bit her lip, wishing she could drag the words back.

Dmitri smiled and it stole her breath away. "Don't worry about offending me. It's practically impossible."

"Sure, you say that now, but wait until I use my dad's favorite cold cure of a whole clove of garlic minced into tomato juice. Then see if you talk to me."

"Garlic is a Hollywood fabrication, as are stakes and death by sunlight."

"Yeah. I figured you wouldn't be serving garlic bread at Sangria if it had been a problem."

"The only things that really can hurt a vampire are dead man's blood, which acts like a temporary poison, and silver or orichalcum, which burn on contact and are unbreakable to a vampire. And explosives. Those tend to be deadly."

"Orichalcum?"

"A metal they haven't made since Plato's time." Dmitri glanced out the window. Faint streaks of daylight were beginning to brighten the edge of the early-morning sky, throwing his carved profile into a mixture of shadow and light, a duality just like the vampire himself.

"As much as I would like to stay with you, I need to return to the clan. I've other duties to attend to."

Disappointment carved out a small space within her chest. Kristin chided herself. Why on earth had she thought he'd stay past daybreak? Writing about her experience as a donor must have scrambled her brain. *Come on, you had to practically beg him to feed off you,* she reminded herself. And the intense push and pull she sensed between

them was probably just all those vampire pheromones or whatever it was that made vampires
ultimately attractive to their donor of the moment.

"I'll be fine. I'm a big girl, remember?"

He phased a cell phone into his hand, then
grasped her hand and slipped it into her palm.
"If you need anything, or see anything unusual,
call me."

"You mean, anything more unusual than vampires." She smiled. He didn't.

He leveled his no-nonsense gaze at her. "This
phone will bypass the security system and reach
me directly."

"Got it." She lifted up on her tiptoes and pressed
a quick friendly kiss to his cheek, trying to
put some distance between him and her heart.
"Thanks, Dmitri."

"For what?"

"Everything."

He stepped back from her, his eyes turning
that mysterious dark shade she'd come to associate with him holding something back. "Don't
thank me just yet. You're in more danger now
than ever."

"But that's not your faul—" Before she could finish her sentence he dissolved into a swirl of dark smoke and was gone.

She yanked a pillow off the couch, flopped down onto the cushions and hugged it close. As she'd been writing the article, she'd started a mental list of pros and cons about being attracted to a vampire.

"Reason six why a vampire would make a terrible boyfriend—he can just zap out of the room whenever the mood takes him."

She dropped her head back against the couch and groaned. How could the most erotic night of her life have left her back at square one? Alone. Again.

Across the room her cell phone started doing a happy dance as it vibrated across the counter. Who in the hell needed to talk to her at five-thirty in the morning?

She glanced at the phone and saw it was Hollander. It figured.

"What are you doing up so early?" she said with a little asperity. If he wanted a proper greeting, he could have waited until she'd actually had some sleep.

"I couldn't sleep. I was waiting for your article."

"And?"

"You've done it! This is going to be huge. Just wait until Associated Press gets an eyeful of it. I've ordered a double print for the next edition. If this hits the way I think it will, it could pull in a ton of new subscribers."

That was good news. Great news, in fact. Her job was secure, her editor happy. But that didn't make her limbs less heavy or her eyes less gritty. It was one thing to be a night owl. It was another to be teetering on the edge of becoming nocturnal because you were hanging out with a vampire. She yawned.

"So does that mean I can have today off?"

"Sure. Sleep in, eat chocolate, do whatever it is you do on your day off."

"Usually I research for another article."

"I like how you think."

Kristin sighed, slightly irritated with the admission. Exactly when had work become all there was to her life? "Are you going to send a photographer to the club tonight?"

"Yes. You'll meet him there?"

"Yep."

With plans for the night already in place, she tossed the phone back onto the counter and staggered to bed.

Somehow she managed to sleep most of the day away, until her ringtone woke her. "Hello?"

"I'm outside Sangria, but I'm not going in until you get here." It was Harry, the photographer from the paper.

"Damn. Sorry. Be there in ten minutes."

In a whirlwind, she dressed, shoved her hair into a messy topknot with a few wispy bits, grabbed her stuff and headed out the door.

She trudged up the street to where she'd parked her car. Her breath stuck hard in her throat. All across her white Honda Accord in what she hoped was only dripping red spray paint were the words FANG BAIT.

Swiping her finger across one of the wet letters on the windshield, she tested the substance between her fingertips, then gave it a sniff test.

The chemical fumes confirmed it was paint. Just paint. Thank God. How could someone have known it was her car? Hell, how did they know where she lived? The article hadn't even come out yet. Her phone buzzed in her hand, making her jump.

"Good evening, Kristin. Did you find my love note?"

She struggled to place the voice. Oh, no. Billy Idol vamp, from the club. What had the girl called him? Vane.

"Did you do this to my car?"

He laughed and it chilled her to the bone. "That's nothing compared to what we're going to do to you."

"Yeah, I saw your handiwork on Balor."

"If you expose us to mortals, his demise will look peaceful in comparison. If you do, we *will* stop you. This is your last warning."

The line went dead.

Chapter 10

Now she was pissed.

Kristin snapped her phone shut and shoved it deep down into her pocket. If there was one thing that got her ire up, it was being bullied.

She wasn't about to let a little thing like tagging by a particularly nasty vampire stop her from a shot at a Pulitzer. Of course, saying that to herself did little to slow the shaking in her hands. If what she'd seen with Balor was any indication, these vamps weren't nearly as into maintaining good relations with humans as the vamps in Dmitri's clan.

Harry, the photographer assigned to her story,

was still waiting for her outside Sangria. Opening her trunk, she took out one of the newspapers she'd been intending to take to the recycling station. Scrunching up several sheets, she strode around to the front of the car. The red paint was still wet, which would make it easier to get off. But it was still going to take work. And time. Which she didn't have.

"Bastards. I don't give a crap *what* you call yourselves." She scrubbed at the paint on her windshield, smearing as much as she removed. "You're nothing but freaking vandals." Vandals who can kill with a single bite. The thought sent a shudder down her spine. "Bullies." She tore off several more sheets and mopped up the paint as best she could. At least enough that she could see to drive.

Cleaning the bodywork would have to wait.

After stuffing the wet newspaper into a plastic bag she kept in the glove box, Kristin finally got on the road. "I'd better not get a speeding ticket because of you, you freak." Thankfully it was almost dark. Driving around with FANG BAIT painted in lurid red on her car was sure to illicit attention.

Every block she drove, the more pissed she got.

She had the phone Dmitri had given her. One call, and *he'd* deal with the vandal. And while it was seductive knowing that a man would go to battle for her, Kristin wasn't the type to run for help. She'd gotten used to proving herself to be as tough, as determined, as any male reporter. Investigative reporting wasn't for sissies. She could handle a phone threat. She'd just be careful and ultra aware of her surroundings. And perhaps she'd find a way to get ahold of some dead man's blood, like what Dmitri had used on the reiver. Better prepared than sorry, she told herself. And Vane and his buddies seemed like the type to make a girl very sorry.

Weighed down by all his equipment, Harry was tall, painfully skinny, and decked out in his usual work attire of faded jeans and a graphic T-shirt. He whistled as she pulled up. "Nice paint job," he gibed, nodding his closely cropped head. "You get that special for tonight?" He snapped a picture of her car and gave her a wide grin as she got out and headed for the front door.

"Shut up."

He snickered as she blew past him and strode inside. The minute she entered, she could feel Dmitri's gaze following her, heated and intense. He moved in her direction, but even ten feet away she could tell the scent of chocolate he threw off was different tonight, spiked with something spicy and hot and unpredictable, like chilies.

"Do you smell chocolate, Harry?" she asked as Dmitri closed in.

The photographer shook his head, sniffing appreciatively. "Nah, but they must cook a killer steak in here."

Dmitri took her hand in his, brushing the back with a kiss that she could feel all the way down to her belly button. "I thought you'd finished your article."

"My editor wants some pictures. Do you mind if we take just a few shots inside the club before it gets busy?"

He stared at her a minute longer, as if he was stripping her. Kristin blushed.

"Why didn't you tell me?"

"Hollander just asked me—"

"I meant about the car."

Kristin glanced over her shoulder, then locked her gaze back on his inscrutable face. "I don't remember giving you permission to read my mind."

He raised a brow. "Perhaps I don't have to. We do have security cameras. I'll find out who did this and take care of it." His commanding tone resonated inside her, the barely leashed restraint vibrating in the warm air inside the club.

The place was nearly empty, except for Anastasia at the bar and a few employees moving about to prep for opening. Apparently just past twilight was still too early for many of the regulars. But it was practically perfect for what she needed. Harry could get the shots without needing a photo release from dozens of people.

As he lined up his shots, Kristin turned to Dmitri. "I know who did it," she told him grimly. "It was reiver Vane."

Dmitri's eyes flashed black fire and Kristin heard the telltale flick of his fangs unsheathing. "Vane." It wasn't a question.

The murderous look on his face forged a huge lump in her throat and she nodded rather than trying to talk around it.

He waved a hand in a clearly dismissive gesture to Harry, his intense eyes never leaving her face. "Take whatever pictures you need." It came out sounding more like an order than permission.

"Um, I—" Harry stuttered.

Dmitri whipped his head around, glaring at the photographer, the tips of his fangs bared. "What?"

"Do vampires show up in pictures?" Harry asked, then gulped, his eyes wide. Kristin bet he'd never seen a pair of pearly whites like that before.

Dmitri sighed with exasperation. "Of course we show up, unless we're moving too fast for the camera to capture it."

Harry nodded, then glanced at her, waiting for direction. "Get a few shots of the decor, the bar and the sign outside," Kristin said. He nodded and hurried away, the pulsating flashes pinpointing his location in the low-lit interior of the club.

She turned on Dmitri. "You scared him, you know."

He swiped the tip of his tongue over one of the fangs in a self-conscious gesture. "It wasn't anything to do with him."

"Yes, but he doesn't know that. So how about you try to keep the twins under control, huh? I want a few shots of a tasting room, if that's all right with you."

"Of course."

With a nod of her head she indicated the crimson curtains to Harry and he started moving toward them. Kristin held Dmitri's gaze for a moment and realized he seemed both angry and distracted.

"We'll be out of your hair shortly."

"Take all the time you need. Just be sure to ask permission from anyone you shoot. Vampires aren't always agreeable about having their picture taken." He grabbed her hand and held it for a moment, as though to reassure himself that she was really there. She gave his hand a small squeeze, then walked away from him, feeling the weight of his stare on her back and lower.

Harry stood beside the curtain, holding his

camera with a white-knuckled grip. "What's in there?"

"The tasting rooms."

Harry shuddered as she swept aside the curtain and let him in first. She stepped directly over to the tall black lacquered cabinet nestled in the corner where the gauze, razor blades and other assorted items were stored, and opened it. "Harry, get a close-up of this, then a couple of wide angles of the room, would you?"

He dutifully pointed the camera in her direction and shot a couple of flashes. The bright light illuminated a corner inside the cabinet and she caught a quick glimpse of dark vials in a holder near the back that hadn't been there before.

Her brain scrambled. What if it was vampire ichor? What if it held some of the secrets Dmitri was still withholding from her? What exactly was in vampire ichor that made it able to medically repair what modern medicine couldn't? And was there something addictive in it? Without blinking she waited for an opportunity to snag one of the small vials.

As the flash pulsed a blinding light in the direction of the room, Kristin used it as cover and grabbed one of the vials, quickly hiding it in her pocket.

Her pulse kicked up a notch, and suddenly she felt the need to get out of the club as quickly as she could. "That's enough, Harry. Let's wrap it up."

She could tell by the look on the photographer's face he'd had more than enough of his experience in the vampire club. For now so had she. The questions, nagging and persistent, were pounding in the base of her skull even as she fled.

Before she could reach the door, Dmitri grasped her upper arm in a firm but gentle hold. "Where are you going?" His voice held a silky hard edge to it, velvet over steel.

The vial felt heavy in her pocket. Or perhaps that was guilt. Could he be reading her mind? Did he already know she'd taken it? "I'm going home."

"Not in your car you're not." There was no mistaking the tone. Authoritative and direct.

Against her better judgment she looked him in

the eye. "I'm not walking, if that's what you're worried about."

His hold on her loosened. "I've taken the liberty of having your car repainted and detailed. In the meantime, you'll use the loaner car I've arranged for you." He held out a key ring to her. Kristin noticed the expensive BMW emblem.

"Thanks." What she really wanted to say was that she hadn't asked him to do anything about the car. A conflicting mix of appreciation and ire surged through her. Deep down she appreciated Dmitri's thoughtfulness. He really did want to look after her. But somehow the feeling got muddled up with a far older gut reaction that said she could take care of herself and didn't need any man, including him, making decisions for her, thank you very much.

"How long do you think it'll take to get my car back?"

"You don't need to worry. I'll take care of it."

That was precisely the part that irked her most. Deep within, she could feel herself becoming more dependent upon him and it made her decidedly uncomfortable.

"Black coupe. Should be waiting at the curb. It has remote entry and start. Just push the buttons on the keypad."

For the moment, the nagging questions in the back of her mind were more insistent than the strange new feelings swimming around in her gut. The reporter in her was deadly curious. She wanted to know if there was an addictive compound in the blood sample she'd just stolen that could be the Love Potion Number Nine of the twenty-first century.

She held up the key in her hand. "Thank you, Dmitri."

"Call me if anything out of the ordinary happens. I mean it, Kristin. I'll deal with Vane. Just because he did something fairly innocuous this time doesn't mean he won't try to harm you."

She nodded. "I know. He called and threatened me if I continue reporting on vampires."

Dmitri's dark eyes flashed black fire. "But that doesn't mean you'll stop."

"You know I can't."

His brows bent. Just because he knew it didn't

mean he liked it. "I'll be careful, I promise." She slipped out the door of Sangria.

There at the curb sat the sleek black sports coupe. It looked so damn expensive, Kristin would have bet it was owned by a high-tech computer executive or a drug lord. The mirror finish on the black paint reflected the strobing red neon of the Sangria sign behind her, bending it into graceful arcs of blazing light.

She opened the door, sliding into the form-hugging sports seat crafted out of buttery-soft black leather. Vampires had good taste. She pushed the key in the ignition and the engine roared to life, like a waking beast.

Just like with Dmitri, she wasn't used to being around something so powerful and obviously dangerous. She drove carefully, toward the one person she knew could help her decipher what was in the vial.

The spectacular view of downtown Seattle's night skyline sparkled like glitter on black velvet when seen from the top floor of Genet-X Laboratories International. As pretty as it was,

Kristin turned away and pulled the vial out of her pocket. She set it on her friend's desk.

Dr. Rebecca Chamberlin was a genius freak when it came to anything biochemical. With a heart-shaped face and a mass of auburn hair that seemed to twist itself into perpetual ringlets, she hardly looked like a superbrain. But Kristin knew her well enough to know that if anyone could crack the secret of vampire ichor, it was Beck.

"What is it?" Beck asked, holding the vial up to the light, tipping it back and forth as her inquisitive hazel eyes peered over her dark-rimmed glasses.

"Not sure. I need you to analyze it for me."

"What am I looking for?"

"Just run a normal blood panel on it. Perhaps a viral and DNA test too and anything else that can tell me what's in it. Cover all the bases."

Beck set the vial down, peering intently at the black liquid inside. "But it's not blood."

"Probably not. I'm trying to figure out exactly what it is, Beck."

Her friend glanced up and shrugged. "It's your dollar."

"Thanks, I owe you one."

Beck smirked, which made her look even younger. "Oh, you owe me a hell of a lot more than that. But I don't have time to go into detail."

Kristin flinched. "For the last time, I'm not setting you up with Bradley Peters. Take my word for it, he's not your type."

"How can blond, good-looking and loaded not be my type?"

"He's an ass."

Beck shrugged. "Most men can be asses. That's why being loaded and good-looking helps."

"Really, I'm doing you a favor not introducing you."

Beck let out a dramatic sigh. "Fine. I'll drop it. But if you aren't going to set me up with him, then how about someone else? Getting a date while working at the lab is like trying to fish with no bait."

"They're intimidated because your brain is bigger than theirs."

Beck grinned in response.

"How fast can you get the testing done?" Kristin pushed.

"What's the rush?"

"It's research for an upcoming article. I need to know what's in it before I can go any further into the investigation."

"Have anything to do with that hush-hush assignment that forced you to turn down dinner last week?"

"Yep. The very same."

"And…?" Beck rolled her hand, waiting for Kristin to add details.

"And you can read all about it in the morning paper."

Beck snorted. "I'm going to bust a gut getting this testing done for you in a rush and that's the best you can do?"

Kristin rolled her shoulders to ease the tension that had been building there ever since they'd found Balor's body. "I suspect that what you've got in front of you is vampire ichor."

"I'm sorry, did you just say vampire, as in *Dracula, Lost Boys, Twilight* and *True Blood?*"

Kristin nodded. "They're real, Beck, seriously, honest-to-God real. I've been to the place where they live here in the city and apparently they aren't just in Seattle, they're everywhere."

Beck sat back in her chair, clearly stunned. She snapped her mouth shut, her eyes coming back into sharp focus. "Do you know what this means? This is going to cause mass panic. Hysteria. People are going to freak. You're unveiling their nightmares for real."

Beck's reaction stung a bit. "I'm trying to do exactly the opposite. I'm not writing this to sensationalize vampires. Actually, I'm hoping the article will help dispel some of the myths and maybe quell the drama."

Beck snorted. "Not damn likely, but good luck with that. So you think this stuff is like vampire blood?"

"If my hunch is right, it's what keeps them immortal."

Beck pulled her glasses down and massaged her temple. "And what, other than for your article, are you going to do with the information of the chemical makeup when I give it to you?"

"This stuff could hold the key to unlocking

some major leaps in health care if we can replicate it or find out how it works."

"Whoa. Back up. You mean you've seen people shoot up with this stuff?" She tapped the vial, making the black liquid within agitate.

"Not exactly. People were being treated in a special clinic with a mix of this with regular blood. According to the physician I met there, it was helping where our modern medical treatments couldn't, curing things like inoperable cancer."

"Can you get me some more to test?"

Kristin shook her head. "I'm nervous enough taking this sample."

"But you'll have details about the healing properties in your upcoming article, right?"

Kristin shook her head. "I'm not writing about this part of it until I know what's in that vial. Then I can get a list of questions from you and ask the vampire doc I talked to, if you want."

Beck nodded vigorously. "Look, if you can get me details, we'll call this an even trade, my testing for the info."

"Sure. You get the results for me, and if this isn't just ink in a bottle and we can pinpoint what makes it tick, then I've got some groundbreaking news to cover."

"Uh, yeah. More groundbreaking than telling the world vampires really exist? You sure know how to pick 'em, Kris, I'll give you that."

An image of Dmitri, with his dark penetrating eyes and powerful build, immediately sprang to mind, making her skin feel suddenly a size too small. "You have no idea."

Chapter 11

Kristin flipped on the morning news and nearly spewed hot coffee across her television screen. People were chanting and marching with signs held high above their heads outside the *Tribune* offices and city hall. BAN VAMPIRES, VAMPIRES SUCK, NO BLOODSUCKERS IN MY TOWN and a few other more colorful variations bobbed in rhythm in front of the cameras.

"…protestors are demanding a citywide search for the vampires, asking for them to be quarantined as a health hazard and threat to public safety until officials can provide citizens with assurances that the vampires mean no harm to residents of Seattle." The reporter spoke in tones guaranteed to incite the people watching the news.

The image shifted to a middle-aged woman with glasses who spoke into a microphone. "We don't know what they're capable of. Until we do, we have a right to public safety. I'm scared for myself and my children."

A man in a red flannel shirt and ball cap appeared next. "Wouldn't surprise me if they're the reason behind the Bloodless Murders."

Kristin flipped the channel, but there was only more of the same. More protestors. More panic. More reporters squeezing every last bit out of the story, just as she had, but from a whole different angle.

Her staff mug shot, which ran next to her byline, popped up on the screen in all its scary full-color glory. *"Pacific News Tribune* investigative reporter Kristin Reed broke the story after spending time with the group of vampires here in Seattle that call themselves the Cascade Clan—"

Another channel wasn't any better. "Now that one of the staples of Halloween has become a real-life nightmare, many are concerned what new developments will occur now that vampires are out of the coffin. Back to you, Phil."

Kristin groaned, letting her head fall back on her couch as she muted the television. Why did people have to overreact? If they'd actually read the article, they would have realized how vampires had been there all along and there hadn't been any mass killings. There was really nothing to worry about. Except possibly from the reivers, which she had purposely left out of the first article. Humans were every bit as dangerous as vampires. The crime rate alone proved that. Why all of a sudden did they act as if vampires were responsible for everything wrong with the world? She'd tried so damn hard to be objective and informative. It was frustrating as hell.

If this public outcry didn't throw the suits at the paper for a loop, the second article would run tomorrow. She could only imagine how these hyped-up vamp haters would react when she gave details about the donor-vampire relationship and described exactly what happened when a vampire bit you. An insistent throb built behind her eyes as morning coverage of the picket line continued. Her cell phone rang and she got up off the couch to grab it.

"Where are you?" It was Hollander.

"I'm taking the day off, remember?"

"I know that, but where are you?"

"Does it matter?" For a moment she wished that she were in Dmitri's apartment. Sure, he'd likely be dead to the world, passed out asleep at this time of day, but that didn't matter. Perhaps it wouldn't be any more secure than her own apartment, but she couldn't help but feel safer, more protected, when he was around.

"You're at home? Good. Stay there. Watch your back, Reed. We've got a bunch of nut jobs down here picketing the place. The phones have been ringing off the hook. And you've already had four death threats phoned in." Hollander sounded excited as hell.

That would have Dmitri wound up when he found out. All it did for her was make her more agitated. She might have to hire security—or stick real close to Dmitri. She glanced at the black phone he'd given her. She had a direct line to him.

Anytime, anywhere. So why did that thought make her just as uneasy as the thought of being without him? She shifted in her seat, tucking her legs underneath her.

"Yeah, I saw all the commotion on the news. A banner day at the *Trib.*"

Hollander chuckled. "Nothing sells papers better than controversy. Your article touched a nerve."

A raw feeling scraped away at the back of her throat, forcing her to swallow. What if the suits who owned the paper saw the next story as too big of a risk? Would she be just a one-hit wonder? And once Dmitri read it, how was he going to react? Worse still, how would her father and Beck react when they found out she'd let a vampire drink from her?

"We're still running the second installment to-morrow, right?" she asked.

"Of course! When can you get part three handed in?"

Just how protective was Dmitri going to be when he discovered she'd stolen the ichor and had it analyzed? Hell, she might need protection from *him*. She shivered and rubbed her arms, a sudden chill sweeping over her. She doubted that anything could protect someone from Dmitri if they were on his bad side. "Once I get some test results back."

"Good. Just send it in as soon as you can."

Right now Kristin had bigger problems than a deadline. Vane and his little band of merry vampires were going to read the article and be out for blood tonight. Specifically her blood—and not as some erotic feeding fest. She flinched as an image of Vane's red eyes flashed in her mind. Balor had been gutted like a deer during hunting season. And Vane had promised to do even worse to her.

Maybe serving the public interest as a journalist wasn't worth the risk. She shook her head. Living in fear wasn't going to get her anywhere, which meant she needed to get the results from Beck, keep that phone on her, get ahold of some dead man's blood pronto and keep her head down and her eyes and ears open. And, if possible, live in Dmitri's pocket.

* * *

In the depth of his daydreams Dmitri sensed Kristin's fear, tasted the bite of it on his tongue, acidic like vinegar. Visions of Vane swooped in and disrupted his far more pleasant images of running his fingers over Kristin's silky skin as he kissed her.

The dreams twisted, became a macabre mesh of the past and the present. Kristin's vivid blue eyes morphed into the frightened green eyes of the blonde village girl Larissa had brought before him and Vane.

Entertainment and snack.

Over six hundred years ago, and the memory of that young girl's terror was still fresh in his mind. Six hundred years and he'd never forgotten his own transfiguration from fledgling to fully formed vampire.

"You need your strength, my fledglings," his maker had crooned, her eyes glowing red in the firelight of the castle's keeping room. "Time to feast."

The blonde had shrieked, her scream echoing

against the stone walls as Vane had leaped at her, nearly breaking her in two as he fed greedily.

Dmitri had turned away, sickened at the reminder of what he had become. But he was weak. He did indeed need to eat. He'd resisted as long as he could, knowing that nothing could undo what he had become. He could try to starve himself, but he'd only become a shell, an immortal, useless shell that couldn't die, but neither could it live.

"Do not resist the urge to feed, Dmitri," Larissa beckoned, her sultry tones smooth and silken as they raked across his skin like barbs, digging in deeper the more he tried to pull away. "She is a virgin. Her blood is so sweet, so fresh it will make you drunk with the taste of it. And once you have killed her, we can rest."

"I will not kill her."

Larissa's eyes flashed. Angry. Haughty. Determined. "Very well." She cast a withering glance at the whimpering village girl. "Then leave her broken. Either way, the little blood baggage will die before dawn. It is up to you whether it is slow and painful, or fast and blissful."

The girl's eyes were so wide with fear and pain

that they speared Dmitri to the core. He knelt beside her. "Do not fear. I promise not to hurt you. You go to be with God, a place much sweeter than any here."

Rendered speechless by the gaping hole in her throat, the girl merely gurgled her terror.

The smell of her bright red blood made his blood lust rise in an overwhelming tide, impossible to ignore. Hating himself for giving in to the hunger that clawed deep in his belly, he'd slipped his fangs into her wrist, allowing the venom to flow, allowing her to feel only bliss as he drained the remaining life energy from her body.

But within the confines of his dream, the green eyes of the village girl turned into the vivid blue seared upon his brain. He stared in horror as the last spark of life left Kristin's blue eyes and she became limp in his arms.

"No!"

He woke in the darkness, his body shaking. Dmitri scrubbed his hands over his face. He blew out a cleansing breath and whipped the sheets off his nude body, unable to bear anything touching him. No matter how he wanted to defend his actions, the truth was, feeding from Kristin put her in mortal danger. Each and every time he'd be less able to control the impulse, the desire to feed. What complicated it even further was that the blood lust was tangled with his desire to protect her, his duty as *trejan* to protect his clan. He couldn't possibly do it all.

By now the mortals of Seattle knew they existed. Kristin had told him the story would be in the morning edition. Unable to sleep after the terrible dream, he phased a copy of the *Pacific News Tribune.*

Damn. Of course. They were front-page news.

No sooner had he scanned the story than the pulling sensation that started at his navel and sucked everything inward began. Dmitri barely had time to phase himself into a pair of black exercise pants before he materialized before Roman's desk.

"Seeing as how you are awake, I thought I would discuss what's happened today, the day of our unveiling."

Dmitri nodded. "The article was fair."

"It is not the article that concerns me."

Roman flipped on the enormous wall-mounted flat-screen television behind Dmitri. Images of protestors flashed across the screen. "The mortals are not taking it well."

As laird, Roman had every right to call him day or night, but a little warning would have been appreciated. Inside, Dmitri boiled, not from the calling alone, but from the knowledge that Kristin was afraid and there was no way he could get to her until Roman was done with him. Dmitri fought to keep his exterior demeanor cool and smooth. "As predicted."

"Yes, as predicted. But that doesn't make the situation any easier. Especially when we have reivers threatening our borders. As *trejan* you know that the welfare of the clan must come first. The reporter is simply a means to an end for us."

His words hit home and Dmitri bristled. "I know my duty, my laird."

"It is not your knowledge or your loyalty I question, *Trejan*. It's your heart. You have already started to form a bond with the mortal reporter."

Dmitri kept his expression bland as he met and

held Roman's intense gaze. "I repeat. I know where my allegiance lies."

Roman reached into his head. *You know it's true, brother.*

It is merely proximity that has endeared her to me.

Roman sighed. *Do not fool yourself, brother. A woman who can bring a* trejan *to his knees comes once in a millennium. And she is just that kind of woman.*

Dmitri locked gazes with Roman. "Then perhaps she's worth the risk."

Roman's eyes flashed red for an instant, betraying his ancient lineage, before they returned to their darker steady brown. "Tread carefully, *Trejan.* If you fail in your duty to protect the clan because of her, I will have the right to execute you both."

Kristin didn't dare leave her apartment that day. There was just too much weirdness happening out on the streets of Seattle. Never in her wildest imaginings had she thought the reaction would be this severe. There'd hardly been a blip on the reader radar when she'd written the first article on blood fetishes and vampire groupies. But apparently, as long as people were just playing at being vampires, nobody cared. They were merely seen as one more strange pop subculture like goths, skaters or grunge.

But reveal the existence of another actual species and the world went bonkers.

After it had rung nonstop for hours, she'd finally shut off her cell phone and sat on the sofa, sipping a diet cola. A knock on her door caused her to jump, spilling the cola down her shirt. Kristin muttered an oath.

She got to the door and glanced through the peephole. Relief flooded her as she recognized her dad.

She unlatched the locks and threw her arms around him in a big hug. Nothing in the world felt as good as having her father hug her back.

"Had to come by to see how you're holding up. You didn't answer your phone."

She closed the door, efficiently turning all the locks. "Yeah, well, it's been a weird day, so I turned it off. Come on in and sit down."

Her dad sat down on the couch, looking far smaller than Dmitri had when he'd sat in that exact spot less than twelve hours earlier. He smoothed the copy of the *Tribune* he held in his hand, then glanced at her. "That's quite a story you wrote, Sunshine. Top-notch reporting."

Heat stole into Kristin's cheeks. Her dad seldom, if ever, gave compliments. "Thanks, Dad. That means a lot coming from you. I always wanted to be a reporter just like you."

But all the warmth she'd seen in his eyes fled, replaced by worry. "You're not seeing one of these vampires, are you?"

"Why would you even ask me that, Dad?"

He slapped the folded newspaper with the back of his hand, concern furrowing his brow. "I read between the lines, Sunshine."

Kristin stiffened at her dad's tone. "I'm not a little girl anymore. And I'm a professional. I'm doing what I need to to get the job done."

"But vampires are dangerous. Surely you aren't putting yourself in jeopardy merely for a story."

"It's nothing you wouldn't have encouraged a young male reporter to go after." It still galled her that underneath it all her dad didn't think her competent enough to compete with the boys. Well, she admitted, perhaps it was that. Or perhaps it was more about her being all he had left of a family since her mother had died.

He rubbed his hands together. "True. But this is totally different." He stood slowly from the couch. "I really don't like the idea of you hanging out with vampires. They're an abomination! Freaks! And I don't want my little girl ending up sucked up and thrown away like an empty soda can."

Kristin folded her arms. "You're overreacting, Dad. You haven't even met one."

"The hell I am! Didn't you read the rest of the paper? Four murders. Four. And several other missing people this week alone. And from what the authorities are seeing, they think it's all vampires. Bastards are eating us like takeout."

She'd never seen her dad like this, almost frantic, and it scared her. She reached out a hand, trying to reassure him. "I know you're worried, Dad. But you've got to understand that the members of the Seattle clan are just as civilized as you and I. If you met the vampire assigned to help me with my articles, you'd see he's just as protective of me as you are. Maybe even more so. They want my help to get their side of the story out. To forge a connection with humans where we can coexist."

"You can't coexist with the devil, Sunshine."

Kristin rolled her eyes with exasperation. "Dad, they aren't the devil."

He grabbed her and pulled her into a tight hug. "You're all I've got. I can't lose you." For several moments neither of them said a thing, he just held her close. His back heaved with a determined sigh. "I can't let you do this. You've got to stop seeing these vampires before they pollute you."

Her fingers skimmed over the spot where she'd let Dmitri drink from her. She pulled the collar of her shirt up a little more tightly. "I knew you'd never welcome them with open arms, but I had no idea you'd be this bigoted."

"Baby, listen to me." The pleading, broken tone in his voice almost made her buckle. She'd never heard her dad beg for anything before. "This a destructive path you've chosen. I can't help you if you choose this. Walk away from it. The story isn't important if it's going to cause you to risk your life."

Kristin thought about the death threats called in to the paper and about Vane. The risks were definitely growing, but then didn't every reporter stuck in a war or foreign country take risks just as big on a daily basis?

This was the break she'd been working her whole career for. It was a chance to be part of history, and she was in deep enough that getting out now wouldn't be easy or pleasant. "It's not that easy, Dad."

His face crumpled. "I can't just stand by and watch you self-destruct. This is going to end badly. I can feel it in my bones."

Her father's words startled her, hitting like a dart from out of nowhere, making her feel numb. "You know it's not fair to make me choose between my career and you."

"This isn't about your career anymore. It's about your soul. If you associate with them, eventually you'll become one of them. And I can't watch you destroy yourself." His eyes had become flat and distant, twisting her pain and making it worse.

Without even asking, Kristin knew he was thinking about her mom. She'd gotten deeply involved in a secretive group while Kristin was little, and one day, her mother never came home. Despite his best efforts, he'd never found out what had happened to her mom until he went out to cover a fire in the mountains. The entire commune and those in it were nothing but char and ash caused by self-immolation.

But he didn't know what he was asking. And he sure as hell didn't know Dmitri. Without a doubt Kristin knew she could trust him to protect her from whatever might happen. Even if he had to protect her from himself. "It's not going to happen."

Sadness dragged down her father's features. "I'm sorry to hear that. You take care of yourself."

"Dad, don't do this."

"I can't watch it happen, Sunshine. I just can't live through it again."

She grabbed his hand. "Dad, don't leave like this. I promise I'll do everything I can to keep myself safe. And you'll be proud of me when this is over. You'll see."

He glanced back at her over his slumped shoulder as he opened the front door, suddenly looking far older than she'd ever seen him, and his hand slid out from hers. "Goodbye, Sunshine."

Kristin was too stunned to move as the door closed behind him. This couldn't be happening. First the protestors, now her own father freaking out.

Hurt and bewildered, she shoved on shoes and grabbed her purse, phone and the loaner-car key. Her hands were shaking. She needed to talk to Dmitri. Hell, she needed to see Dmitri. He'd know what to do. She opened her door, looking both ways, pulled the hood of her jacket over her head against the growing chill of twilight, then walked as quickly as she could to where she'd parked Dmitri's black BMW. The streetlights were just flicking on, casting pools of yellow in regular intervals along the cracked sidewalk.

Kristin pushed the button on the remote to start the car. Three seconds later she was thrown back against the building by a blast of heat and flying shrapnel as the car exploded.

Chapter 12

"What in the hell do you mean it 'blew up'?" Dmitri demanded, wishing the clan's security captain wasn't at the other end of the phone. When he got bad news, he wanted to see the person's face, read their body language.

"Detonation occurred approximately three minutes ago," James said tightly.

"Where?"

"The 900 block of Eighteenth between Marion and Spring."

Kristin.

"Get back to me with the details once you find out what triggered it." Without waiting for an affirmative, Dmitri hung up as he transported. Pressure built into a throbbing mass at the base of his skull. Something was wrong. Very wrong.

If he had a beating heart it would've stopped cold as he materialized outside Kristin's apartment building. "Where are you, woman?" His voice sounded strained even to his own ears.

The stench of burnt rubber and hot metal permeated the evening chill as he searched for her in the debris. Drifts of heavy black smoke rose from the charred remains of his hundred-thousand-dollar car turned into a blown-out barbecue in six seconds flat. Under the acrid assault of smoke, he caught a whiff of the familiar dark scent of Vane. Inside, his vampire ichor began to seethe and bubble like hot lava, running in explosive rivulets through his veins.

How could anyone survive a blast of this magnitude? Especially a frail human with creamy skin and guileless eyes.

He moved fast, rage and fear giving him wings as he circled the wreckage to the sound of the approaching emergency vehicles. He overturned a crumpled door with his bare hands, a twisted blackened fender with a vicious kick of his booted foot. Even as he swiftly scouted the area, his eyes were ever vigilant looking for any sign of her.

Not dead. Not dead. Not dead.

The words buzzed inside his head like a mantra. Hell, a prayer.

He smelled her blood first, that blend of vanilla and cinnamon totally at odds with the stink of the burning car. His fangs descended instantly with an audible flick. Relief flooded him when he saw her limp body twenty feet away from the blast. Dmitri was beside her in seconds. *Not dead. Please.* He hadn't prayed in five hundred years, but he didn't think God would care if he was rusty. God would know this was not for his sake, but for hers.

She'd been thrown by the blast and had probably hit the wall of the building with enough force to break most of the bones in her body. He didn't need to see the blood running down her temple; he smelled it, viscous and warm, seeping the life from her. Kristin's unique fragrance saturated his senses, making him hyperaware of her.

Despite his rage at Vane, he gently placed two fingers against her throat.

A pulse. He closed his eyes briefly as unfamiliar emotions flooded through him. *She's alive. Thank you, God.*

Alive, but hurt. How badly? He ran his hands over her body, searching for God only knew what. He wasn't a physician, but he knew to be concerned over internal injuries and concussion. The sirens drew closer. He couldn't wait. Pain, deep and bullet hot, pierced his chest. *Damn you, Vane.*

He gingerly scooped her up in his arms, trying not to jar her. She was far too light and too fragile. Blood dribbled from a gash on her head and multiple smaller lacerations on her hands and face. The scent of it swamped his senses, clouding his thoughts. He fought the craving to feed from her. Keeping her alive mattered more than anything else.

Focusing, he transported her back to the emergency room of the Cascade Clan medical unit. Zarah met them in the clinic emergency entrance. Her dark eyes met his with a flash of worry.

What happened?

Car bomb. The blast threw her against a brick wall.

She pushed up the sleeves of her lab coat, her fingers feeling for Kristin's pulse. Dmitri was astounded anew at the doctor's ability to ignore human blood in favor of healing. Her fangs didn't even extend. "Pulse is weak, but there. We'll need to stabilize her— Yes, Dmitri," she said reading his mind, "and check for internal injuries."

With silent efficiency the medical team brought out a stretcher and he gently laid Kristin down on it. Within his chest his stone heart shattered.

Zarah turned away briefly to speak to a nurse. "Check his hands. Don't take no for an answer." She gave him a stern look. "I'm going to do my job. I don't need your help. By the time Mary's attended to you, I'll have news. Go."

He closed his eyes and clenched his singed hands in an effort to stave off the wave of helplessness encroaching on him as Zarah and her team wheeled Kristin away. When had this mortal become more than just another assignment? His fear for her was real enough to make him ache marrow deep.

Dmitri? Zarah's voice sounded in his head, clinical, emotionally detached, while inside him everything was a seething mass. *She's sustained a few broken bones and has some internal bleeding. We are going to administer ichor to stabilize her condition. Do you know what blood type she is?*

Type O.

Thank God he didn't need to speak to communicate with Zarah. As tight as his throat was, he wasn't certain he'd be able to. As much as he hated the idea of her being infused with ichor without her consent, he knew it would heal her more quickly than anything else could. As long as too much wasn't administered, she'd still be mortal. That was a big if. But he trusted Zarah implicitly. She'd make sure the balance was maintained.

There was, of course, nothing to be done with his hands. The burns had healed already, leaving his skin filthy, with new pink, quickly fading scars, but otherwise unmarked. After thanking the nurse for directing him to the restroom where he scrubbed his skin, he teleported back to the club.

Standing around useless like a lovesick swain wasn't going to help anyone. Least of all Kristin. She was in excellent hands. Behind the closed doors of his office Dmitri phased in a set of signature sensors and programmed Vane's imprint into their alarm code. If the vile bastard so much as curled a lip within walking distance of Sangria, he'd know in an instant. Kristin was protected within the confines of the clan complex. Vane would be unable to reach her there.

He paged Achilles. The head of security transported to his office, his chest stripped, his face half-shaven. "I'm assuming this is important or you would have called James?"

"Vane is leading the reivers. He just blew up my car in an attempt to kill the reporter." Dmitri stuck to the facts. Achilles had no business knowing how his emotions were in a tailspin after seeing Kristin broken and bleeding. "If she dies…" He managed to speak without clenching his teeth with rage. "If she dies—especially now—it will look as though the Cascade Clan sought revenge for her articles revealing our existence. We've got to keep her safe."

Achilles eyed him critically, phasing away the remaining shaving cream on his face and phasing in a clean black T-shirt. "So there's nothing personal in this?"

"Exactly."

"Glad to know. For a moment it sounded as if you were asking me to divert clan security from border protection to personal bodyguard duty just to protect your mortal plaything."

Dmitri glared at him. Physically assaulting Achilles would accomplish nothing. "She is *not* a plaything."

"But she *is* special to you. Admit it."

"She is…important…to all of us."

Achilles shook his head, then looked deeply into Dmitri's eyes. "You are bonding with her, aren't you?"

Dmitri looked away, not liking how keenly his mentor saw through him. "Not of my free choice."

"That's even worse."

"Roman has threatened to sign an execution order for both of us should I fail in my duties."

Achilles touched his shoulder, and they stared for an instant at each other, Achilles's penetrating gaze saying far more than he ever would. Friends. Brothers. Warriors. Vampires. Achilles would stand by him when none other would, even if it came down to defending him against the clan council and Roman in a tribunal. "I've got three words for you, brother. Don't. Screw. Up."

"Sterling advice. Thanks."

Achilles slapped him on the back. "How did you determine Vane was leading the reivers?"

"He's the one who passed Kristin the note leading her to Balor's body. He's the one who had her car tagged. He's the one with a personal grudge against me. It's only a matter of time until he moves directly against the clan. Up till now, he's been toying with us."

"You should know."

Dmitri grimaced. More than he hated having been made a vampire, he hated the fact that he shared a maker with Vane. It placed them on equal status. Two halves of the same demented coin. He'd been the cleric, Vane the aristocrat. He'd loved his human life. Vane had been grate-

ful to be rid of mortality. He loved— He wanted
Kristin safe. Vane wanted to destroy her.

His security phone buzzed with a message from
the clinic. Kristin was awake. Zarah must have
been too busy to reach him telepathically.

Dmitri turned back to Achilles. "I have signature sensors posted around the club, but I want
24/7 surveillance on Vane."

Achilles raised a brow and squared his thick
shoulders. "Is that an order, *Trejan?*"

"Yes, dammit. That's an order," Dmitri barked.

The *trejan's* order was law within the clan. He
was second in command; only Roman could gain-
say him. And with the official order to watch
Vane, he'd bound himself even tighter to Kristin.
In fact, he'd sealed his fate with her.

Kristin blinked against the ultrabright glare of
the overhead lights. She raised her hand to shield
her eyes and found an IV taped to the back of
her hand, one tube of a reddish-black substance
and the other clear. She wrinkled her nose at the
acrid smell of freshly cut lemons that seemed to
permeate the room.

"Welcome back." The confident quality of Dr. Al Kashir's voice rubbed out some of the tension building behind Kristin's eyes.

She struggled to focus. Wow. She could see every pore on Dr. Al Kashir's café au lait-colored face from across the room, but couldn't adjust to see her whole face. She squeezed her eyes tightly shut and blinked again. "What's—" She swallowed against the dryness coating her throat. "What's wrong with me?"

"Close your eyes for a moment and I'll adjust the lights."

The lights dimmed, making it considerably easier for Kristin to focus properly. She scanned the room, instantly recognizing the wall of frosted glass with a gentle diffused light coming through it. She was at the clan's medical center. Pristine sheets and a blanket covered her on the narrow bed.

She grasped the cut-crystal glass of water from the bedside table and sucked on the straw. Tepid water flooded her parched mouth and throat.

"Is that better?" the doctor asked with a slight smile. Her dark eyes were keen and penetrating, as if she could actually x-ray Kristin just by look-ing at her.

Kristin nodded. "Yes. Thank you, Doctor."

"Please, as I've told you before, call me Zarah," she said as she approached the bed.

Kristin frowned at a loud and unfamiliar sound. It was as if someone were rubbing a sheet of paper over a microphone inside her head. Could a concussion affect her hearing this intensely? It took her a moment to realize that the sounds she was hearing were those of the doctor's lab coat rustling against her slacks as she moved.

Kristin covered her ears with her hands. "Why is everything so...*intense* all of a sudden?"

Zarah nodded, scribbling a note on the chart in her hands. "You were in an accident. Trejan Dionotte brought you to us. The effects of the ichor will wear off in time. Until then, your senses may be heightened."

May be heightened? Her senses were on super-steroids. She could probably pick up interstellar radio signals if she focused on it. Instinctively she tried to connect the dots. She'd walked out to the car. Pressed the remote start button. But everything after that was a blank.

"How ba—" She swallowed, her throat still dry. She took another sip of water. "How badly was I hurt?"

"You had four broken ribs, a shattered vertebra and pelvis, a punctured lung, and assorted cuts and abrasions."

Kristin glanced down at her body, her hands roaming over the hospital covers and gown. No body cast. No bandages covering stitches. How was it possible? Her eyes met Zarah's in silent question.

"It's the ichor. You've almost completely healed from your injuries, although I wouldn't advise running any marathons or going rock climbing in the next week." She grinned, her glance flicking to the monitors beeping and humming loudly just behind the head of Kristin's bed.

"Healed? From all that?"

Dr. Al Kashir shrugged. "Ichor is quite powerful when administered properly."

That was an understatement, Kristin thought. Wait until she told Beck. She'd be all over it.

She heard the slight brush of a footstep outside the door a few seconds before the tumblers in the lock clacked and clicked as the knob rotated and the door opened.

The scent of rich dark chocolate spiked with brandy filled the room, more intensely than she'd ever smelled it before, but it was underscored with something spicier, like chili peppers. Dmitri. For an instant Kristin's vision shimmered and all she could see were his dark brown eyes. The room filled with the color, absorbing her completely.

"Ciao, tesoro." The deep timbre of his voice resonated through her in a completely new way, making her feel as though he'd stroked her intimately. Her toes curled under the sheet, and her heart picked up a rapid, excited beat. "How do you feel?"

She couldn't stop the goofy grin that widened across her face. "Much better. Especially now that you're here." Oh, God, had she said that? And in front of the doctor? Her pulse sounded unnaturally loud to her own ears, like the roar of the ocean. It mixed with the rumble of conversations she could hear in the hall and in the room next to hers. When she didn't see the doctor's mouth move, but heard her voice as if she were talking to another person, she suspected she was hearing thoughts too. Holy crap. She shook her head, trying to escape the wave after wave of new sensations assaulting her senses.

Dmitri grasped her hand gently. She felt the brush of his thumb over the back of her hand all over her body, focusing her senses on him alone. Good grief. This must be what that girl donor she'd interviewed had meant by feeling as if you were some kind of superhero. Ichor was certainly heady stuff, but far too intense for her liking.

Kristin knew one thing for certain. She was sincerely glad she didn't have to deal with this sensory overload on a daily basis like vampires did. God, if this was what being a vampire was like, they could keep it. It was hard to think when every sound was amplified a hundredfold. Even more impossible to concentrate when a simple touch aroused her like foreplay.

"How do you deal with this day in, day out?" she asked.

Dmitri's eyes narrowed. "Deal with what?"

"All this." She slipped her hand from beneath his and felt her body contract with need. "The intensity of the light, the overwhelming smells, the loudness of sound, having to block out other people's thoughts."

His gaze flicked to the doctor, questioning.

"It's only temporary. Once the ichor has been impacted by her immune system it'll readjust to her normal levels," she reassured him.

He gave Kristin's hand a small squeeze. "It's different for a full vampire. We have the ability to control our sensory input."

Kristin shut her eyes, suddenly exhausted by trying to cope with so much at once.

"Her reaction is slightly elevated." Kristin could feel the doctor's gaze lingering on the twin puncture marks near her collarbone that were nearly healed. She also swore she could hear gears moving in the doctor's brain during the long stretch of silence, and the minute cracks as her spine stiffened. Kristin shifted uncomfortably at the sudden tension in the room. "Feeding has left her more susceptible. She needs to rest until the effect is more normalized." The pen scraped and scratched against the paper as Zarah made several more notes on her chart.

"I want her moved to my quarters when you feel she's able."

Kristin cracked an eye open. "I want to go home."

Dmitri's face turned so dark that both Kristin's eyes popped open as she felt the blast of heat he radiated. "Not until we apprehend Vane. I'm not taking another chance on you being easy prey. You're under protection of our clan now." The bitter edge to his voice caused a sudden tightness in her chest, making it hard to breathe.

She swallowed reflexively against it.

"It will be as you wish, *Trejan,*" Zarah said, inclining her head in a bow.

Kristin's head was now throbbing so badly she wished she could just wrap it in a big fluffy towel and stick two or three pillows over it to block out all light and sound. Tears swam in her eyes as she tried uselessly to block the cacophony assaulting her senses.

Dmitri's brow furrowed as if he sensed her pain. "Is there anything you can give her?"

Zarah nodded and fiddled with the tubing at- tached to Kristin's IV. Like a warm blanket being slowly pulled over her, a soothing relaxation claimed her little by little until she drifted off into a dreamless sleep.

When she woke, she found herself in the center of Dmitri's massive bed. It was pitch-dark, but her eyes were still able to see clearly. She listened intently, wondering if he was still there. When not a whisper of sound reached her, she threw off the comforter and staggered out of the bed, her legs far weaker than she'd anticipated.

"Running marathons. Very funny. Right now I'll be lucky if I can stumble to the bathroom."

After brushing her teeth and drinking a little water, she decided she might be able to make it to the kitchen. Her stomach rumbled loudly as the scent of fresh doughnuts and coffee tweaked her nose, giving her a burst of energy.

Dmitri sat at the kitchen table reading the eve- ning edition of the paper. He looked drop-dead gorgeous in a crisp burgundy shirt, the sleeves rolled up to expose his strong, muscled forearms, the collar open, giving Kristin a tantalizing view.

"You look far too normal doing that," she said, leaning against the door frame as she looked her fill at the gorgeous, sexy vampire in front of her. There was nothing normal about him, or their relationship, or about her attraction to him.

He looked at her over the edge of his newspaper, his espresso eyes dark and inviting. "Better than Taylor Lautner?"

"Oh, you have it way over him."

A killer smile broke his face and melted her heart as he folded the paper and placed it on the table. "I intended to bring you breakfast in bed." He stood up and pulled out the chair beside him.

Kristin padded closer, her bare feet whispering on the floor. "Careful or you'll spoil me. Those doughnuts smell good." She sat in the chair and shivered as he gently pulled her hair aside and kissed her lightly on her nape. Arrows of need shot straight through her. Her breasts tightened, begging for his attention.

"Not as good as you smell, I assure you." His murmur tickled the edge of her ear. The telltale flick of his fangs extending caused a delicious shiver to race from head to toe. He wanted her.

She leaned her head back to gaze up into his eyes. "I take it you're hungry for breakfast too?"

Bold desire darkened his features, bringing the angles of his face into stark relief. The power of him swirled around her like a living thing. "I'm hungry for you."

He held out his hand and she slipped hers willingly into his, her skin so much paler against his Mediterranean complexion. The friction of their skin set off sparks inside her. Raw need sizzled and snapped along her nerve endings as he drew her up against him. She gasped, spreading her hands out along the broad plane of his chest, reveling in the feel of his muscles under her fingertips. His sculpted firmness fit her softness to perfection.

"After breakfast I'm giving you a bath." The hunger in his eyes was unmistakable. The thought of being naked with him made her skin burn.

"Let's skip breakfast," she managed to whisper roughly before he covered her mouth in a swift, possessive kiss that shook her to her core.

Without effort he lifted her into his arms. Her body became one giant heartbeat, each pulse throbbing throughout her entire frame as she clung to him, her arms around his neck.

"As my lady wishes."

Rather than transport them, he carried her slowly, gently, as if she were some kind of fragile porcelain doll that could shatter at any moment. Endearing as it would normally be, right now all it did was piss her off. She didn't need protecting from the fire raging inside her. She wanted to revel in it and know that she was alive. She wanted to feel all of him now. Hard and fast.

She leaned forward, rasping her lips over the tantalizing roughness of the light shadow covering his jaw. Possessed, she bit his bottom lip, suckling it for a moment. He growled, the sound vibrating deep within him, his eyes locked on hers. The heat inside her spiked.

"I'm not going to break."

"But the accide—"

She crushed her mouth to his, cutting off his concern. When she pulled back she gave him a feral smile. "You talk too much."

He gave her a devastating grin in return. "Must be the ichor," he muttered, sounding almost bemused by the heat of her passion.

"Who the hell cares?" She tightened her arms around his neck. "And why am I still dressed?"

Dark fire blazed in his eyes. An instant later it wasn't an issue. He'd phased away their clothing, leaving them both tantalizingly naked. Skin against bare skin. He let her slide down the naked length of him, feeling every ridge and ripple of his body, until her toes touched the floor. A tortured breath hissed slowly between his fangs. "God help me, woman, but you are the devil's own temptation."

Look who was talking. She'd never seen him naked, only imagined what he looked like. Reality far surpassed any fantasy. He was like a marble statue of some Greek god personified, all rock-hard, perfectly sculpted muscle brushed with sleek, dark hair and touchable skin. She tipped her gaze at the arrow of hair trailing down the firm ridges of his abdomen and bit her lip.

"Wow. Just wow." She grazed her fingers along the thick length of him that jutted proudly, flexing under her exploration. Dmitri's head fell back, his eyes closing. He groaned.

"That's quite impressive," she purred.

His eyes snapped open, burning her in their intensity.

She blinked and suddenly felt the warm water falling over her skin. He had transported them into the black-tiled Vichy shower in his bathroom. Five separate showerheads cascaded water over them from all directions like a waterfall, encasing them in warm decadent wetness. It was glorious. It felt divine. And the best part was—he was right beside her. She shivered, not from cold, but from the absolute rightness of feeling him so close.

"I believe you requested a bath." He stared intently at her, his mouth begging to be kissed. He pressed a gentle kiss to her mouth, his fingers threading through her wet hair as he massaged the shampoo into a fragrant lather that trailed over her shoulders and down her back in a ticklish counterpoint to the blazing heat in his gaze.

"Mmm, that feels fantastic," she murmured.

He chuckled, the sound of a man thoroughly enjoying himself. She was perfection beneath his fingers, all soft skin and sensual curves. He followed the lather with his hands, slippery and smooth as they caressed her uptilted breasts and slid down over her dainty ribs, coming to rest over the flair of her hips. She was fragile and powerful all at once, making everything within him twist and turn in a desire to suit her every whim. He pulled her toward him, her breasts sliding against his bare chest, her hips cradling his hard length. Saints, she'd be just as slick inside.

He bent low, kissing, tasting her, his fangs scraping slightly against her lips. Gliding on her wet skin, his hands slid around the curve of her derriere to cup her searing hot flesh in his hands. She parted, opening for him. Her arousal saturated the steam around them, surrounding him so thoroughly that all he could think of was her, the center of his known universe. She filled his mind, drew every sense to balance on a razor's edge.

"Without a doubt you are a force to be reckoned with."

She panted. "That's romantic?"

"No, it means you're sexy as hell." With deliberate slowness he edged his fingers into the wetness of her, teasing her, reveling in every small pant and groan he elicited from her. Hot and fierce need pounded at him, demanding he take her. He held it back, waiting for her.

Beneath her lashes, a shot of white-hot lightning lit her eyes and a devilish smile curved her lips. Her hands grasped him, slid him down across her wet belly, between her slick thighs. It was the ultimate torture, the ultimate bliss. She drew him into her like a breath, consuming, needy, vital to her next heartbeat, and shuddered.

"Oh, God, you feel good. Don't stop, Dmitri."

The silken glove tightened as she bucked against him. Unable to hold back any longer he drove home, lifting her up into his arms, pressing her against the cool tiles as her legs wound around his waist. She shattered in his arms, her body undone by a series of small tremors that rocked him to the very center of his empty soul, calling him to join her. And he willingly followed her over the edge, growling her name.

Trejan. Why are you not here? Roman's voice scraped like a scalpel, deep and unwelcome.

No, dammit. Not now. Not ever.

I will be there as soon as I am able. He glanced down at her as she lay her head against his chest, her breathing still faster than normal, but slowing gradually. Her heartbeat echoed loud and enticing, shushing just below her skin in a cinnamon-scented confection that made his mouth water and fangs ache. But more than he craved a drink, he craved more time with her. At this moment he didn't give a damn what Roman wanted. All Dmitri wanted, all he needed, was the woman in his arms.

She sat at Dmitri's kitchen table, head in her hands, staring at the hand-written notes she'd made. Looking at the computer screen still hurt too much, even though she'd lowered the brightness and contrast. And who could focus anyway after the man giving you the most amazing sex of your life suddenly vaporized with nothing more than a kiss and a whispered promise that he'd be back soon?

What was far worse than feeling like a wham-bam-thank-you-ma'am was the deep-down sensation that this wasn't just lust roaring through her system at warp speed. Dmitri touched her deeper than that. He'd somehow wormed his way into her very heart.

Dad had been right. She'd gone and screwed up all her fine objective reporting by falling in love with Dmitri.

Her cell rang and Beck's number came up on the caller ID.

"Hey, Beck."

"I tried calling you at home and didn't get an answer."

"Yeah, I haven't been there much."

"I've got your results. You want the good news or the bad news?"

"Which is worse?"

"Probably the good news."

Kristin winced. "Ouch."

"Yeah. Good news is you're right. The stuff is some kind of blood by-product that's been mutated somehow by a virus that's prevalent in the sample."

Kristin tensed. What if she now had the virus swimming around inside her after her stint under

Zarah's care at the vampire clinic? She shoved the thought aside, forcing herself to focus on what Beck was saying. "So you think the virus causes the change in blood?"

She grimaced as Beck flipped through papers as she talked. "Bingo. At least that's what the results are showing me. It seems to have regenerative abilities when combined with human blood, but in the proper ratio can overtake it and mutate it all into the viral form."

The shushing sound in her ears grew louder as her heart pounded against her ribs. "Wait. Are you telling me vampirism is caused by a *virus?*" A virus that was even now circulating inside her?

"I'm just giving you my preliminary test results. That assumption is inconclusive until it's tested thoroughly on some subjects, but theoretically speaking, yes. It's a virus that causes the mutation."

Kristin choked on her own saliva and launched into a coughing fit.

"Are you okay?"

"Yeah," she gasped. "Just swallowed down

the wrong pipe." She took in a deep gulp of air. "What about the DNA?"

"That's the bad news."

Kristin's vision started to shimmer with black sparkles around the edges.

"I cross-matched the DNA from the ichor with another sample I was working on. It also has the same viral signature."

An unnatural skittering sensation crept up her neck, telling Kristin this was bad. Not just bad, but the worst-case scenario. But her reporter gut told her to find out what it was, regardless. "Where did you get that sample?"

"Police forensics. Seems whoever tapped off this little black bottle also had a hand in at least one of the Bloodless Murders, possibly more. The saliva sample they scraped out of one of the bodies turns out to be some kind of venom that can liquefy human flesh, just like a flesh-eating bacteria or spider bite. This is some seriously nasty stuff you're wading around in."

Dear God. Whoever had given that vial to Dmitri was involved in the Bloodless Murders, which meant that whoever he was, he was close to Dmitri, and Dmitri didn't even know it. Either that, or Dmitri had known all along and he'd been lying to her about the reivers being the murderers to protect someone close to him, perhaps even himself.

Her heart, which moments ago had been so full and near bursting, now shriveled at the thought that he may have betrayed her. Used his supernatural sexy amazingness to keep her off the track of the real killers. Why did she keep putting her trust in the man? God knows, he bent her inside out. "Anything else?"

"Yeah. You need to be careful."

Considering that she'd just been blown to hell and back by a car bomb, the advice was well founded. "I will."

"I'm serious, Kris. If this virus gets out into the blood supply, there's no telling how many people are going to turn into those bloodsuckers and not even realize it's happening. The consequences could be disastrous."

For a moment she had second thoughts about telling Beck about the ichor treatment she'd received. What would happen if Beck freaked out?

"You know, it's not as bad as all that."

"What? Are you hearing yourself? It's a virus. Who knows what it can do."

"Actually…"

Beck sucked in a startled breath. "Oh, no, oh, hell no. Please tell me you haven't used any of it."

Kristin sighed heavily. "It wasn't like I had a choice. I was in a pretty bad accident."

In the background a chair crashed to the floor, probably as Beck stood up too fast. "What! Why didn't you say anything? Are you all right?"

"I'm fine. That's the amazing part. That vamp doctor wasn't kidding, Beck. The stuff this ichor can heal is pretty amazing."

"How bad was it? Are you suffering from any side effects?"

"You mean like a craving for an extra-rare steak?"

"Exactly."

She laughed at Beck's serious demeanor. "Beck, I'm fine. I had broken bones, a punctured lung—"

"Oh my God. That's not fine, that's critical!"

"Yeah, but that was less than forty-eight hours

ago. Now it looks like nothing even happened to me."

A heavy silence stretched between them.

"Beck, you still here?"

"Wow," Beck said, clearly stunned.

"Know how there's a black and white to everything? I think this is the bright side to this ichor."

"But how do you know you won't become a vampire from it?"

Kristin shrugged. "I don't. Not really. Dmitri and the doctor both said there's more to it than just a treatment and that my immune system will break it down and get rid of it eventually."

"But you've got it in you at the moment?"

"Yeah."

"Do you think you could come in and give me some blood?"

Kristin snorted. "Now *you* sound like a vampire, Beck."

Beck groaned at her attempt at humor. "This is for science, so please don't compare the two."

Deep down, Kristin realized that Beck's quest

for knowledge would override any squeamishness she had about vampires.

"Let me see what I can do."

Chapter 13

With plans set to meet Beck later at Sangria, Kristin called Hollander. She could practically feel his hot breath on the back of her neck. He was going to swallow his freaking tongue when she told him this latest development.

"Are you putting me on?" Hollander asked, his tone wary, but underscored with excitement. "No shit?"

Kristin grinned. "You heard it here first. Vampirism is caused not by a vampire bite as everyone has been led to believe by Hollywood, but by a virus. Not only that, but I have lab evidence of a DNA connection directly to the Bloodless

Murders." Damn, she was good. Better than good. *Pulitzer* good.

"Great job, Reed." He sounded as pumped as Kristin felt. "Get me your article ASAP. I'll stop the presses and have this run in the morning edi—"

Her elation had the lifespan of a mayfly. "No can do. We can't run it until I can get more concrete details on who's behind the DNA connection to the Bloodless Murders."

"What? You can't seriously expect me to sit on something this big." She heard a pencil snap between his meaty fingers, then another. Hollander broke a hell of a lot of pencils when he was pissed.

"No. I repeat, *hell* no, Reed. What if someone else snatches it from under us?" She could picture his face turning that particular shade of purplish-red that happened right before she thought he might pass out from hypertension.

She felt for him, she really did. This wasn't the way she wanted to play it either. "Trust me, there's no chance of that happening. I don't want anyone challenging my sources or doubting my facts. Not until I'm one hundred percent positive I have all my ducks in a row."

"Settle for ninety percent, and your ducks in the same city block. I want this story, Reed, and I want it now."

That made two of them. "Let me get solid leads on who's behind it first. If we run the piece now, there's every chance the person will disappear and I'll never learn what's really going on. I can write up the part I know about the virus, but not the Bloodless Murder connection just yet."

"We've run stories on less." Another pencil snapped, and he was talking through clenched teeth.

"Nothing of this magnitude." Nothing that would earn the reporter a Pulitzer. "Be patient," Kristin told him soothingly. Like that would ever happen. "A day or two more at the most. Then you can put it to bed."

"Twenty-four hours."

"Forty-eight."

"Twenty-four and not a second longer."

Which was what she'd hoped he'd say. Hollander

hung up on her and the dial tone drilled all the way through her brain.

Twenty-four hours. That wasn't a lot of time to find out exactly what was up with the ichor at Sangria, who it had come from and what was being done with it. What made the waiting worse was that she was still sitting in Dmitri's apartment, envisioning the inevitable confrontation between them. It made her jittery as hell.

She didn't bother to turn on the lights. The computer lit up the room enough for her heightened sense of sight. Just how long were the side effects of the ichor treatment supposed to last? She wished she knew. She hadn't wanted to get too into it with Beck. Visions of becoming Beck's guinea pig, poked and prodded with needles in a test-tube hell, flitted across her mind.

When Dmitri finally came home in the wee hours of the morning he didn't bother coming through the door. Instead, an instant before he transported into the living room, the small hairs on her body all rose to attention as though she'd raised a supercharge of static electricity and was just waiting for something to set it off with a *snap*.

In this case that wasn't too far from the truth as Dmitri was a trigger for just about everything for her. And that was before the ichor. The aftereffects of the treatment only made everything more acute.

The smoky appearance knitted into solid matter and a moment later he was standing there staring at her with those dark eyes that made everything within her sit up and take notice.

"I thought you'd still be sleeping," he said as he phased away his tailored jacket, leaving his white shirt, which was not as crisp or neat as it normally was. He undid the top three buttons, revealing the dark V of his throat and making Kristin ache to touch him. Her gaze drifted down. Just thinking about his killer abs and the dark hair that trailed down beneath the edge of his waistband made a tingle spread like wildfire through her, heating up all her erogenous zones and putting them on high alert.

Down, girl. Focus on the story. Focus on getting the facts.

She tucked her hair behind her ear. "Busy day at the office?" she gibed. She tried to keep things light, but she didn't know where he'd been or what he'd been doing since he'd left her.

His half-tilted smile slid straight to her heart, making it double bump thump. God, he was gorgeous. Kristin clenched her hand, her fingernails pressing small crescents deep into her palm. He was also holding out on her, she sternly reminded her libido.

"We need to talk," she said with no preamble.

His eyes narrowed. "Why does that sound like something dangerous?"

"I want to know the truth about the ichor I found in your cabinet at Sangria. Whose is it?"

His brows bent into a deep V. "I suspected you'd stolen it." Dmitri unbuttoned his cuffs and began rolling them upward, exposing thickly muscled forearms. Kristin's attention wavered and her temperature rose. Actually having seen Dmitri in the buff made just looking at him fully clothed an erotic experience.

She worried her bottom lip with her teeth. Her ramped-up response to him was tempered with the knowledge that she'd abused his trust by taking the ichor without his consent and having it tested behind his back. But she'd been desperate to understand how it worked, especially now that it was circulating in her system. She was hoping against hope that he'd be understanding instead of insanely pissed. Of course, he had every right to be, but she crossed her fingers behind her back all the same.

He caught her staring at him. "So, are you going to explain why you stole it?"

His even tone agitated the guilt already churning in her chest. Her stomach shriveled into a tight, hard knot. Apologies were in order. "I'm sorry for taking it without asking, but I had to know what was actually in it so I could understand it for the article. How big an infraction was taking it? Was that ichor designated for someone in particular? Oh, God, Dmitri, tell me you didn't need it for medical reasons!"

He pinned her with a serious look. "Luckily for you that isn't the case. You could have asked me. I would have let you take a vial for testing or you could have asked Zarah. Either way, I expect you not to go behind my back again for your investigations. The situation is too dangerous. Are we clear?"

She nodded, but couldn't stop herself from blurting, "Where do you get it from? Why do you even have it?"

His eyes turned smoky and he moved away from her toward the wet bar. "Zarah provided me with a small amount of recreational ichor for our customers. I'm not certain whom she procured it from and I don't approve. But I've been overridden by the council who say the quantity is not enough to cause a spontaneous conversion process." He poured himself a glass of brandy and swirled the deep amber liquid. The sharp sweetness of the liquor blended with the dark chocolate and citrus scent that seem to fill the room whenever he was around.

Kristin swallowed hard. Everything about him shouted sex, but he was cool and reserved and standing across the room as if she somehow smelled bad. It completely confused the hell out of her, especially when she was fighting her own desire to touch him. All if it combined to tie her tongue in knots. "Well, you shouldn't be.

Overridden, that is. There's a virus in it, Dmitri. Were you aware of that? It causes people to become vampires."

He twirled the liquid in his glass, his gaze unreadable. "Sometimes."

She rubbed her arms, trying to stave off the chill that seemed to be growing in the room and the strange sensation that her skin was getting tighter. "Look, I've got this vampire blood circulating through my system and I've just found out that there's a virus in it that could potentially cause me to turn into a vampire. Define *sometimes*."

"Won't happen to you." He took a casual sip of his brandy as if they were merely discussing the weather and not her potential death or undeath.

An angry heat stole into her cheeks. How could he act so blasé about this? "How do you—"

"Zarah knows exactly how much she can administer to heal mortal patients without causing the conversion to begin." Dmitri took another long, slow sip of the brandy and let it sear a hot trail down to his stomach. Her eyes were too bright, nearly luminous. The ichor was still affecting her more than he'd seen in others. Zarah had hinted that it might be because he'd fed from her just days before. He wasn't sure. But he did know he shouldn't have fed from her in the first place. That was his mistake and he damn well wasn't about to repeat it. No matter how badly he wanted to. He tore his gaze away from her and concentrated on keeping his fingers on his glass instead of reaching out for her.

"But I still have a virus in me, right?"

He nodded. "For the moment." He took another drink, working hard to keep as far from her as he could without raising her suspicions. The air vibrated with a heady mixture of female sexual desire and something that was purely Kristin and as addictive to him as any opiate.

Since she'd had the ichor treatment her scent had altered slightly. She now emitted a vampire mating pheromone that was changing to suit his most intimate fantasies, to lure him in. Dmitri steeled his resolve.

"What do you mean? It's a damn virus. Once it's in there, it's in there!"

Saints, he prayed it wasn't so. Because if it

was, he was screwed. She had already broken through the reserve he'd tenaciously clung to all these centuries. And that was when she'd been fully mortal, not a walking, breathing package of seduction in a powder-blue sweat suit that molded itself to every curve and swell of her exquisite body.

He couldn't touch her. Dared not taste her no matter how strong and elemental the compulsion became. The least he could do was calm her fears from a safe distance.

"Not with this virus. Once the virus has done the work necessary, your body's natural immune system neutralizes it, unless, of course, you don't have enough blood left in you to actively fight it off."

Curiosity sparked in the depths of her intelligent eyes. Saints above. She was breathtaking. Streams of golden hair spilled softly over her sloping shoulders, but her chest and chin were held high with determination. For an instant his vision faltered and he saw the panic-stricken green eyes of that young maid replacing Kristin's far sharper blue ones.

"That's how you create your kind, isn't it?"

Dmitri snapped himself out of the memory, stiffened and nodded. She made it sound almost like catching a case of the sniffles. The details of his own turning were still deeply etched into his brain like acid on glass. Being drained slowly, being used up and then filled up with the ichor Larissa had poured into his open mouth. The wounds seared as if hot acid were being siphoned into his veins. The intense hunger, the overwhelming sensations that had flooded him until he'd completed his first feed and slept overnight covered in deep dark earth. "It's not a pleasant process."

Six hundred years and the memory still nauseated him, had the power to make him shake with anxiety and bone-deep fear. He'd never put another human through the painful process, and he'd be damned if he ever would. It was simply too horrifying a memory for him.

"What about the murders? My friend Beck says the DNA from the ichor and a DNA sample from Balor's case are a match. Are the murder victims people who didn't fare well in the conversion process?"

Dmitri wished. "Frankly, I hate the comparison between those of the Cascade Clan and what the reivers are perpetrating. So, no. That's different. That's murder. Vampires don't have any reason to remove the organs, and conversions in our clan are tightly monitored."

She kept pressing, her dogged determination something he both admired and loathed. "Do you think that perhaps someone in your clan is in on it?"

He straightened his shoulders. "No. I'd know. The Bloodless Murders are firmly laid at the reivers' door." Achilles had been working on ferreting out their nest without any success. They were like the Scottish border reivers of several hundred years ago, striking in small groups, taking what they needed and vanishing without a trace until they struck again, causing havoc in their wake. Vane was the only solid lead they possessed.

"I thought you said the clan council would be taking care of the reivers. But they're not, are they?"

He clenched the snifter in his hand too hard and it shattered, spraying shards of glass and droplets of brandy across his shirt and the floor. He growled in frustration and phased the mess away, whisking away his sodden shirt in the process. He heard her small gasp and without glancing in her direction, assumed he had scared her with his display of anger.

He couldn't look at her. It just hurt too damn much to know that their bonding was doomed from the start. She was mortal—and going to stay that way. She had no business being with a vampire and he had no business wanting her with every fiber of his being. "Sorry. It isn't that simple. There's more involved than just subduing them."

When she didn't reply, he did cast a quick glance in her direction and the sight nearly drove him to his knees. Her eyes were the luminous electric blue of a summer sky, her skin flushed a delicious pink and smelled like cinnamon icing.

She drifted toward him, as if she was mesmerized, almost floating rather than walking. And when she reached out and stroked his bare shoulder, he flinched, the feeling akin to fire licking his skin. Need, raw and primal, surged through him in a crashing wave so intense it nearly caused his knees to buckle.

"Don't touch me." His words came out a harsh whisper.

Her caress skimmed over his chest, making the muscles bunch and flex, cry out for more.

"Why?" The sultry tone in her voice caused him to shudder thinking of how wet and slick her skin would feel.

"Because all this—the reivers, you and me—it's all far more complicated than you can possibly imagine." He blew out a harsh rattled breath that had nothing to do with oxygen and everything to do with maintaining his control.

She leaned into him and the scent of aroused female and vampire bonded, filling his sense with the pheromones swirling in the air, and weakening him further. He closed his eyes and visions of her wet skin sparkling with water drops appeared before his eyes. Hell. He couldn't escape the need that raged through him or the extension of his fangs any more than the aching erection she'd aroused.

"It doesn't have to be complicated, Dmitri," she said softly, her words a whisper of hot breath fanning against his bare skin. God, she was a temptress. And he was definitely no saint. "You just need to tell me the truth."

He opened his eyes and gazed at her. Big mistake. Huge. The blue sucked him in like an endless inviting pool and he felt himself drowning, gladly. Saints above, he was totally screwed.

"Let me guess," she said as she twisted a finger into the hair at his nape, setting off a chain reaction of need in his body. "Do those vials of ichor at Sangria have something to do with the complexity of this situation?"

As much as he wanted to sink into her touch, feel every inch of her sweet softness, he couldn't. If there was any hope of breaking their bonding, he had to initiate it now. Control it now. He pulled away from her fingers, instantly feeling the loss like a punch in the gut.

"We've always restricted illicit trade in ichor to ensure that conversions aren't random or unintentional. The rest of the complexity in this situation is strictly about the bonding happening between us. I can't be with you. And you shouldn't want to be with me. It'll never work. You're mortal. And I'm—"

She reached a finger forward as if to shush him and instead gave his right fang a long, deliberate stroke from root to tip. Dmitri shuddered, the sensation shooting straight through him, igniting his hunger into a full-fledged demand to have her.

"Don't tell me what I want. I already know," she breathed.

Unable to resist her, Dmitri pulled her in to nestle against him, reveling in the feel of her, even as he hated himself for giving in to temptation. "Do you know how difficult this is? Do you even realize how close you are to death? Just being here, being with me, being involved with this problem we have with the reivers, is reducing your chances of survival. I hate being the cause."

She pressed her mouth against his in a kiss that started as light as the caress of a butterfly's wing and then grew more lush and full until he was utterly lost. The kiss was so pure it tasted of sunshine. How could he ruin something so utterly perfect? And ruin it he would.

She'd never be the same if he fully bonded with her. No mortal ever was.

He'd seen some of Achilles's bonded mortals wither away into empty husks, because their desire consumed them so fully they could neither eat nor drink. He'd heard of mortals dying of insanity in the bonding experience, unable to control the onslaught of their heightened sense. And that alone scared him when it came to Kristin.

Without a doubt he knew he would do everything in his power to protect her, even if it meant keeping her away from himself. For her own good. He broke the kiss, pulling away from the very thing that made him feel the most human, most alive in centuries.

"Some things are worth dying, or becoming undead, for." She pulled his head down to hers, her eyes shining with promise as she licked a damp trail across his lower lip.

He shoved her back, the temptation almost more than he could bear. "No! Not this. You don't understand."

The roughness of his words hit her like a physical blow, causing her to stumble back a step. "Then help me understand."

His shoulders bunched into tight coils of sinew and muscle as he wrapped his hands around the back of his head and began to pace. "The truth is, everything's changing. And it's all happening because now mortals know about us. But it's more than that. The reivers want to fundamentally change the way the world works, with vampires at the top and mortals—"

"Somewhat lower down the food chain." Even as she said the words, panic started to flutter and beat behind her ribs like a frightened bird trapped in a cage.

He sighed, staring at her with defeated eyes. "Exactly."

"Crap."

He closed the centimeter of space between them. "You can see why we'd be concerned. This isn't just about a few murders, or even just about the survival of our clan. It's about the survival and freedom of mortals as well."

Adrenaline spiked through her system.

"Concerned? I'm completely freaked out! You're telling me we're about to become freakin' fast food."

"We're trying not to let that happen."

Determination once again surged in her. "How do we beat those reivers?"

Dmitri shook his head. "You aren't fast enough to beat them, and unless you have a significant supply of dead man's blood, or access to the silver stored in Fort Knox, or a few extra atomic bombs lying around, you have nothing."

Power and anger pulsated off him in dark, shimmering waves, like mirage heat, that filled the small space between them. This was bad. Really bad. Kristin's knees gave out suddenly and she plopped down on his couch, her stomach a tumble of knots, fear prickling her skin. "Why didn't you tell me about this sooner?"

He looked up, his glare menacing, but alluring to her all the same. "Would you have understood?"

"I think I would have. And even if I didn't, you could have trusted me." Her defensive tone instantly softened his features.

"I do trust you. The problem is, I don't trust the rest of the mortals out there. My position in the clan demands that I keep certain things secret."

She stood up and stepped toward him. "Not between us. Not anymore."

"It's not that easy."

Kristin spun away and groaned with frustration, fisting her hands at her sides. God. What a mess. They were worse off than Romeo and Juliet. *They* only had warring families. She and Dmitri had different species. "Stop saying that! Look, I'm going to write about the virus, whether your leaders approve it or not. Humans have a right to know what they're up against and the potential that ichor has to heal. They also need to know about the reivers. But that doesn't have to change what's growing between us."

"Actually, yes, it does."

"Why?" It came out more a plea than a question.

"If I can't maintain control of the mortals' reactions, if I can't keep the members of our clan safe, my laird has the right to execute us both. And I'd rather be beheaded than let him kill you."

Kristin just stared dumbfounded. She'd be damned if some vampire she'd never met was going to change the course of her life and her kind. Suddenly this was far bigger than any Pulitzer. This was her one shot to change the world.

"Bullshit," she muttered hotly. She locked her gaze on his, intense and determined. "If the reivers were gone, would any of this be an issue?"

"Yes. You'd still be mortal."

"But we might have a chance?"

"Slim to none, but yes, a chance."

"I'll take it. If we get rid of the reivers, then we can work everything else out. We'll prove they're behind the murders, and let the human authorities take care of them."

Dmitri shook his head. "You're betting that mortals will rally to this cause."

"You don't think they will?"

He shook his head. "If six hundred years has taught me anything, it's that all vampires are alike to most mortals. If one of us is a threat, we're all a threat."

Chapter 14

Even after a full eight hours of sleep, Kristin still wasn't one hundred percent. Ichor or not, she fortified herself with caffeine and forced herself to work frantically through the day. She needed to write as fast as she could to have the article in to Hollander by the evening deadline. Touting the ichor's enormous benefits while acknowledging its vampire-causing virus proved to be harder than she'd anticipated. She hoped against hope that Dmitri was overestimating just how bad a reaction humans would have once this story hit the newsstands.

She blew out a breath as she emailed the file to her editor.

"Finished?" Dmitri stood in the doorway, sexy as hell in a drawstring black pajama bottom and nothing else. Kristin felt her breath catch at the sight of his well-defined chest and ripped abs gloriously bare. He'd slept the day in his room. Once or twice she'd tried the door, wondering if she could just catch a catnap curled up beside him. But the door had been locked, just as before.

She nodded as she rose from her chair and stretched out the kinks in her neck. "Don't like being disturbed when you sleep, do you?"

She'd fallen asleep on the couch watching television sometime during the night while he'd been working and woke in the morning to find his bedroom door locked once more.

The corner of his mouth lifted. "I don't think sleeping in dirt would really appeal to you."

Deep down, part of her disagreed. Sleeping with him was the least of what she wanted to do with him in a big wide bed. Finally his words hit her. "Dirt? But you've got a bed."

"That's purely for show." He crooked a finger and she crossed the short distance to him willingly, her fingers itching to touch the broad expanse of hard muscle she found so irresistible.

His fingers curled over her hand and he led her into his bedroom. Awareness arced between them, causing her heart to start pumping harder and the tips of her breasts to harden. It was getting more difficult to see in the dark and Kristin surmised that the ichor was beginning to wear off.

He snapped on a lamp with a push of a remote control in his hand. A second button caused a series of metallic clicks. Panels over the headboard slid open to reveal a huge gap in the wall. The entire bed lifted from the floor and folded neatly into the space, revealing a large square hole that had been carved into the rock below and spread with black satin.

She eyed the space, then eyed him. "I kind of expected a coffin. But you sleep down there?"

He shrugged. "It's not plush, but it works."

Kristin shivered and he pulled her closer. The fact that it resembled a double-wide grave wasn't lost on her. She pressed her cheek against his chest. It was far too easy to forget that he was undead, especially when he made her feel so utterly alive. "But your bed would be so much more comfortable."

He chuckled as his fingers lazily stroked her hair. "With you in it, I have no doubt."

"So why bother with a bed if you actually sleep down there?"

Beneath her cheek his chest stiffened ever so slightly. "It's a small connection to whatever humanity I once had. A reminder."

"Have you ever wanted to be human again?"

He closed his eyes, sighing deeply, as though the thought alone caused him great pain. "Countless times."

"Well, isn't there some kind of antivirus, some way to undo the damage?"

He shook his head. "Once a vampire, always a vampire. Only once every thousand years does a plague come that mutates the virus, putting us all at risk. And that threat has already passed."

But if the virus could be activated and deactivated naturally, then it could be done artificially too, she thought. Beck could do it, given enough time and resources. "What if you could create an antivirus of some kind?"

"Why are you so intent on finding a solution?"

She looked up into his eyes and felt her heart trip over itself. Somewhere along the line reality had snuck up on her and delivered one heck of a sucker punch. She loved him down to the tips of her toes. She'd take even the slimmest chance if it meant they could be together. And, as much as she wished he felt the same way, she knew her being a mortal and his being a vampire was a major issue for him. But she wasn't ready to tell him about her newly discovered feelings yet. "I just wanted to see if there was any way to be with you."

A flash of vulnerable yearning gleamed for an instant in his features. He tenderly kissed her forehead. "Saints bless you for that."

He hugged her fiercely, then let her go, not trusting himself. If his heart had still been beating like a normal mortal's, it would have stopped. In six hundred years he'd never felt truly wanted like this, and the depth of her feelings for him were humbling. He didn't deserve them.

He knew precisely what she was thinking. She believed herself to be in love with him. Since their physical joining, her thoughts were far more accessible. Too bad it could never last between them. He deliberately turned, leading her away from his bedroom, and from temptation, before he did something he regretted even further, like bonding with her completely by feeding from her in the midst of sex. That would forge an unbreakable tie between them that would last through the cycle of mortal life, death and rebirth.

"I know you wouldn't want this life. And I have no choice in the matter," he told her. "By this time tomorrow, the world as you've known it will change."

What he didn't say, couldn't say, was that once she saw the raw, uncivilized side of vampires at war, she'd never feel safe with him again. And it was coming. It was inevitable. And then she'd regret being tied to a monster whose essence would be imprinted upon her soul for eternity.

He tucked her to his chest, selfishly absorbing every moment with her. "I still have a few hours before I can go out."

She nodded, her skin rubbing against his bare chest, amping up the heat between them. "I'd rather stay and spend it with you, but I've got to meet Beck at Sangria to get some final details for my article."

He stroked her hair. "Take the security phone."

"I will. There's just one thing..."

She tilted her head up, looking at him with those soft baby blues in a way that pierced his heart harder than any stake. He realized in that very moment he'd do anything, be anything, if he could just have her beside him. But it was merely a dream. A fantasy. He couldn't have her for his own and never would. Not without taking the choice out of her hands. And he'd never do that.

"I was wondering if my car was ready," she finished.

Dmitri phased the car keys into his hand and dropped them into hers. "It's in parking space number sixty-six in the garage."

"Thanks."

Saints, she was so damn fragile. And he had no idea how he was going to protect her from the firestorm about to rain down once her article ignited people's deepest fears—that they were vulnerable to a pandemic they had no hope of controlling.

Even as he watched her prepare to go, he knew she had plans to stay away that evening. She was questioning his deliberate distance after their night together, and he couldn't blame her. As much as he wanted to explain the grave conse-quences permanent bonding presented, it was just easier to let her push away, for her own good. Letting her go burned like dead man's blood, a stinging fire that ached in every pore, but it was for the best. And he'd do anything to protect her.

"Don't talk to any strangers."

She grinned at him. "Wouldn't dream of it." She grabbed her purse and headed out the door.

She found Beck sitting at the bar in Sangria nursing a martini, wearing a nondescript black backpack. A spring of relief welled up inside her. She could always count on Beck. "Hey, stranger."

Beck glanced at her, an errant curl from her ponytail bouncing as she moved her head. "Hey yourself." She motioned to Anastasia. "My friend will have—"

"A Vampire?" Anastasia asked, popping her gum.

"Sure," Kristin nodded, smiling. "Thanks."

Beck's face scrunched up. "It sounds disgusting."

Kristin shrugged as she took the red drink in the hurricane glass from the bartender. "You shouldn't knock it until you try it."

Beck gave a mock shiver and snatched up her martini. "No, thanks. They're not my taste." She glanced around the club. "You know it's kind of creepy in here, right?"

Kristin laughed. "You get used to it. Come on, let's sit over here." Beck followed her toward the tasting room. Kristin held back the curtain.

"You're sure we're all right going in here?"

"Trust me."

She cast a suspicious look over her shoulder at everyone else in the bar. "Oh, I trust you. It's the rest of *them* I'm not sure I trust." She leaned in a little closer. "That bartender is one, isn't she?" Beck whispered.

"Anastasia, yeah. But one of the good ones." She hoped. For all she knew the bartender could just as easily be the secret connection Vane had inside the clan. Despite what Dmitri said, she was sure somebody was.

Beck flopped into one of the leather couches in the tasting room as Kristin pulled the curtain closed then sat beside her. "Were you able to get it?"

Beck put down her martini and shrugged out of the backpack, then pulled out three large plastic pouches filled with dark brownish liquid and set them down on the coffee table.

"Blood from a corpse, as requested. Although what the hell you'd plan to do with it, I have no idea. My friend at the county coroner's office was curious too."

"If I tell you, you can't tell another soul."

Beck's eyes sparked with curiosity. "Spill it."

"It's a security measure. Dead man's blood is like poison to vampires. If it gets into a cut or they drink it, they're immobilized like they've taken a tranquilizer."

"Good to know."

Kristin picked up the cold squishy packages, putting them carefully into a special bag she'd packed inside her purse filled with ice packs.

"Time to pay up," Beck said.

Kristin started rolling up her sleeve. "What are you planning on doing with it?"

Beck pressed her arm searching for a vein then stuck in an IV. "More tests. Now that I've tested the pure stuff, I want to know how it's interacting with your blood chemistry."

Kristin watched her darker-than-normal red blood dribble into the container Beck held. "You know your fascination with science borders on weird, right?"

Beck grinned. "At least I just want to analyze the blood, not drink it like your other friends. Besides, this is for scientific research." She pinched the tube, sealing the packet and taking out the IV and putting a cotton ball and bandage on Kristin's arm. "Your boyfriend isn't going to be pissed I took your blood, is he?"

Kristin shook her head. "Don't worry about it. I'll make more. Thanks for bringing the stuff to me."

"You know I'd do anything to help you. Well, almost anything." Beck grasped her hand for a second. "Are you sure you're all right? The thought of you being a supersnack around a bunch of vampires really worries me."

"Trust me, Beck. Dmitri isn't going to let anything happen to me. He isn't a monster. Deep down, he secretly wishes he was still human."

Beck looked startled. "Really?"

Kristin nodded and helped Beck pack up her things. "Call me if you find anything truly wrong with my sample."

Beck gave Kristin a hug. "Take care of you. Okay?"

When Kristin left Sangria, she headed back to her apartment. Sure, it would have been safer at Dmitri's, but she couldn't bear the thought of spending the night alone there without him next to her, touching her, knowing that instead he was right below her encased in a crypt in the earth.

More than that, his coolness after their love-making in the shower had left her hurt and bewildered, just like his reaction when they had first kissed. She knew he was attracted as hell to her, just as she was to him, but something else, something he wasn't sharing, sat silently between them, shoving them apart. Whatever it was, it had to be big. Guys like Dmitri didn't sweat the small stuff.

Which didn't make her feel any better. She refused to be some needy female who ran to him with every tearful moment. She was as strong and capable as any man. If he wanted distance, she'd do that. Spending a night in her own bed, perhaps with a quart of Ben & Jerry's Cherry Garcia, sounded like a good way to self-medicate her aching heart.

By the next morning, Kristin didn't feel any better. Spending the night without Dmitri nearby had only made her miss him more. His solid strength, his steady reassurance had made the rest of her crazy life seem somehow saner. She only hoped his dire predictions about how people would react to the news of the virus were over the top.

She grabbed a cup of coffee spiked with cream

and sugar, picked up the small pile of newspapers stacked by her door and stumbled into the living room.

Hollander had splashed the huge headline Virus Causes Vampirism across the front page of the paper along with her story. Kristin cringed. Great. Leave it to him to sensationalize the hell out of this.

Sure enough, when she turned on the morning news, she realized with a sinking sensation in the pit of her stomach that the true monsters weren't the ones with ichor flowing in their veins.

People were panicking. Several blood banks were broken into by angry mobs, their storage rooms decimated by fanatics who thought them all tainted by vampire virus.

Throughout the day it got even worse. Hospitals were now on high alert because of bomb threats. And then the real mob began to form, making her feel terribly responsible for the chaos she'd created. The mob swelled in the streets of Seattle, bending over lampposts, shoving over parked cars. They broke windows, and ultimately they took hostages.

* * *

Dmitri watched the television with horrific fascination. In a rush it all came back. The frenzied wild eyes, the avid interest of the onlooking throng intent on seeing their dose of blood. It might as well have been six hundred years ago.

He focused on appearing to breathe. In. Out. In. Out. The ancient rhythm calmed his mind enough so he could think. But the pounding in his veins didn't come from a working heart slamming blood through his system at record speed. It came from something far deeper: the elemental urge stamped into the *trejan* at the moment he took the oath to protect.

He watched the scene flickering on the television with furious anger. First one vampire, then another were bound in silver chains and shoved to their knees in an execution-style lineup along the city street. And there was no time to stop it. Nothing he could do without inciting further violence and misunderstanding.

The mob acted as jury, judge and executioner with no trial and no appeal. The police stood aside, holding back the surging onlookers, but not stopping the actions of those on camera.

One after another, the vampires had their heads tilted back and their fangs exposed. A jubilant cheer swept the crowd as the first vampire was executed, then another. Dmitri's gut rolled in protest. The spilling of ichor did not bother him, but the lifeless eyes staring plaintively from the screen did him in. He should have known they needed him. He should have protected them. But he'd been utterly absorbed by Kristin.

Now seven vampires lay in the street. It was only a few minutes until they combusted in a flash of fire, disintegrating into bone dust and ash. The crowd pushed back, away from the heat and flames, but even through the television Dmitri could sense the crowd's increasing savagery. This was far from over. In fact, it had only just begun.

Across town Kristin had nibbled a raw scrape into her lip as she'd watched the news unfolding. Her gut twisted at the images she viewed.

A pounding knock at her door made her nearly

jump three feet off the couch. Her heart thundered in her throat as she crept toward the door, waiting for another knock. But it never came.

Instead, something much worse happened.

A black oil slick crept beneath her door. Even without opening the door, Kristin knew she didn't want to see what was on the other side.

She peered out the peephole, but saw no one. Carefully she pulled back the door, leaving the guard chain attached, and glanced through the slim crack.

Crumpled like a discarded newspaper, Dr. Al Kashir lay on the floor, a shiny brass-colored spike sunk into her chest and a folded white paper in her mouth. Kristin swore and turned away. An invisible vise squeezed her chest and throat, making it impossible to take a deep breath. "What the hell?"

By now Vane's calling card was unmistakable.

She wanted to puke. But that wasn't going to get her anywhere. She pulled herself together, unlatched the door and took the slip of paper out of Zarah's mouth, trying hard not to think about what lay in front of her or glance too long into her sightless eyes. She gently closed Zarah's eyes with a brush of her fingers before she opened the paper.

WANT THE TRUTH ABOUT THE BLOODLESS MURDERS? SEATTLE DOWNTOWN POST OFFICE BOX 2476 COMBO 9–18–27.

"Vane, you are one sick twisted vampire," she muttered.

Kristin glanced up and down the hall, checking for neighbors who might have seen anything, then dashed back in her apartment to the hall closet where she fished out a queen-size sheet. She put her brain and stomach on autopilot, trying not to look too closely as she carefully wrapped the body in the sheet and dragged it into her apartment.

She grabbed a bucket and filled it with water to clean the puddle of ichor at her door. But as she knelt beside it, the dark liquid already seemed to be disappearing. She gasped as she watched it evaporate completely. A crackling sound caused her to whip around. Behind her, Zarah's body was in flames, quickly disintegrating into nothing but a pile of pale gray ash and the brass spike that thumped to the floor.

Behind her the phone rang and Kristin jumped, her nerves already raw and frayed. Everything in her was hoping it wasn't Vane.

"Reed?" Thank God. It was Hollander. She'd never been so glad to hear his gravelly voice before.

"Good afternoon to you too."

"I need you to come in today. We need to plan out how we're going to break the Bloodless Murders once you've met with your contacts." From his voice alone she could tell he was distracted. Happy, but totally distracted. At least he wasn't breaking pencils.

"But I don't have—"

"See you at five." The phone buzzed in her ear. Kristin glanced down at her cell phone. She had only an hour. Time enough to go to the post office and still make it to the *Tribune*.

She dug for the silver charm bracelet her father had given her when she'd landed her job at the *Tribune* and snapped it around her wrist as a precaution, then shrugged into a jacket. She glanced at the brass spike and snatched it up, stuffing it into her purse. If it had killed Zarah, then it could kill Vane. She double-checked to make sure that Dmitri's black phone was in there too, then took a deep breath and headed to the post office.

Late-afternoon sunlight slanted through the two-story wall of windows and smells of industrial wax, metal and paper tinged the air inside the building. The walls were lined with row after row of identical little brass boxes, each with a miniature window and a small rotating knob in the center. Kristin looked for box 2476.

Her fingers shook as she turned the combination dial. Inside was a thick padded envelope. She took it and glanced around to make sure she wasn't being watched. Better to open it in a public place just in case there was something insidious hidden in it. All that came out was a glaring red cell phone that matched the color of Vane's eyes. No note. No directions.

Kristin flipped the phone open. There were no numbers in the contacts list. The phone was clean. Obviously he'd call her when he was ready. A twisting, uncomfortable heat bubbled up inside her. She hated waiting, hated feeling as if Vane was calling the shots. But what else could she do at this point but follow the trail of slime he was leaving behind? Disgusted, she tossed the phone into her purse, where it clinked against the brass spike, and headed for the *Tribune* offices.

She walked in to wild applause. Glancing across the floor at the people popping their heads above their cubicles was like looking at a village of prairie dogs all standing on their hind legs with only their top halves showing and clapping their little paws with enthusiasm.

"Great job, Reed!" Anderson yelled out. A few of the guys whistled in agreement. Never in her life had she felt as if she'd actually belonged in the testosterone-fueled floor of the newsroom. And never had she wanted it less. What saddened her deeply was that her stories had led to so much unnecessary violence.

She nodded brusquely, and waved in acknowledgment, then headed as fast as she could toward her own cubicle. She sure as hell didn't feel like talking about it with anyone. If she could just keep busy, in a half hour the place would be nearly deserted with only the production crew working, then she could feel as though she could breathe again.

She threw her purse under her desk, grabbed a Snickers bar for fortification and downed it in four bites as she headed to Hollander's office. The door was open, but she knocked on it all the same.

"Hey, Chief."

"Come in, come in." He gestured to a seat without stacks of paper on it. Oddly, as stressed as she'd been a week earlier in this same office about her job, she could hardly believe how relaxed she felt now. Maybe it was the chocolate. Then again maybe it wasn't. Spending a week with vampires and getting blown to hell by a car bomb could certainly change a girl's perspective. The job certainly wasn't everything. Not anymore.

"Great job on the article. Sales have soared." He smiled, sort of. Kristin wasn't sure if she'd ever seen Hollander actually smile full out and was certain his face might crack from the strain of disuse. But he seemed happy enough.

"You think it's good enough to enter for a Pulitzer?"

"Already submitted it."

Kristin beamed, but despite the good news, it somehow seemed a hollow victory. What good was a Pulitzer if she couldn't get people to see the reality that vampires had peaceably lived among them for centuries?

"So how's the article coming on the vampire connection to the murders?" Hollander asked, leaning forward, his hands clasped together.

Inside, Kristin sighed. That was the business. Always chasing the next story and only as good as your last byline. Fame was fleeting, but all the same she'd thrived for so long on always reaching and striving for the Pulitzer Prize that she wasn't sure what to do with success now that it appeared within her grasp.

"There's been a new development this afternoon. I'm waiting for a source to contact me." She thought about the red cell phone in her purse. Vane could hardly be called a source, more like a root cause, but Hollander didn't need to know that. The less he knew, the safer he'd be from all the weirdness unleashing all over the city.

"Good. Will you have it to me by tomorrow?"

"I can try, it depends on what turns up."

"I need something hard-hitting for the Sunday edition."

Her mind flashed to the horrific images of the mob in the city that afternoon. "We could cover the execution of those vampires today downtown."

"Already have Peters on that."

"Well, one way or another, you'll have an article. That I can guarantee." If nothing else, she was going to expose the reivers and their plans for humans. That would be headline enough.

The phone rang and Hollander grabbed it. Kristin took the opportunity to slip out of his office and head back to her cubicle.

There was only one other person she wanted to talk to right now besides Dmitri, and that was her father. His familiar voice picked up on the second ring. *"Maple Valley Herald."*

"Hi, Dad, it's me."

"Hi, Sunshine. I was wondering if I'd hear from you."

"I take it you saw the paper?"

"Yeah. Quite a stir you've started. I'm proud of you, Sunshine, real proud. That's one heck of a story."

A warm feeling swelled in Kristin's chest. "Hollander sent it in for a Pulitzer."

"He should have." A heavy pause stretched between them, punctuated by static. She could tell he wanted to say something else.

"So, this vampire, was he just part of your investigation?" he asked, an uneasy edge to his voice.

"Yes and no. I'm working on a follow-up story right now."

"But—" A tired sigh echoed in her ear. In her mind she could see him shaking his head. "Oh, never mind. What I really want to know is, are you okay?"

"I'm better than okay, Dad."

A sense that he accepted what she was doing, even if he didn't approve of it, relaxed the tension between them. "Good," he said. "That's all I need to know. One more thing, are you going to save me a seat when you win that Pulitzer?"

Kristin smiled. "Of course, Dad. You know it."

"Stay safe, Sunshine."

"I will."

She'd barely hung up when Bradley Peters peeked over the cubicle wall and ruined everything.

"Nice score, Reed. Pulitzer nomination, huh? Who'd you have to screw to get that story? Anyone I know?"

Kristin scowled at him. "It's called reporting. You should try it sometime."

He gave her a cocky grin. "Been too busy. Wanna see what I got this weekend?"

She rolled her eyes, imagining him flashing some new Rolex or iPhone that Daddy had paid for. "Not reall—"

Brad flashed her a full-on smile, complete with fangs. *Holy crap!* Kristin leaped out of her seat. "Please tell me those are dental enhancements." His eyes flashed red in reply and all the air fled her lungs in one big whoosh.

She crumpled back into her desk chair and it creaked in protest.

Bradley came around the edge of their shared cubicle wall and crowded into what little space she had. His hands grasped onto the hard plastic arms of her chair, hemming her in, his eyes back to their familiar blue, but still feral. He was far more filled out than she remembered and had a far more menacing air about him. "Actually, I have a message for you. You've got a dinner date tonight."

"Not with you," she muttered.

Bradley chuckled, but there was something off about it. Something not entirely Brad. Something darker, more powerful and a hell of a lot more evil.

"My God, Brad, what have you done?" The words slipped out, but she already knew. He'd gotten a conversion.

"Traded in a life of mediocrity for one that rocks."

God, he was still an idiot. Seems converting into a vampire didn't automatically endow one with common sense. "I noticed you're still here." She gestured to their abysmally small cubicles.

He pulled back as if he'd read her thoughts. "Yeah, I'll be taking care of that soon enough."

Kristin crossed her arms. "Then what do you need me for?"

"You're the down payment."

Down in the depths of her bag, the red phone began to play "Follow You Home," by Nickelback. A chill swept through her like a blast of icy winter wind.

"Go ahead. Answer it. It's your date calling." Bradley rubbed the back of his hand over his mouth in anticipation and ended up with two long thin red scratches from his new fangs.

She briefly touched the spike for reassurance; it was still there. Then she dug out the phone and flipped it open.

"Hi, Kristin. I was wondering when you'd get my invitation."

The rough quality of Vane's voice rubbed her completely the wrong way. A shiver of distaste skittered over her skin. She swiveled in her chair, deliberately putting her back to Brad.

"What do you want?"

"I want a chance to be alone with you."

Like hell. "Well, you kind of blew that when you tried to blow me up in Dmitri's car."

"Tsk, tsk. You aren't going to hold that against me, now, are you?"

She stood up, the chair shoving back on its casters. "Hell, yes, I am."

"Look, I'm trying to help you, but my boss wants you dead. You can see how that would put me in an awkward position."

Bastard. Kristin wanted to strangle him through the damn phone. But she knew that wouldn't do any good. If Dmitri was right, only a sharply honed blade separating Vane's head from his shoulders would do the trick, that or a bomb to shatter him into a million pieces. "You wanna help? How about you start by leaving me the hell alone."

He chuckled and it was all wrong. Dark and sinister. "The Bloodless Murders are happening because a particular Cascade Clan member has been pumping ichor into the local blood supply for profit. They're making vampires out of people who are looking for a cure, not an entirely new lifestyle. I've been trying to stop them."

"Yeah, so you and your group can make takeout of the rest of us."

"That's only their side of it. I'd like to be able to share ours as well. You're still an objective journalist, aren't you?"

As much as she hated to admit it, Vane did have a point. She'd heard the party line from the Cascade Clan, but hadn't really done anything about finding out what had initiated the reivers' actions.

"You want details, don't you? The truth?"

God, as much as she hated it, Vane's offer tempted the journalist in her. She knew whatever he had to say would be a twisted version of the truth, but still there might be something he knew about what was happening within the clan that could help Dmitri stop the illicit ichor trading. "Sure. How about we start with why you killed Dr. Al Kashir and left her on my doorstep?"

"I should think that would be obvious to a reporter like you. She was part of it. Just like Balor."

"So you killed her?"

"She was a threat to mortals and vampires alike."

"That's crap and you know it."

"No, what I know, dear Kristin, is the truth of what's really going on in the dark underbelly of the Cascade Clan."

Kristin's head spun so hard with thoughts it made her dizzy, and her knees started to buckle. What if Dmitri knew? What if he was the one conducting the transactions? What if that was the big dark secret that seemed to be perpetually wedged between them?

"Meet me where they found Balor's body tonight at 10:00 p.m."

"No."

"Do you want the details or not?"

"You may think being blonde and mortal makes me stupid. I'm not. Let's meet somewhere neutral. What about Sangria?"

"Sangria isn't neutral. It's crawling with Cascade Clan."

"Name another public place, then."

"Ivar's on the waterfront—9:00 p.m."

Before she could answer, Bradley snatched the phone from her hand and had the audacity to wink at her. "She'll be there."

Chapter 15

A posh restaurant with starched white linen table napkins hadn't been exactly what immediately jumped to mind when Kristin had planned to meet with the lead reiver. But at this point, anything extremely public would do.

With vampires out of the coffin he could hardly put a move on her without others noticing. But she had to be careful she didn't allow him to glamour her. It didn't help matters that Bradley still had ahold of her arm, his fingers gripping so hard they practically popped through her skin, as he escorted her to a table where Vane sat waiting for them. Kristin kept thinking about that spike in her purse. The weight of it caused her straps to dig into her shoulder. Just knowing it was there made her feel more confident.

"So glad you could join me." Vane lifted a glass of red liquid in greeting and drank. Kristin shuddered with revulsion.

"I'm guessing you aren't ordering off the main menu." She yanked her arm out of Bradley's grasp, threw him a nasty glare and slid into the booth opposite Vane.

Vane smiled, showing off his matched set of dagger-like teeth. "I only brought an appetizer. Bradley and I will be going out later to eat."

Kristin's heart had lodged itself firmly in her throat, throbbing somewhere just below her tongue, making her nauseous.

"In that case, how about we skip the run-around and get right to it. You said Dr. Al Kashir and Balor were both in on some ichor-trading scheme you're working to stop. How does it work?"

"Aren't we eager?"

She tipped her head and gave him a tight smile. "I'm on deadline."

Vane flicked his gaze to Bradley, who nodded.

Something had just gone down that she wasn't privy to. She wasn't sure if the ichor had completely worn off, or if they were masking their mental communication from her with vampire voodoo. Either way, she couldn't read their thoughts. "If you're going to talk to each other, can you please let me in on the conversation?"

Bradley fixed her with a gleaming smile, his fangs bared. God, for what she was certain his parents had paid in orthodontics, wouldn't they be pissed if they knew?

"Keep your shirt on, Reed. Wouldn't want you flashing the customers. Those double Ds might draw too much attention." The tip of his tongue rolled over the edge of one of his shiny new fangs like a guy polishing the chrome on an expensive new car.

Kristin bristled. "Go on, errand boy. I've got important things to discuss with your boss."

Bradley instantly lost his smile and lunged toward her. In the time it took her to blink, Vane was on his feet, his hand pressed against Bradley's chest, the look between them intense.

Kristin grabbed on tight to her purse, her fingers brushing against the spike.

Her skin contracted, feeling tight and uncomfortable. For the first time Kristin gained a new respect for the change in Bradley. He wasn't just an egotistical spoiled rich kid in the newsroom anymore. He was a vampire. She sat a little straighter, refusing to acknowledge her fears in front of them.

Bradley shot her a withering glare then turned on his heel and left her alone with Vane. He swept the tails of his long black leather duster aside before he sat back down.

"The young ones don't know how to control their impulses yet."

She swallowed past the thickness in her throat, going for brash to convince herself, if nothing else, that she would be okay. "So did you turn him from a mere asshole into a terminal one?"

Vane's face was smooth, unemotional, but his eyes remained eerily red. "I'm his maker, if that's what you're asking." His finger circled the rim of his glass of blood as he stared at her. "I can see why Dmitri is so interested in you."

Kristin shifted uneasily in her seat. Hunger, blood hunger, pulsated in the air around Vane. He obviously was serious about going out for dinner and she wondered if that was the real reason she'd been brought to meet him. "I thought we were here to discuss the murders."

"Doesn't it worry you that your boyfriend might find your talking with me to be a betrayal of his trust?"

Inside her the truth burned, churning uncomfortably in her stomach like an extra-large blazing chili dog with onions and sauerkraut. She knew Dmitri wouldn't tolerate her talking to Vane. But ferreting out the truth behind the Bloodless Murders was something that had to be done, especially if the people involved in it were hidden within the clan and operating behind Dmitri's back. He'd need to know to protect the clan, and that would be reason enough.

"So why aren't you part of a clan like Dmitri?" she asked Vane. "You said the reivers have a reason for being involved in this."

"I chose a more ancient path." He paused a beat,

his eyes boring into hers. "Has Dmitri told you he and I are brothers?"

At her quick intake of breath, Vane's smile widened, the twin points of his fangs growing more prominent. "Ah, I see he hasn't."

Confusion and doubt crowded into the back of her brain, little insistent voices that refused to be silenced. "But he was a priest."

"And I was an aristocrat. But the same vampiress, Larissa, created both of us at the same time, making us blood brothers."

Kristin wasn't sure how to take the news. Part of her was pissed Dmitri had deliberately withheld that bit of information from her. It explained why Dmitri knew Vane so well, but it also called into question his motivations for keeping this information to himself. Just how much of what was happening between him and Vane was a personal vendetta and how much of it was really about the clan? More importantly, how much did he *really* know about the Bloodless Murders?

"Doesn't that make you wonder what other secrets he's been hiding from you?" Vane asked.

Of course it did, but she wasn't about to tell

him that, nor doubt Dmitri without a damn good reason. A spark of anger flared in her gut. "He's been up front with everything I've asked."

"And what about the things you've neglected to uncover as yet?" He sat back, steepling his fingers. "But no. Of course not." He chuckled, but the sound came out oddly mirthless and somewhat sinister. "You are merely a tool to further the clan council's objectives."

His twisted game was beginning to annoy her. "Which is?"

"They want to control the ichor trade in this region."

"I understand that conversions are happening to patients who only wanted help, not a vamp-my-lifestyle makeover."

He shook his head. "That's not the real reason behind the Cascade Clan's monopoly. You didn't think that they gave those treatments at the clinic free, did you? No, my dear, the ichor trade has become a large cash cow for many clans. Just like mortals get money for donating their blood to the blood bank, vampires are reimbursed for donating their ichor. Those in the human medical field who know about it are clamoring for it."

"But why would vampires need the money? I mean, aren't most of you wealthy just by virtue of being around long enough?"

Vane took a sip of his blood, kicking back the glass and draining it in one gulp. His long tongue snaked out, licking a few thick drops from the rim. He set the glass down and shrugged. "Another myth perpetuated by fiction and film. Fortunes are made and lost every day. Not all vampires are wealthy, in the same way that not all mortals have vast sources of wealth. The headlines only focus on the ones that do."

Kristin glanced at her watch. "Look, this has been real educational, but if you can't give me something solid regarding Dr. Al Kashir and Balor's connection to the Bloodless Murders, then I'm afraid our interview is finished."

Vane's superior smirk faded. "Why don't you ask him?" His gaze zeroed in over Kristin's shoulder and she turned to look at the man who Bradley had escorted to their table.

Kristin gasped, but quickly covered it.

"So glad you could join us." Vane scooted out of the booth and Mayor McCallum slid in. Vane snagged a chair and positioned it at the end of the booth so he could survey them both.

"Miss Hartman, wasn't it? We met at Sangria." The mayor held out a hand, and Kristin shook it as briefly as possible.

"I see we're not the only one with secrets." Vane glanced from the mayor to Kristin. "Mayor, may I reintroduce you to Kristin Reed, reporter for the *Pacific News Tribune,* the one who's been doing such a wonderful job revealing the truth about vampires to the public."

The mayor's eyes flashed red, then turned back to his normal hazel. "So you're the reason my city is in an uproar."

The hairs on Kristin's nape stuck straight up, an uneasy feeling swiping down her spine. *Holy crap. The mayor was a vampire too. And obviously not one of the Cascade Clan.* She was getting the distinct feeling of being outnumbered, and in hostile territory, to boot. So this is what war journalists felt like.

She glanced at Vane and his eyes seemed to stare straight into her buzzing brain.

"Yes, Mayor McCallum is one of us. You see, after a series of unfortunate health problems, the mayor was seeking out the kind of help only Dr. Al Kashir could provide," Vane said. She could feel him savoring her surprise, drinking her confusion and fear like a rare vintage.

"In exchange for his treatments and to cover his mounting medical debt, he set up an extension of the Cascade Clinic's services to the local hospital where his surgeon, Dr. Chung, started using the ichor with excellent results. So excellent that Mr. Paulson, the hospital administrator, saw the ichor as a profitable, although hardly medically sanctioned, new revenue stream. Unfortunately some of the medical staff was too eager in their use of the ichor, and a few unintentional conversions did occur."

She glanced back at the mayor. "And where does Balor fit in?"

He ground his teeth. "Some of the patients were very unhappy and ended up complaining to the Centers for Disease Control. For a rather large cut of the profits, Balor was willing to turn a blind eye."

"So why kill him?"

"He got greedy, which made him stupid," Mayor McCallum said.

"And what about the other murders, Vane? What about the missing organs?"

"A few members of our operation, particularly Dr. Chung, decided that in addition to ichor, transplant organs would be profitable as a sideline. Especially if provided by those who were threatening the profitable little venture we had been working on so diligently."

"And you let them?"

"Why not? They were going to go to waste otherwise."

Yes. That made perfect sense. Why question it? Thoughts, clearly not her own thoughts, were pushing at her brain, trying to take over. Those stoplight eyes sucked her in until all she could see was red. Kristin began drifting toward Vane, letting go of her purse, unable to stop herself. Everything else around them faded, the restaurant, the people. A white fog had taken their place.

"Good. Now take my hand." He extended a hand toward her.

The hand without the silver charm bracelet extended as if she had no free will. A small voice in the back of her mind took it all in and said with utmost detachment, *So this is what a glamour feels like.* Another part of her, deeper still, silently screamed bloody murder.

Vane captured her hand in his viselike grip, and suddenly the fog lifted and they were outside the restaurant in the moonlight. Her purse and the spike were gone. Water slapped against the piers beneath the buildings and traffic streaked by with a *whoosh* two stories above them on the Alaskan Way Viaduct across the street.

"Let go of her." Dmitri's voice echoed hard and commanding off the walls of the building behind them.

Vane yanked her so hard against him that the action slammed the breath from her body and made her shoulder socket burn.

"What's wrong, Dmitri? Don't approve of my bargaining chip?"

"She has nothing to do with our border dispute. Let her go. Your argument is with me."

"Wrong, *brother*." He spoke the word like a curse. "She has everything to do with it. If it weren't for this nosy little bitch, we'd have taken over from your clan already."

"Changing mortals without their consent is illegal in this clan and every other on this continent."

Vane growled. "That's why I don't belong to any of them. When are you going to figure it out, Dmitri? The blood bags don't want us here. They'll kill us all the moment they get the chance. There isn't going to be any peace now that they know. The sooner we establish who's in control, the sooner we can live in the open."

"You and I both know this comes down to power. You and your nest want it."

"Is that what you think? That this is just my pitiful nest looking for hunting grounds? God, you are an imbecile. We serve Eris, *Trejan*. Do you know who she is?"

Dmitri's jaw clenched so hard he thought the bone might crack. He knew, all right. Eris, daughter of Ares, was chaos incarnate, the literal goddess of discord. She was one of the first, who had become one of the worst. There was no need to compare her to Lucifer because she was, in fact, the reason the devil came to be. Part vampire, part fallen angel and all ancient god, she was hell personified and put on earth to torment, causing strife, heartache and misery in her wake. She thrived on it. Fed from it. No vampire with two brain cells to rub together would be stupid enough to go against Eris and believe he could survive.

For over two thousand years she'd been locked up in a special cage underneath the Parthenon, created from silver and orichcalcum, just waiting to be set free. Then, just before the beginning of the First World War, someone had freed her. Had Dmitri realized during his studies with the priests that the beast to be unleashed during the end times was really Eris, he would have been completely demoralized and given up any hope right then and there. With Eris on the prowl, World War Three was just waiting around the corner. This was far worse than he had ever imagined.

"Of course. But it still puts us at odds." He

stared down Vane. "You have something I want. And if you aren't going to give it to me, then I'll have to take it."

While they argued, Kristin carefully slipped the silver bracelet off her wrist, letting it pool into her palm. She waited a moment or two for her heart to stop beating so wildly, then took a deep breath, turned and slapped the coiled silver onto the back of Vane's hand.

A pale wisp of smoke, ripe with the odor of burning flesh, curled from the contact. Vane shouted, his hand opening, momentarily releasing his hold on her. That was all it took. She bolted at the same time Dmitri rushed at Vane like a linebacker.

She glanced back over her shoulder. Though total opposites, the two were equally matched. Vane jumped upward, launching himself fifteen feet in the air to escape Dmitri's charge. Kristin gasped as Dmitri coiled and sprang, grabbing Vane by the ankle and whipping him around like a leaf in a gust of wind.

Both stayed suspended in the air, like actors

on flying wires. All Kristin could do was stare slack-jawed at the scene. There were no wires. Hell, there were no cranes. The two vampires were fifteen feet up, hanging above the sloshing water of Puget Sound as they circled each other. Several bystanders quickly joined the thickening crowd on the pier as both Vane and Dmitri snarled at each other, then sped together, fangs bared and weapons drawn.

Dmitri's silver knife glinted in the moonlight. Vane pulled something shiny from the depths of his duster and threw it at Dmitri. It was going so fast it seemed to disappear completely, landing a second later with an audible *thunk* in the side of a building just inches from the head of a woman watching the fight. Kristin caught a glimpse of the sharp points of the ninja-style brass-colored throwing star protruding from the wood just before the woman fainted.

Dmitri barely had time to register that the mortal below him was unhurt before Vane came at him once more, another star already palmed in his hand. "You almost hit that woman," he growled.

"If you'd only stay still then they wouldn't be in any danger."

Dmitri dived, the sound of the deadly orichalcum star buzzing past his ear in a hum so loud it vibrated in his skull. He stretched himself, shot upward and grabbed Vane by the wrist, wrenching it backward with a twist hard enough to break bones.

Vane howled and spun a kick, catching Dmitri in the side with the steel toe of his pointed boot. Dmitri grunted as pain blasted through his side. One broken rib, possibly two. He switched the knife to his other hand.

Come closer, you bastard. Let me see your pretty neck. He swung his blade at Vane, a speeding silver arc. It struck Vane's flesh with a satisfying slice. Vane's eyes, a pulsating blood red, glowed. "Lucky shot, brother."

"I. Am. Not. Your. Brother."

He heard the whizzing of the star an instant before it caught him in the bicep, shooting pain down his arm so intense he dropped his knife. Down below, the mortals screamed.

Vane twisted, his fangs gleaming long and white as he smiled, even as ichor dribbled in a thickening black patch from his chest. "I'll have her one way or another. It's just a matter of time."

Dmitri roared, launching himself at Vane.

In a flash of light Vane vanished. A gasp rose from the crowd. For the first time, Dmitri really looked below at the people gathered. He telescoped his vision, searching for Kristin's face among them. He found her, pale and sweating, but unharmed.

He couldn't reach her to transport her with him back to the clan buildings. There were too many people, and they looked just as angry as those who had slain the seven people from his clan. He didn't want to implicate her in any way and possibly put her in danger.

"Kill the vampires!" one shouted, shaking his fist at Dmitri, still out of reach twenty feet above them. A screech of breaks and squealing tires were followed by the crunch of metal as two cars collided on the viaduct. Dmitri saw the faces of the drivers staring at him as he floated in midair, near level with the highway. *Dammit.*

Roman was going to have his head for this. Literally.

Chest lifted, Dmitri focused on his destination.

From below all the people saw was a puff of smoke and light, and a man who floated in midair disappear, like some Chriss Angel magic act. A collective gasp came from the crowd, followed by a growing chant. "Kill the vampires!"

Clearly they were freaked out by what they'd seen. Kristin couldn't blame them. How often did you get two vampires battling out in the open, especially when you only found out vampires were real a few days before?

The sound of sirens filled the air as several police cruisers arrived at the edge of the crowd now spilling out into the main road along the waterfront.

A news van from one of the major television channels pulled up, a cameraman and reporter hopping out and doing a lightning-fast setup before the crowd vanished.

Kristin did her best to stay at the back edge of the crowd, sticking closer to the shadows of the buildings as she walked away from the scene. But a hand snaked around her wrist, yanking her close.

"Don't say a word." Bradley's voice held a shimmer of fear.

"Afraid they'd turn on you?" She twisted to look into his shadowed face. "Look, I'll help you get out of here if you let me go."

His eyes glowed red in the shadows. "Why would you help me?"

"Let's just say that unlike any of the vampires involved in this, or these idiots—" she nodded at the crowd "—I don't have any interest in seeing anyone harmed."

"Aren't you scared?"

Kristin shrugged. "Of you? No. What scares me is how this is all going down the highway to hell."

"So what's your brilliant plan?"

"Have you learned to transport yet?"

Bradley smiled, and for the first time that day, it looked normal, just like his orthodontist had planned it. "That was one of the first things I tried to master."

"And?"

"I don't have enough focus to make long distances, but I can do it."

"Can you read thoughts yet?"

"Sure."

"Great. Then all you have to do is concentrate on what I'm thinking about and we should be able to transport out of here."

"What are you, half vampire or something?"

"Let's just say I've been doing some in-depth research."

He snorted. "I bet."

She smacked him on the chest with the back of her hand. "Come on, vamp boy. Focus." Kristin closed her eyes and thought of the dance floor at Sangria.

The familiar pulling sensation of transporting centered in her gut. The music thumped and blared as the multicolored spotlights swiveled overhead. She wrenched her wrist out of Bradley's grasp. "Welcome to Sangria. The local vampire hot spot."

Bradley glanced around, beads of nervous perspiration dotting his brow. "But this is Cascade Clan."

She patted him on the shoulder. "And if you behave yourself, nobody will care that you're here, or that you're a vampire. You look like you could use a drink." She gave him a light push in the direction of the bar.

"That was well done of you. I would have just ripped his throat out." The soft Italian lilt tickled her ear as Dmitri's firm hands slid around her waist, making her stomach tighten and quiver.

"Stupidity is not a reason to kill someone. Any more than an overgrown ego." She leaned back into his chest, letting him sway her hips against his to the music. Heat drenched her skin as she soaked up the sizzling sensation of his muscular form intimately pressed up against her. Maybe it was just the adrenaline or remaining ichor in her system talking, but she was definitely in the mood to listen.

"We found Zarah missing."

"Vane admitted his group killed her. She disappeared in a fireball just like the others executed downtown. Only the brass spike was left."

"Orichalcum. It's what killed her."

Kristin added that information to the growing list inside her head. "Dr. Al Kashir was his link inside the Cascade Clan. She was releasing ichor into the medical system."

"And they were making a profit from it."

"Exactly."

"Poor Zarah, so intent on helping mortals that she couldn't see how their greed might twist it."

Kristin wiggled back against him. She didn't want to think about Zarah now. Or Vane. Or any of this craziness she'd stumbled into. Right now all she wanted was to feel Dmitri.

The hard ridge of his erection pulsated against her butt, making her insides contract remembering the exquisite fullness and sensation he offered her. She wiggled against it just enough to elicit a hungry growl from him. "But that, that I might be tempted to kill for." Her body grew damp at the feel of him so close and yet so far from where she wanted him most.

In an instant, a swirl of white mist wrapped

around her as his arms did, and he turned her, pressing her breasts against his rock-hard chest. He lifted her against him, tilting her world so that there was nothing but the heat, the scent, the feel of him surrounding her. A moment later she regained a solid foothold and found herself wrapped around him in utter darkness. Not the cool black of a cave, but a warmer musty darkness that spoke of age and hidden secrets. She clung to him not caring where they were, only that she was with him.

His hands cupped the curve of her bottom, pressing her against him. Saints, the scent of her warm desire filled his nose, demanding a response.

Dmitri could see every delicious curve of her even in the deepest darkness. He traced her cheek, his fingers lingering as they trailed over the lush, wet softness of her mouth. She slid her tongue out, pulling his finger into her mouth.

A rocket of pleasure mixed with pain shot to his groin, throbbing and aching. Saints above! The cavern of her mouth was hot, wet and exquisite.

His fangs extended, aching, fanning the hunger boiling up inside him. He pulled his finger out, fighting to maintain his composure, his focus, against a surging tide of hunger and desire. He'd brought her here for a reason.

"Where are we?"

He phased fresh linens and candles into the room for her. Then with a flourish of his hands, the flames leaped to life on each candle, throwing dancing shadows along the stone walls. "My ancestral home in Italy, or what's left of it."

He kept kissing her, indulging in the feel of her warm, pliant mouth as the room grew brighter until it was ablaze with light. Candles of all sizes and shapes covered every surface, crammed together on the stone window ledges, spread over a great wooden table dark with age—everywhere but the enormous bed with four posters that twisted upward to hold an arched red velvet canopy.

The sweet smell of warm beeswax mixed with dried lavender, reminding him briefly, with a bit of heartache, of a time long ago. A time when he could have loved her as a man rather than a monster. This had been his mortal home, the last place he'd lived happily before he'd been given to the church by his parents, before he'd become Larissa's pawn.

He'd brought Kristin here, to this place, a place where he'd never brought another, to bond with her. He'd come so close to losing her twice now that he could think of nothing else. He crushed his mouth to hers, as if he could extract that element that made life possible from her kiss alone.

As she gazed up at him, her eyes reflected the flames like stars scattered across an endless blue sky. And he was lost in a swirl of time and space. Nothing else mattered but this woman. Her unique blend of spicy sweetness branded itself into his skin, filling him up and making his chest ache with the utter rightness of it.

He pulled back. "I don't know what tomorrow will bring," he murmured.

She looked at him, her eyes bright with fevered need. "I don't care. Just don't stop kissing me."

He captured her slightly swollen lips, desire a hungry, clawing animal inside him. She responded, her mouth just as hungry, devouring him. Her tongue traced his fangs, first one, then the other, as her hand slid down his chest and over his stomach, grabbing his aching length with deliberate pressure. He growled, his fangs extended beyond mere desire, enough for him to feed the blood hunger spiraling up inside him.

He grabbed her about the waist, lifted her and took her to the bed. Grasping her hands from around his neck, he laid her back on the red velvet.

Her hair encircled her head in a golden halo, but a devilish delight lit her eyes. She reached down and began to unbutton her shirt from the bottom upward until it lay open, exposing the creamy swells of her breasts, cupped in black satin. Her fingers traced a path from her bra to her pants, and his gaze willingly followed. She slowly unbuttoned and unzipped her pants, revealing a scrap of black satin and lace that covered her silky damp curls.

He reached forward to rip the clothing off her. She put up a warning finger. "No. No hands."

Dmitri cocked a brow, then knelt and bit into her pants, his fangs popping straight through the material. She gasped, her eyes glowing with unabashed desire. She lifted her hips as he pulled the pants off with his mouth.

On the way back up, he grazed a path up along the inside of her calf and then her thigh, enjoying the tremble that shook her. Her panties were damp and he nuzzled her mons, making her groan. But her femoral artery, so close to his ear, throbbed. The rapid shush of her blood caused his body to contract with another kind of painful need.

He resisted it. Instead, his tongue brushed a warm, damp path down the inside of her thigh as his fingers skimmed the edge of her panties, slipping past to rasp against her sensitive flesh, making her groan and thrash. Her hips arched as he stroked and dipped, faster and deeper, until she shook.

"Dmitri, please."

Hunger and desire fisted deep in his gut, demanding release.

"Let me see you, Dmitri," she coaxed.

Good God. She was spread like a feast before him that would drive a man to his knees, let alone a vampire, and she was all his. "You are too much temptation, even for me. I want you all to myself. Forever."

"I'm yours." Her words staked him in the heart. He slid over her, phasing away his clothing, reveling in the slide of her satin skin against his as he brushed against her. The panting moan that poured from her tightened everything within him another precious inch closer to meltdown.

He circled the pink tip of her breast with his tongue. She groaned, wrapping her legs around his waist in response, pulling him in tight against her wet heat.

He threw his head back and let out a fierce cry. Sparks ignited in his veins as his vision turned red. Need, raw and deep, took him to the edge. He pulled back for an instant, afraid of what he might do to her, the monster inside him too great to control.

"Don't stop. Don't you dare stop now," she growled as she pulsed against him.

Unable to hold back the avalanche of sensation falling in upon him, he sank into her, giving her everything he had.

For Kristin, it was as if a bolt of liquid lightning

connected them. She felt it vibrate from the spot where he lay sheathed inside her to the spot where he sank in his fangs now. She felt as if she was being lifted off the bed, spun out into the air in thousands of shattering shards.

Dmitri took everything she had and she arched, letting him in deeper still, so deep that it seemed as if he touched her very soul.

His hands and his mouth touched every bit of her at once, electrifying every nerve. All the universe coalesced into one shining star centered within her, between them. For a moment she couldn't even breathe. She was overwhelmed with rightness, the total completion, as if she'd only been half a person, missing half her senses and oblivious to the immensity of the universe around her.

When it was over, she lay her damp head on his chest as he stroked her hip with his fingers. "Are you okay?" His voice penetrated her, rumbling inside her.

She ran her fingers through the dark hair on his chest, loving how it felt against her flesh. "I'm not okay. I'm amazing. This was different than the other times, wasn't it?"

He nodded. "We've bonded. That changes everything." He looked down at her, his eyes so full of love that it made her heart stutter. She glanced at the spot near her breast where the two puncture marks dimpled her skin. He bent down and laved them with a quick swipe of his tongue, and her body sat up and took notice, coiling and ready to go all over again.

He dipped his finger into the red liquid that welled to the surface, tracing it on her bare stomach. Three interwoven circles, each crossing the other at the center where they met at her navel. "What is that?"

"It's our mark. Our way. It represents an interlinked web of life and death." He retraced each of the circles as he spoke. "One circle for life, one for death, one for vampire. All complete, all connected, all dependent on one another."

"That's the symbol on the dance floor at Sangria."

"Yes."

"You said we're bonded. What does that mean?"

"It means you're mine. Now. Always. Forever. We'll always share a connection of mind and heart with each other, even across lifetimes."

"And that frightens you."

He curled his arms around her, hugging her fiercely to him. "The only thing that truly scares me is the thought of anything happening to you."

Chapter 16

How had his entire existence gone to hell in the short time he'd known her? Now, not only did he have the reivers to contend with, which he would do with relish, especially since Vane had it coming, but he also had the added weight of having bonded with her. He'd divided his loyalties when he most needed focus and resolve.

He'd been stupid. Rash. Completely blown away. Completely enslaved to his desire for her.

She was a temptation so complete, so utterly perfect, he'd been unable to resist. Saints above, Eris couldn't have planned his downfall any better herself. Roman had been right. A woman able to tempt a *trejan* from his duty came along only once every millennium, and Kristin was that woman.

Roman's command to hightail his butt back to Seattle had come through loud and clear as he'd held a sleeping Kristin against him, refusing to let the real world ruin perhaps their last moment together before the coming battle.

War with the reivers was imminent. Achilles had been able to extract enough information from the reiver they'd captured at Balor's murder to know where the battle would take place, but not when.

Dmitri had transported with Kristin back to Seattle, but settled her in his apartment where she'd be safest, and himself in Roman's office to receive his briefing.

"Reivers have been spotted gathering in smaller groups within easy transport distance of the confirmed battle location. We've already got warriors posted in the Fremont district," Roman said as he pinpointed the details on his computer screen for Dmitri.

"Hell. Are you telling me they are going to strike during the street fair?"

Roman glanced up at him. "High concentration of mortals, huge chance for casualties, easy ability to blend in to the costumed crowds. Can you think of anything better to take down the reputation of our clan and cause mass chaos?"

Dmitri shook his head.

Roman clasped his shoulder. "We need you with us, *Trejan*. Remember that."

Dmitri straightened, offered Roman his salute of his hand across his chest, then transported to his assigned position in the field. The fighting members of the Cascade Clan waited, barely having to cloak themselves in the eclectic mixture of costumed people attending the annual Fremont Fair. They waited for the signs the reivers were coming, and had been given strict instructions not to incite panic among the mortals.

The reivers came out of nowhere, a great mass of black and menace. At least that's what it looked like as they transported en masse upon the street fair in progress. There was no time to warn the mortals. The members of the clan saw them moving quickly through the streets, dodging behind cars, jumping over them and swooping down from the buildings like enormous birds of prey.

The reivers braced in a line against the mortals on the opposite side of the clan warriors, so that the hapless humans were surrounded by vampires. But the mortals could not know that on one side were the vampires that fought to save their kind and on the other were the ones who sought to subjugate them. Which was just what the reivers had counted upon. Panic, confusion and ultimately blind fear caused people to rush in every direction, filling the air with screams.

As if they operated with one hive mind, the reivers advanced, pressing the mob of mortals back toward the clan.

Without any warning, Kristin materialized by Dmitri's side. *Vane.* The bastard wasn't going to miss a chance to throw him off balance in this battle, so he'd targeted his one weakness—Kristin.

"How the hell—" Kristin glanced at him, her eyes wide with fear as she stared with raw terror at the advancing reivers. "We're dead. We're all dead. Aren't we?"

"Not if I have anything to say about it." His silver knife in one hand, he phased a sword into the other, as did Achilles beside him. The only thing that would stop the reivers now was the edge of a blade.

He fixed his gaze on hers. "Stay behind the mortals," he ordered. There was no time for her to argue. Not now.

He and the others moved among the mortals like smoke, weaving their way between them quickly. In no time the clan was out in front of the mortals, facing the vampires advancing on their group.

The time for words had passed.

As the clan sliced through the reivers, Dmitri zeroed in on Vane at the back of the reivers, his red eyes both a warning and an incitement to battle. As the war started, the mortals fled in fear, running from the melee, their screams piercing the air.

Several of the reivers went down in a spark of light followed by a flood of black ichor, looking like an oil slick on the road before evaporating into a swirl of smoke.

A few of them simply exploded, taking some of the advancing clan members with them in a blast of heat and red light. But in the end there were far more reivers than the clan had counted on. They surged through the lines, vampires slashing at vampires and unfortunate mortals getting in the way.

He threw a quick glance back at Kristin to find that she was in the thick of it, swinging wildly with an eight-inch bowie knife drenched to the hilt in dead man's blood. While his heart nearly exploded out of his chest in fear for her, the reivers around her were dropping to the ground. Everyone she touched was destroyed. Everyone but Vane.

His nemesis had transported closer to Kristin an instant before Dmitri's sword had cleaved home against Vane's neck. Now Vane stalked her, his duster billowing out behind him. Six reivers transported around Dmitri, blocking his path to Vane and Kristin.

Kristin kept swinging at anything with fangs. Let the vampires sort out who was who from among the poisoned. Thank God she'd been able to persuade Beck to get her several quarts of dead man's blood. She kept dipping and slashing, her arm burning now from the effort.

From the corner of her eye she caught a flash of platinum and black bearing down on her.

She faltered, her legs immobile, a scream frozen in her throat. Vane stepped over a fallen body at his feet and closed the gap between them in the time it took to suck in a startled breath.

"Now it's your turn." He picked her up by the shoulders and flew fifteen feet up in the air. He could have dropped her, let her splatter over the pavement below, but something told her that would be too easy, too simple and not nearly frightening enough for Vane's taste.

"I'm going to enjoy eating you." He closed his eyes and took a deep inhale of the air. His eyes snapped open, glittering like dark rubies. "No wonder Dmitri likes you. You're sweet enough to be virgin's blood." He alighted atop a building overlooking the chaos below.

Kristin didn't—couldn't—think. She was more scared than she'd ever been in her life. Her hand tensed around the handle of the bowie knife still clenched in her fist. There was no way she could let this guy win. She pulled herself together and slammed the knife covered in dead man's blood hilt deep into Vane's gut.

He howled and grabbed her before she could scream, his fangs sinking like hot spikes into her throat. Pain exploded out her eyes, her heart pounding so hard she thought it might burst. Everything within her curdled and burned. Kristin could feel her life slipping away, her side drenched in hot stickiness. Her blood.

She had only one last thought. *Dmitri.*

Dmitri finished off the reiver he was fighting with an orichalcum star to the forehead, then raised his eyes to search for Kristin.

She was nowhere to be found among the fighting. Neither was Vane.

He reached out with his mind, searching for the link that bound them, and found it so weak it had nearly vanished.

Dmitri.

She was dying. Panic slammed into him with the power of a jet plane.

He focused everything within him to take him to her. He found himself on a rooftop. Both Kristin and Vane were sprawled out on the flat roof.

Vane was unconscious, but still very much undead. From ear to collarbone Kristin was savagely torn open, her skin in shreds, her shirt soaked through with bright red blood.

He fell to his knees beside her and scooped her into his lap knowing there was nothing he could do to save her—unless he converted her right then and there. For a moment he faltered as he stared at her angelic face, the smears of red violently stark against the pallor of her smooth skin. Never, in all his existence as a vampire, had he ever changed another person. To do so now, without her knowledge, without her consent, would violate the very last thing he'd held sacred. The last shred of his humanity.

But she was worth all that and more.

If it worked.

Blind panic and fear turned to determination.

He'd never done it before. Had no idea how much to give her or how to keep her from the pain he'd experienced during his own conversion, but he'd do it nonetheless.

He lifted his wrist to his mouth and opened himself to her, giving everything he had left in him.

His ichor flowed into her slack mouth, staining her lips dark. She coughed, sputtering. His gut seized into a hard, hot mass.

"Drink," he pleaded.

She swallowed and coughed again. He vividly remembered the suffocating sensation of ichor sliding down his throat, so he moved his arm to let the ichor flow into the wound at her neck. Still she struggled to breathe.

He knew she knelt on the threshold of death's door.

Dmitri strained everything within him reaching out to her as he listened to the slow fading *ka-thunk, kaa-thunk, kaaa-thhhunk* of her heart. And then there was nothing. It simply stopped.

Chapter 17

For a moment Dmitri couldn't think, was helpless to move. He pulled Kristin into his arms, her form limp and heavy, and held her close. He had twenty-four agonizing hours ahead of him, not knowing whether she'd survive the conversion or not. Regardless, he needed to get her into the earth as soon as possible to ensure every chance at success.

"I'm sorry, *tesoro*. I didn't know what else to do," he whispered into her ear. He sent up a silent prayer that she'd survive, quickly followed by another that she wouldn't hate him for what he'd done to her *if* she survived.

Surely God could understand his fears. It was one thing to suffer damnation for one's own stupidity and pride, as he had. Quite another to have damnation forced upon you without your consent.

He stood, lifting her still-fragile mortal body in his arms. Strands of her flaxen hair floated ethereally around the dirty curve of her cheek, brushing against the lips that had already faded from a soft rosy pink to a dull purplish-mauve.

From down below, the moans and cries of the injured could be heard drifting up from the city street, but the battle had stopped. He glanced only long enough to confirm that the clan had been victorious and the mortals were being helped. Achilles's bright hair stood out and he called to his brother.

How did we fare?

Achilles raised his head, shielding his eyes as he looked up toward the building where Dmitri stood. *There are several poisoned and a few beheaded, but the reivers are gone. How is your woman?*

I don't know yet. Deep in his chest an ache radiated outward, painful and unnerving, paralyzing him as effectively as dead man's blood. Dmitri took a breath, thinking it might ease the pain.

Was she hurt?

She was dying.

Did you...?

Yes. The pain intensified and he finally identified the burning ache as a mix of guilt and fear.

Bury her quickly. The longer she's in the earth, the stronger she'll be.

If she makes it.

She's a strong woman. She'll make it, brother.

He prayed Achilles was right. *Vane is up here. Can you—*

I'd be happy to take out the garbage. Just go.

Dmitri stood on the building's edge, the wind coming off the bay lifting and slapping his trench coat like dark wings. He focused with everything inside him on his bedroom and transported there, Kristin's body cradled in his arms.

The bed was still secured in the hidden panel. He hadn't bothered to reset it after he'd shown her where he truly slept each night. He knelt at the edge of his crypt, laying her gently down upon the black satin where he'd always slept alone.

Her scent of cinnamon and vanilla had faded, only a faint whiff in the air around her. Dmitri shoved away the fear pounding insistently at the base of his skull. He'd assume nothing until the time for her conversion had passed.

He phased away her tattered blood-soaked clothing and the grime, and clothed her instead in a fresh white gown. His trembling fingers traced over the soft curve of her cheek. He tried to make her comfortable, phasing a bandage over the wound Vane had caused, adjusting the pillow beneath her head and crossing her hands over the concave curve of her stomach. There was enough room that he could curl up beside her. And God knew he wanted to. But the danger was not over this night.

He'd have to face Roman and the council over the brutal battle they'd waged. The fault for it lay squarely on his shoulders. He should have been able to fend off the reivers before the mortals had become involved. It should have stayed an internal matter. And he would take responsibility for it, if only the council would spare Kristin, if she survived the change.

He lit a candle on the nightstand in hope that she would wake. If she did before he returned—if he returned—she might want the comfort of the light.

Achilles, he called.

Yes, brother?

I am reporting to the council. If I do not return, see after her.

For a moment there was silence from his mentor. As head of security, Achilles knew exactly what was at stake during the tribunal. Tension pressed between Dmitri's shoulders like a sharpened blade.

I will.

Dmitri took one last gaze at Kristin. With her hair spread on the pillow beneath her head, she looked like an angel cast in stone. He tamped down the raging ache inside him and seared the memory of her into his mind, in case it was all that remained.

Achilles would see to her welfare and training if she awoke and he was gone. But his mentor would not love her. Not as he did. No one would love her more. Not now. Not ever.

Trejan. *We are ready for you.* Roman's voice echoed in his skull like a bell struck to announce the last steps of a man to the gallows.

A barely audible moan came from her throat. He froze, every cell of his body focused on her.

Kristin awoke suddenly from one hell of a nightmare. In the confines of her mind she'd screamed and writhed trying to escape the searing pain that radiated in burning waves through her body as it felt the destruction of each living cell one by one. But she couldn't move, couldn't speak. It was as if she'd had instant-set concrete poured over her.

She stared at the room, realizing she was in Dmitri's room, but her perspective was wrong. She glanced to either side at the vertical hewed rock. A cold chill slithered through her. She was lying in Dmitri's crypt. How in the hell had she gotten there? She tried to sit up and realized she still couldn't move, though the piercing pain had faded. Her lips and throat were frozen, unable to give voice to the scream inside her head.

A heavy arm crossed over her side, a warm

hand covered hers and the dark sweetness of chocolate stirred the air. Instantly her panic subsided. Dmitri. He was with her and she wasn't alone. She wasn't dead.

"Try not to move just yet. You are too weak still," he rumbled, his voice heavy and tired.

Kristin found her mouth still wouldn't cooperate. She focused hard with her thoughts. Now that they were bonded, surely he could read them.

What happened to me?

Dmitri looked down at her, his eyes twin fathomless pools that swirled with remorse and anguish. The air feathered against her mouth, making her lips tingle for an instant before the smooth firmness of his mouth reverently touched hers. But her damn mouth wouldn't move to return his kiss. Her body still refused to obey her. All she could do was stare at him.

What's wrong with me?

You were dying. I had no choice. He closed his eyes, anxiety creasing his brow and forming tight lines around the corners of his eyes and mouth.

What? Do you mean— Wait. You mean I'm a vampire?

He nodded slowly, opening his eyes. They swam with regret and agony, as if he'd committed the gravest of sins against her. *I'm sorry. There was no other way to save you.*

It took a moment for the reality of it to sink in. The nightmare had been real. Vane had attacked her, the pain blinding and fierce as he'd torn out her throat and left her to die.

Kristin's eyes pricked with heat. Hot tears welled up and spilled past the edge of her lashes to trickle down her temples into her hair. Dmitri wiped them away with an infinitely tender sweep of his fingertips.

I'm sorry I failed you. I'm sorry I've pulled you into this existence without your permission.

"Don't," she croaked, her throat incredibly dry, the word a thick paste in her mouth. "You saved me."

He shook his head. "I've condemned you. And I can't forgive myself."

It was too hard to speak. With tremendous effort she focused all her will on lifting her arm. It seemed to weigh fifty pounds as it inched up slowly so she could place her hand against his cheek. *There's nothing to forgive. You did every-thing you could. You saved me when no one else could.*

"It was selfish as much as anything else. I couldn't let you go. I didn't want to lose you." *You don't hate me for doing this to you, do you?*

Understanding dawned clear and bright. She brushed her fingers into the thick strands of his dark hair, reading the fear in his eyes, hearing his thoughts. Strength returned in a rush, flowing into her limbs, flooding every cell so that each hair became a nerve ending sensitive to the slightest movement.

The dancing flame of the single candle seemed to light up the entire room like midday sunshine. His unique scent of chocolate had changed, mixed with musk and bergamot, the faint smell of salt water, the scent of blood and battle cloaking his skin. And she could hear the grinding painful sound of Dmitri's heart breaking in two. All her senses were even more acute than when she'd woken from the ichor treatment. So this was what waking up vampire felt like.

As much as Dmitri reviled his own maker, sh

couldn't have chosen a better one. She couldn't think of another vampire she'd want to be tied to for however long this lasted. She put both hands on his face so close to her own, and looked deeply in his eyes, seeing for the first time the flecks of gold that sparked in the dark brown. "How could I hate you? I love you."

He pulled her fiercely into his arms, holding her tight like a lifeline.

Dmitri! You are summoned before the council. Now, Trejan. Roman was furious. Too damn bad. The moment he'd known Kristin was coming through her transition and awakening, he didn't dare leave her side.

"I must answer the council's summons."

"No. We'll go together." She reached out her hand, her fingers intertwining with his in a perfect balance of light and dark. Hand in hand they transported to the clan council's chamber.

Candles flickered in the ornately scrolled golden candelabra high on the walls, casting shadows on the crimson velvet that hung along the rock walls. Nine chairs sat in a semicircle around a black stone dais with the clan's interlinked three-circle mark etched in a contrasting red against the smooth black stone.

Roman occupied the center in a slightly larger intricately carved cherrywood chair upholstered in crimson. With a motion of his hand he indicated Dmitri should step up to the dais.

Dmitri took his place facing them, hands fisted behind his back, feet braced apart and chin held high.

Roman stood, his cloak pooling around his feet. "Trejan Dionotte, you are called before this tribunal council to discuss your recent conduct. The charges are conduct unbecoming to a *trejan,* resulting in the loss of seven members of our clan. You have not protected your kind before mortals, as is your solemn oath. How do you answer these charges?"

"I accept them as stated." Dmitri took a deep breath. "I was occupied saving the mortal reporter's life. Her death would have ruined our peaceful efforts at reintroducing our presence."

Roman's eyes flickered with distaste and pain.

In accepting the charges, Dmitri had accepted his own death sentence.

A heavy silence filled the chamber, pulsating and growing larger. Dmitri waited for their verdict even as he could hear them mentally debate with one another.

In turn, each council member turned to look at Roman. Roman bowed his head. "The council has reached a decision. In failing to protect the clan and the vampires within this clan in your duty as *trejan*, you are to be executed at sunset."

Dmitri resisted the terrible urge to glance at Kristin. If he showed so much as a flicker of emotion before this group, they would know his true feelings for her. Any chance of survival she had rested squarely on him and that mattered far more than anything that might happen to him. "And what of the reporter?"

Nine sets of eyes bored into him, piercing him. "She has become vampire herself, and is therefore under protection of our clan and shall be spared."

Dmitri's heart crumbled to dust. In saving Kristin, he'd lost his chance to be with her and now condemned her to an eternity as a vampire.

"How dare you!" Kristin shouted. Dmitri couldn't stop himself from glancing at her. Her eyes flamed an electric blue as she levitated off the ground six inches.

Every one of the council members stared at her as if she had just transported into their midst. In the buzz and hum of their thoughts he could tell they were unsure what to make of her.

"This man has done more to save this clan and advance it in the past few weeks than any one of you. How dare you condemn him!" A hit of pepper stung the air strong enough to make eyes water.

"You speak out of turn, young one." Roman crossed his arms, causing his silk cloak to rustle ominously, his eyes blazing a dark vicious red.

Undaunted, Kristin took a step forward in midair, her hands fisted tightly at her sides, no longer afraid of anyone or anything. "I don't give a crap! If you're stupid enough to kill him, then you deserve whatever happens. The only reason you're still around is because he and I have managed to convince mortals that you aren't a threat."

She was every inch an avenging angel. Dmitri's

heart swelled with pride for the amazing woman beside him and stung with terror for her survival.

From the far side a council member with streaming white hair to his waist and pale blue eyes stood up to speak. "But there have been executions—"

She turned, matching his icy stare. "Yes. That's because just like the reivers, there are mortals who have no objection to destroying what they don't understand. But I'd been led to believe that this clan was better than that. But you're just as bloodthirsty as the reivers. The only difference is you hide behind a veneer of civility and legitimacy."

She raised her chin a notch and stared them all down. "If you choose to take this man's life in exchange for all that he has accomplished for your clan, despite the setbacks, then you may as well kiss your clan goodbye. There won't be enough of it left to salvage once your enemies and mortals are done with it."

The council members glowered at her. The buzz of their overlapping conversation filled Dmitri's mind, but he only had eyes for the extraordinary woman beside him. His mate. His love. Kristin.

Roman glanced at the council members, but Dmitri was certain Kristin had heard them as clearly as he himself had. She was vampire now and her powers were already extraordinary.

The council put the matter to a vote.

Roman squared his shoulders. "Your protest has been duly noted, young one—"

"Kristin Reed."

Roman raised a brow. "The council has decided to spare Trejan Dionotte. In return, and because of your knowledge of the mortals and their media, we would ask that you and he become official ambassadors of our clan to the mortals."

Kristin sucked in a startled breath, even though she knew she didn't need the air to fill her lungs any longer. She couldn't stop herself.

Dmitri reached over to her. His hand covered hers, big and warm and solid. The very air seemed to sparkle as she looked into his eyes, and she suddenly felt the hysterical need to laugh and cry at the same time out of sheer happiness.

Does this mean I can still write about the clan? Be an inside reporter?

That and much more.

What do you think? Should we do it? she asked him.

He winked. *Only if we do it together.*

She smiled at him, letting everything she felt in her heart show plainly on her face. Turning, she straightened her shoulders and schooled her features into a more professional appearance. "We accept."

"My laird," Roman added.

Dmitri leaned over, whispering in her ear, the words sending a shiver down her skin. "It's his official title. It's considered proper for you to address him as such."

"We accept, my laird." She gave a brief bow of her head.

Roman nodded in approval. "And when will you two be mated?"

"Mated?" Had she still been mortal she knew she would have been in a full-out blush. It was ne more reason to be grateful she was now a mpire.

"It is obvious you have bonded. And if I am not mistaken, Dmitri has already claimed you as his own."

Dmitri pulled her in close, his arm around her shoulder, and she felt the strength of him flow through her all the way to her toes. "She *is* mine."

In a twinkling, the rest of the council vanished, leaving Roman standing there alone in front of the two of them. "And may I say, you've chosen well, brother. She has the heart of a *trejan*."

"Yes, mine."

Dmitri had eyes for her alone. The force of his full power directed at her sent a delicious rush of desire coursing through her. A cloud of white surrounded them and Kristin felt the familiar tugging sensation in her belly as they transported. She wrapped her arms tightly around his neck, kissing him for all she was worth.

When the mist cleared, she realized he'd returned them to the bedchamber of his ancestral home, away from the clan, away from the tumult of Seattle. Candles blazed, bathing the room's arched stone walls and intricately carved headboard in golden light. She found herself encircled by Dmitri's arms. Gently, by infinite degrees, he lowered his head to hers, his lips nearly touching. "You don't have my heart. You *are* my heart. My reason to exist."

Outside, Kristin heard a nightingale sing. She could feel the moonlight pouring into the air, the very roots of the plants extending into the earth. And she could feel the depth of the love this man possessed for her. "Are you trying to tell me you love me?"

His eyes darkened with passion, with devotion, and blatant desire. "Yes."

"Good. Because I love you too."

Stretching out with her mind, Kristin focused on Dmitri being completely naked. She gasped with delight as his clothes disappeared like smoke. Gliding her fingers over his bare skin and taut muscle, she grinned. "I think I'm going to like being a vampire very much." An unfamiliar sensation pressed against the upper edge of her gums and with a flick her fangs extended for the first time.

"That's very impressive. Most young ones take

several months to learn to phase material objects into and out of existence."

She phased away her own clothing as well, pressing herself against him, hunger sluicing through her. "I'm a quick study."

Hunger flared in his eyes in response. "Good. We have a lot of catching up to do." He crushed his mouth to hers in a kiss that seared away all rational thought.

She pulled back, trying to breathe. "Not so fast."

Relax. You don't need to breathe, you only think you do. I've waited an eternity for this, for you.

"We have forever, don't we?"

He brushed the tip of his tongue down the length of her fang in a slow, circular motion. A chain reaction ignited, melting her body to the core and leaving her craving him in a thousand different ways. He hadn't been kidding when he'd said they were sensitive.

"My darling vampire, when it comes to you, forever is not nearly enough."

* * * * *